ALIENATION OF AFFECTION

<hr>

By
H. D. KIRKPATRICK

<hr>

Library of Congress Control Number: 2010927676

ISBN: 978-1-59712-431-7

Cover design by H & S Media, LLC.

Cover photo by Ann Ehringhaus.

First U.S. Paperback Printing: May 2010

This edition published by arrangement with Catawba Publishing, Charlotte, NC www.catawbapublishing.com

Printed in the United States of America.

For ordering information, contact:
Ms. Carol Beebe
clbeebe@carolina.com
704-377-8872

Dedication

To Robert Galloway Kirkpatrick, Jr.:

"He ain't heavy, he's my brother."

This one's for you. I miss you.

Disclaimer

High conflict divorce cases are real. The story and characters within this novel are entirely fictional. Any resemblance to persons living or dead is coincidental.

'I have taken a full revenge for your unnatural feast.'

--Percy Bysshe Shelley

Acknowledgements

To reach the point in writing a novel when it is time to thank all the people who aided me along the way is exciting and daunting. To try to thank everyone means I did what I set out to do: write a novel. This feat still blows my mind. The daunting part is there were many people who helped. I know I've left out someone in my efforts to express my gratitude. Please forgive me if I did, for it was unintentional, and let me know and I'll try to make amends.

I am indebted to Louise Friedlander, who pushed me to pursue my forensic specialization and who instructed me that other psychologists write murder mysteries too. Many years ago, Beth Loeb kept telling me I could do this. Many people read early drafts of the manuscript for this novel: Susie Kornegay, Camille Ventrell, Karl Rohlich, Glenda Gilmore, Candace Barr, Tom Pettus, and Judy Stock. A number of friends and family were kind and patient enough to listen to me read aloud chapters that were rough and clumsy, but they smiled and offered nothing but encouragement: Henry Plum and Charm Klyve, Ellen Holliday, Jean Holliday (may she rest in peace), Cecily Hines, and Pamela Kirkpatrick. A special thanks, too, to Leslie Heimov and Reid Wilson. I am deeply grateful for the encouragement and investment from Jim Schiavone. Teshia Weeks and Woody Weeks were generous with their time and efforts to help me learn about New Bern, North Carolina, and introduced me to some wonderful people who educated me about their city: Sheriff Ike Strawbridge and attorney Bob Thompson. A special thanks to Ted Fillette, whose reading of the manuscript and crafting of the Ocracoke scenes were invaluable. Worthy, one might say.

There's a technical side to this novel, as might be expected in a forensic book. Mike Hervey of the Charlotte Mecklenburg Police Department taught Calder how to safely handle and shoot a Glock, as well as think like a cop. Paul Vadnais edited some of the coroner's wares. Ann Ehringhaus offered Ocracoke aesthetics and history, as well as the cover photo. Tommy Nations took me into the cyber world and got me rocking on the bass. Matthew Swift and John Crowley put me on the web.

I had two fabulous editors—Mela Kirkpatrick, my niece, and Judith Simpson, my mentor. If I have any talent, it was Judith who brought it out and kept pushing, and for those many pushes, I am eternally grateful. We have lost a bard. May she too rest in joyous, eternal peace. Judith's wingwoman was Aletha Hart. It is an understatement to say without her generosity and support, I could not have finished. I am indebted too to Leslie Shiel for her artistry and generosity in the book cover.

No forensic psychologist strays far from legal eagles, and I have some of the best. My gratitude to Jean Lawson, Ed Hinson, Justin Bice, Bill Diehl, and Mickey Aberman.

I could not have written this book without the editing, organizing, and focused skill of Carol Beebe.

To my beloved wife, Katie, a heartfelt boatload of love and gratitude for the many edits, challenges, and for believing. You are fine to me.

Chapter 1

Tell Me about Your Daddy

September 2005

Emma fluffed her hair and checked her look in the mirror one more time. Her friend Bill always told her she had more dangerous curves than a James Bond car chase. She adjusted her Versace sunglasses and stepped out of her room into the motel breezeway, hauling her small cooler and beach bag to her favorite chair by the pool. The strap of the beach bag pulled her bikini top down on that side, exposing more skin than she generally showed. Emma smiled. She was aware of the problem and the attention she was getting from the young men around the pool. Until she reached the recliner, she made no effort to modify her breast's exposure. Let them look. Emma covered the chair with her beach towel and adjusted the back rest. She slipped off her sandals and lay back. Comfy. She was deliberate in how she applied the oil to her tanned body and could feel the eyes of several men run up and down her torso. Oh, how they'd like to touch her. Emma wiped the oil off her hands and pulled her pen, journal, lighter, and cigs from her bag. She lit a Camel and popped a Coors.

Emma's new therapist insisted they approach her mental condition with an open mind. Emma liked Dr. Cooper's metaphor of being on an archeological dig into the realms of her soul. As she dug around in her childhood, Emma kept a detailed journal of what she could recall. Much of it had to do with her sexual victimization and her so-called repressed memories. The journaling she was doing as part of her new therapy with Dr. Cooper was useful and excruciating, to say the least. The analytical psychotherapy was bringing a painful clarity to the family table.

After a few moments, she opened her journal to her recent excavations and drummed the top of her pen on the page as she focused her mind. She had written the notes a few days before, recalling her first round of therapy with her former therapist that began when she was five years old. There was nothing repressed about these memories. She remembered that first appointment very well.

Dr. Hughes had taken Emma back to the therapy room. It was filled with lots of stimulating and exciting objects. A doll house, crayons, Muppets, dolls, paper, scissors, markers, cars and trucks. Too bad she's got boy stuff, Emma thought to herself. Who'd want to play with a stupid tank!

Dr. Hughes sat on the floor with Emma with her back to the door. She didn't tell Emma there was a video camera above the door, in the corner. One of those cheap kinds, like they have in convenience stores. Black and white. Dr. Hughes gave Emma some paper and a box of crayons. Emma wondered what she was supposed to do with them. Dr. Hughes began by asking about her momma and daddy. Did Emma know what divorced meant? Emma remembered thinking about this a minute. She'd been watching and listening to her parents. She'd heard that word. Divorce meant her parents were mad at each other and she and her sister had two houses. She didn't like having two houses. She remembered how much she hated how angry her momma and daddy got.

Dr. Hughes asked Emma to draw a picture of her house. She recalled thinking she wasn't sure if she liked this lady because she should know she had two houses. So, Emma drew a house she'd like to live in, one she'd seen on television. It had a pool and a tree house. Emma drew this house in great detail. She hadn't talked but had been very active in her drawing. Emma recalled Dr. Hughes making lots of notes on a pad. As Emma had drawn, Dr. Hughes asked her whose house that was. Emma couldn't remember the name of the family who owned the house. Dr. Hughes then asked her, "Who lives there?" Emma remembered thinking, and then saying, "All of us." This seemed like a very satisfactory answer. That was what she wished for. She wanted her momma and daddy, her sister and her to live there. It was a nice house and the family could have been happy there. Probably less angry. Dr. Hughes then asked, "Who's all of us?" Emma thought she ought to know. Emma said, "Me, Momma, Daddy, and my sister." Dr. Hughes looked at the drawing. She apparently noticed that Emma drew her daddy last. She also noticed Emma had drawn her daddy with black legs.

Emma looked up from her reverie and surveyed the pool. One of her not-so-subtle admirers was attempting attention-grabbing flips from the diving board. She took a couple of swigs from her beer and went back to her journal. She made a note in the margin about her daddy's black legs. She closed her eyes and recalled Dr. Hughes' voice.

"Tell me about your daddy, Emma. Has he ever done something to you that you didn't like?" Emma thought about this. She nodded her head. She didn't like it when her daddy made her brush her teeth. She especially didn't like it when her daddy made her sit in the child seat, because that was for kids. These were the things Emma was thinking about that she didn't like. Then Dr. Hughes asked, "Tell me what your daddy did you didn't like, Emma. Did he ever touch you in a way you didn't like?" Emma recalled that she had thought about the time her daddy popped her on the bottom for darting across the parking lot at the mall. He had been really mad. She had nodded. "Tell me what he did, Emma."

Funny how years later she could still recall the panic that had set in when Dr. Hughes asked her that question. She took another sip of her beer.

She remembered thinking she didn't want to get her daddy in trouble and she didn't want him to be mad at her. He'll be mad if I say, she told Dr. Hughes. Emma remembered very clearly her doctor's response. "Don't worry, Emma," Dr. Hughes said. "I can protect you. I am very good at protecting children. That's what I do." Dr. Hughes then asked, "Is what happened supposed to be a secret?" Emma remembered Dr. Hughes staring at her, watching her.

Emma had gotten fidgety. She decided she'd clam up. That's what she'd heard somebody say when you want to be quiet. Clam up. She knew how hard it was to open a clam. She'd seen her cousin try one at the beach. Emma remembered her decision back then. *It had been time to clam up. Emma remembered she'd begun scribbling on the paper. Dr. Hughes then asked, "Is it hard to talk about this?" Emma became a clam. Nobody can open me. Emma recalled her defiance. Dr. Hughes said, "You can tell me your secret. It'll be safe. I'll protect you." Be quiet, Emma had said to herself. She had a bad feeling about all this.*

Emma looked up and watched the guy on the diving board through the darkness of her sunglasses. Surfer jams. Kinda cute, she thought. She snickered to herself and wrote "half-baked" in the margin next to the clam memory. She adjusted the towel in her lounge chair and envisioned Dr. Hughes making her own notes. Emma's imagination defined what they were. Her recent research and her new therapy with Dr. Cooper were giving her a good idea of what Dr. Hughes had been thinking.

Dr. Hughes probably wrote some more things down. "Sexual secret? Dissociative process? Trauma symptoms? Need more history."

Emma remembered Dr. Hughes had said, "That's probably enough for today, Emma. You've been terrific. You're very brave. It takes a lot of courage to do what you're doing. Here's a lollypop for being such a brave girl. Now, I'm gonna spend a few minutes with your mother, will that be all right?" Emma the Clam hadn't said anything. Dr. Hughes had interpreted her silence as consent. "Okay, then," Dr. Hughes said. "Let's go to the waiting room and find your momma. I'll see you next week. Thanks for sharing."

Emma imagined Dr. Hughes had discreetly pushed the remote control button and paused the camera she had been using. She remembered Dr. Hughes had said how proud she was of Emma. Emma opened a second beer.

Dr. Hughes led her into the waiting room where her momma, Ruth McPherson, sat with Emma's sister, Starr, on her lap. Dr. Hughes said to her momma she had an inclination to see Starr next, but she wanted to speak briefly with their mother, whom Dr. Hughes knew was quite anxious. The waiting room, too, had been kid-friendly, so she and Starr played over in the corner quietly while the two adults stepped into the hallway and talked. Even though they had been in the hallway, they left the door open, and Emma overheard every word.

"So, did she say anything?" her momma wanted to know. Dr. Hughes then recounted what Emma had said and what she observed--what had later come to be known as her disclosure. "It was subtle and contained more in what she didn't say than what she said," Dr. Hughes had stated. "She wasn't very verbal, which probably means she's scared and feeling conflicted. There's something there, though. A secret, I think."

"Do you have to report it?" her momma asked excitedly.

"No, not at this point," Dr. Hughes said.

Dr. Hughes then said something about North Carolina law, but Emma wasn't sure if she had heard that back then or had this memory because she now knew the child abuse reporting law. It didn't matter, Emma thought.

Dr. Hughes said to her momma, "The law says I have to if I suspect abuse has occurred, I have to report it. At this point, I have an impression, more of an intuitive hunch, well, more of a clinical hunch. Emma's drawings are interesting. Let me show you. See how her daddy's legs are black? This is possibly significant. She drew him last, I think, because of his lack of importance. It was clear when I began some questions about touching, she became very withdrawn, as if she couldn't bear to process the emotions. I'll need to see her again—and soon I should think. This session was hard for her. She's a brave little girl, your daughter, and you were right to bring her in. There's something there. I can feel it."

"Did you get it on tape?" Momma asked. What tape? Emma recalled wondering. Emma knew about tape, especially the kind for wrapping presents. She hadn't seen any tape.

"Oh yes," Dr. Hughes said. "I haven't looked at it yet, but I think I got a good forensic record. If he's done something, we'll get to it. It just takes a little careful probing, but she's begun the disclosure. The secret's just below the surface. It'll come."

"Thank you so much," Momma said.

Emma remembered the lilt in her momma's voice.

She remembered Dr. Hughes then said, "You are very welcome. You can schedule a time for Starr and another appointment for Emma with my secretary. She'll take your check, too. It was a pleasure meeting you. I appreciate your confidence in me."

Emma could imagine the two women shaking hands. They had bonded. It was going to be a good team. Emma had a clear image of her momma and her momma's thoughts.

Ms. McPherson smiled. "Yes," Momma had probably thought to herself! "I needed a trump card. I knew he was perverted. Well, let's see his fancy lawyer deal with this. My poor babies."

Emma recalled not understanding why her momma sounded so happy. Her momma had been unhappy and crying for weeks. She remembered her momma had said, "Have a nice day, Dr. Hughes."

"You, too, Ms. McPherson," the doctor said. "My secretary's name is Sally." Dr. Hughes had smiled too.

Emma made some more notes, clicked her pen, closed her journal, and pulled on the beer. It was time, she thought. Time to get busy.

Chapter 2

Floater

August 2006

Chief Detective Zachary Kenilworth Brown was troubled. Troubled the way a homicide detective's mind gets when he's called out of bed in the middle of the night to investigate a suspicious death. It may have been an accident. Maybe. Too many unanswered questions. Too early yet. Worth, as his friends called him, pulled on the cup of acidic roux the North Carolina ferry system sold as coffee. He'd been awakened by a telephone call from his colleague, Sheriff Bill Garrish, who lived on Ocracoke Island, off the North Carolina coast. Garrish called and told him the body of Mildred Hughes, a psychologist from Wilmington who owned a vacation home on the island, had been found floating just outside the island's harbor entrance. She had some nasty head trauma that, to Garrish, looked too severe to be accidental.

Worth had met Bill Garrish in his formative, post-military years when Worth was chasing fish and women with his friend Calder on Ocracoke. All cops seemed to know one another. Garrish knew Worth was one of the best homicide detectives in the state. As an

African-American raised in the South, Worth had discovered early on the secret to clearing racial hurdles. He simply made sure he was the damned best at whatever he did.

Worth had graduated from Morehouse College in Atlanta in 1976. Magna cum laude and Phi Beta Kappa. Starting middle line-backer on a fine football team. His joining the army had gotten in the way of his law school plans. Army intelligence fit his personality and temperament. Worth had never revealed much detail about what he had done between the years 1976 and 1979 when he was gathering military intelligence, but he'd logged time in Asia, South America and Eastern Europe. He'd once told Calder he conducted White House approved covert ops. Various law enforcement agencies across the country had sought to recruit him after his discharge, but Worth's love of the South and fishing led him to the PD Homicide Division of New Bern, North Carolina, a small city situated approximately half-way between Raleigh and the coast. When he wasn't fishing, in-terrogating reluctant or resistant suspects had become his specialty. And murder investigations, in particular, had become his passion.

He had been up since 4 a.m., driving from New Bern to Cedar Island, the nearest of the state's ferry terminals. Sheriff Garrish pre-ar-ranged with the Ocracoke ferry's captain to get Worth's car on board at short notice. Worth situated his car alongside many others aboard the *Governor Hyde*, one of the classy ferry boats plying the waters be-tween the North Carolina mainland and the Outer Banks, the barrier islands strung like a chain of sand along most of the coast.

Worth was going over in his mind what Garrish sketched out during their brief telephone conversation. What was the doctor doing out at night on her powerboat? What made her fall? Garrish had said she was a seasoned sailor. Garrish also had said a bad storm had been threatening all day. Forensics might suggest something about the cause of death, but it was her lack of rain gear that smelled. Garrish said they found her gear bag in her car. Worth knew no sailor leaves his rain gear on shore when a nor'easter is brewing. Ocracoke sits out in the Atlantic all by itself. It's a two-hours-and-change ferry ride from Cedar Island, and it gets rocked with some powerful storms. God and the Army Corps of Engineers play one-upmanship with each other annually about the fate of Highway 12 that runs the length of Ocracoke. Even if the victim had been going out at night, and apparently sometimes she did, she wouldn't have left her gear in her car. No, based on what he'd been told so far, Worth thought maybe she'd gone to her boat for another purpose, maybe to tie things down. Or maybe for a meeting. Maybe a meeting she didn't know about.

The ferry's diesel horns blasted the air. Worth felt the boat's change in momentum as she slowed to enter Ocracoke's harbor. He walked out of the ferry's cabin and stood at the bow as she made her way into the charming little harbor known as Silver Lake. Worth was practiced in the art of being a well-dressed man who caught other people's attention. Today was no exception. He was dressed in casual mode. Black jeans, starched white cotton shirt with an open collar, and a pale yellow linen sport coat. Blue tinted Revo sunglasses, a black belt with a silver buckle, and soft Italian loafers with no socks finished his statement. His jacket concealed his right-side, pancake type belt holster where he kept his Glock 27. His black hair was kept in a short, military fashion. Worth adjusted his shades on his nose, as a chorus of seagulls trumpeted the boat's arrival.

As the captain maneuvered the *Governor Hyde* into the dock, Worth reflected on the changes he'd seen on this island. In the past twenty years, Ocracoke had been "discovered" by moneyed people, but the island remained a haven for individualists. In the 2004 presidential election, it had been the only town in Hyde County that carried the day for John Kerry. A blue dot in a red sea. Sheriff Garrish told Worth that Dr. Mildred Hughes had a clinical practice in Wilmington, another North Carolina seaport, and for years kept her boat at Ocracoke near the Jolly Roger, a funky bar and restaurant overlooking the harbor. Silver Lake was a little like Friday Harbor on San Juan Island off Seattle, but smaller and less crowded. Along with examining her corpse and her boat, Worth knew he needed to check Dr. Hughes' house, located in Oyster Creek, a residential area about a mile and a half from the harbor. Ocracoke offered isolation, few distractions, and solitude. Except for a few B&E's and an occasional bike theft, the island had little crime. Boating accidents happened, but the sheriff didn't think this looked like an accident. As far as Worth knew, there hadn't been a murder on the island since 1980, when a nice old lady everyone called Aunt Jane, who lived by herself, was found brutally beaten to death. Worth hadn't investigated that one, but he often thought about it. Unsolved murders grabbed and held Worth's attention like a bikini on a jet ski.

Ocracoke's two cops, Sheriff Garrish and his deputy, made their real living at carpentry. The natural wear-and-tear from the effects of an island climate, plus the storms that occasionally pounded the island, kept that business alive. Their crime scene investigation skills were limited. The Coast Guard station crew at Silver Lake had a battle-ready zodiac from some post-September 11 largess, so the victim's boat was first boarded and examined by them. Garrish also had told Worth the commercial fisherman, who found the victim's boat drifting in the harbor, had called 911 right away on his cell phone. Hughes' boat, the *Empathy*, was familiar to them, so they began their search for her body in the harbor. The blood on the port gunwale suggested she'd hit her head on the side of the boat, and gone overboard. Once they found her body, the deputy saw the trauma to her skull was massive. Her body was found floating about a half mile southwest of the entrance to Silver Lake, in the area known as Teach's Hole, a place where Worth had caught many trout.

Worth fired up his police cruiser and eased up and over the ferry ramp onto the island and headed for the Jolly Roger restaurant where the sheriff was waiting. He parked his car across the street and walked down the gangplank past the Jolly Roger where he saw Garrish. Sheriff William Garrish was a fourth generation 'Coke resident. His speech retained the unmistakable English brogue that traced back to the island's original inhabitants, shipwreck survivors from the British Isles.

"Morning, Sheriff."

"Detective. 'Ow's life in New Bern? Keeping the miscreants in irons?"

"Can't complain, Bill. Life treating you right?"

"Not bad. We 'ad our fair share of 'urricanes last season, though. Blowed through 'ere pretty 'ard last August. All in all, things 'ave been good 'til yesterday." Garrish cut to the chase. "I really appreciate yer comin' so quickly and 'elping us out on this, Worth. I may 'ave ruffled a few feathers in some of the other jurisdictions by asking yew in on this, but I wanted some good 'elp I could count on."

"Not a problem, Bill, glad to do what I can. I talked with my chief this morning and he told me to assist you in any way I can. You and he go back a long way, I gather. So, what's your take on this?"

Garrish leaned up against the dock railing and pounded his pipe on the heel of his boot, knocking out the stale tobacco. Nearby, a commercial fisherman was tossing into the harbor the heads and guts of the morning's catch he'd just cleaned for some of his customers. Pelicans and gulls were having a major food fight.

"This don't look like no accident to me, but I'm guessing."

"Bill, most of your guesses are a whole lot better than what most folk claim is gospel, so lay it out for me."

"Yew probably oughta talk with Captain Nash at the Guard station, since 'e got there first, but as yew'll see, it looked at first like she 'it 'er 'ead on the gun'ale. First thought, naturally, was she'd slipped, maybe, 'it 'er 'ead, and fallen over the side. But, it moight 'spose to look like that."

"Meaning?"

Once I saw 'er boat, "I figured if she'd 'it 'er 'ead where we're s'posed to think she'd 'it it, she'd still be in the damn boat."

"Why's that?"

Garrish was studying his pipe, alternately blowing air through the stem and popping its bowl into the palm of his other hand, knocking out bits and pieces of ash. He then said, "The blood on the inside of 'er boat's too low."

"You mean, you think if she hit her head that low in the boat, unless she stood back up, she'd have crumpled up inside the boat?"

"Yup. As yew'll see, the soides of 'er boat are pretty 'igh. So, 'lessin she got up and pitched forward, which is possible, but ain't likely, and ain't my favorite theory, then she mighta 'ad some 'elp."

"Like pushed?"

"Yup. Or dumped. Either a real possibility. Also, her skull looks crushed, much more damage than yew might expect from a slip and fall. They're 'olding 'er body for you to look at over at the 'ealth Clinic. Soon as yew get done with yer exam, we need to get it on the next furry to Swan Quarter. Normally, in cases of natural death 'ere on Ocracoke, the deceased is picked up by Twiford's Funeral 'ome out o'

Manteo, but in this case, there'll need to be an autopsy, so I'm sending 'er to Raleigh."

"Who's transporting the body?"

"May sound strange to an outsider, but the most available refrigerated van is from the local florist. The owner, a trustworthy fellow, will take 'er."

Garrish dipped his pipe into the bag of Dunhill's tobacco, packed it with his thumb, and lit it with the practiced flash of a single match, despite the ocean breeze. He looked at Worth.

"Couple other things. When the Coast Guard crew boarded 'er boat, and later, me and my deputy, too, we weren't thinking 'bout murder, so we probably messed up some possible forensic evidence. Our prints are all over 'er boat. I feel bad 'bout that."

Worth responded, "Don't worry about it. At that point, everyone thought it was an accident scene. We'll sort it out. You said there were a couple of things?"

"The other thing. As I was takin' pictures of 'er 'ead, I saw she 'ad something in the back of 'er mouth. Almost in 'er throat, really. We took it with forceps and photographed it. Thought yew might want to look at it before we send it on to the Medical Examiner's. It looks like a drawing or something."

"A drawing? Of what?"

"Dunno, fer sure. Like a child's drawing. Damndest thing I've ever seen." Handing Worth a large manila envelope, the sheriff said, "'Ere's copies of the photos. I figured yew'd want these. Stop by my office and I'll show yew the drawing. I'm 'eaded back there now. Captain Nash towed 'er boat to the guard station. 'E's expectin' yew. I've got to start locating 'er next of kin. 'Lessin I'm wrong, Worth, looks like the oiland got its second murder."

Chapter 3

Dr. Calder Miro

August 2006

The night was often Calder's worst enemy. Sleep argued with him, refusing to allow him to lie in its embrace. He'd always been that way. He had hyper-vigilance in his hardwiring, and it was difficult to turn off since there was no switch. Growing up in a volatile family will do that to a person.

Calder was the only child of George and Virginia Miro. His mother met his father while she was traveling in Europe after college. His father was stationed in Germany with the US Army. His mother was from North Carolina, and his father had been born and raised in Philadelphia. By his parents' account, they married in Paris, and Calder was conceived in Barcelona when his parents were on "R&R" as they liked to call it. Once she knew she was pregnant, his mother convinced his father to name their son after her most favorite sculptor—Alexander Calder—who had been born in Philadelphia. His mother was convinced her husband was related to Joan Miro, the famous Spanish sculptor, ceramicist, and painter; but there was no evidence of that, except for the fact both father and son had dark hair and olive complexions, supporting his mother's romantic notion. Virginia Miro was fond of saying that Calder Miro was the poetic marriage of names and art. Apparently, his parents never settled on a middle name, so Calder went through life explaining to people that he truly only had a first and last name. Ironically, Calder later learned during his own undergraduate studies of art history that Joan Miro actually had three names, and his full name was Joan Miro Ferra.

The volatility of his parents' marriage surfaced after they returned to the states, first to Philadelphia, then to New Bern. Calder's mother became a relatively successful businesswoman, running an antique and art boutique and selling real estate. She made more money than her husband. Calder's father had settled into a low-paying sales position. He apparently resented the fact that he never went beyond high school and became increasingly angry. Anger he took out on others. His sudden rages at his wife, or even more frequently at Calder, fused the hyper-vigilance into Calder's neurons and synapses. Calder's pursuit of psychology was in part an effort to sort through his own history.

As an adult, Calder tried a combination of Woodford Reserve bourbon, channel surfing, and then maybe a few pages of a good murder mystery until he felt drowsy. Occasionally, he resorted to a sleep aid. His physician prescribed something when Calder was subpoenaed as an expert witness in a high-pressure forensic case and depended on a decent night's rest. The latest pharmaceutical was the little blue pill being advertised on TV in the company of soothing green butterflies. He muted the sound but thought the butterflies were cool.

Calder's natural alertness to his surroundings was a two-edged sword. It allowed him to process his environment at a high rate of speed, but it also caused him to hear every sound. Being tuned into the world around him was a great skill to have, until it was time to go to sleep. An owl hooting deep within the national forest surrounding his house could wake him up or keep him awake.

Somewhere from a great distance, there was an odd strain of music. The butterflies were pinning Calder's arms and legs to the bed, but the music was zapping him to consciousness. Man, these were some tough butterflies, he thought. His eyes snapped open and his ears cleared, like he'd just come up from a sixty-foot scuba dive. His cell phone was going off. Blackjack the cat, curled up at the foot of the bed, gave Calder a look out of his one open eye that said "Answer the damn phone!"

Calder's brain found his voice and he hurled "answer" in the phone's direction on the night stand. The voice-activated system in his phone sprang to life. In either one of his cars, the jeep or the Jag, Calder was as fast as Billy the Kid, because he didn't have to touch anything to answer the phone. Sometimes he used this feature at home. It was handy when he was still trying to get the butterflies out of his head and to let go of his hands.

Calder cleared his throat. "Calder," he said.

"White bread, I need your help." It was the unmistakable baritone of Kenilworth Brown.

Calder threw his legs off the bed and planted his feet. The coffee he was anticipating would have to wait.

"Whuz up, bro?"

Worth was always amused at Calder's thirst for cool but ultimate honkiness.

"You at yo crib?"

"Just woke up, Detective, how nice of you to call. To what do I owe this honor?" Calder slipped on his boxers as he talked.

"I'm calling from Ocracoke," Worth answered. "Fisherman found a floater early this morning outside of Silver Lake you might know. A child psychologist, Dr. Mildred Hughes."

"Shit," Calder said. "That's terrible." In a split second, he had his wits. Calder stretched his eyes as widely as he could to further bring himself to consciousness. Blackjack jumped off the bed. He knew something was up. Calder lifted his phone, grabbed a t-shirt off the floor that said "Big Sky", and followed the cat down the carpeted stairs to the kitchen. Jonah the wonder dog, who was sleeping in the kitchen, hardly looked up.

"And why are you involved?" Calder asked. "Does someone think it was a murder?"

"Yep, Sheriff Garrish. He asked me in on this. At my chief's request, I'm doing what you might call a courtesy consult. Did you know Dr. Hughes?"

"Not well, but I've known her for years," Calder said. "Why do you think she's been murdered?"

As Worth recounted the troubling scene on Ocracoke, Calder held his cell to his jaw and ear with his shoulder and made a strong pot of Peet's coffee. The plastic magnetized flap of Blackjack's cat door snapped open. The Maine Coon had returned from his morning constitutional, jumped on a bar stool, and then onto the maple block counter in the center of the kitchen. He was now at his command post.

Calder put a large amount of skim milk into his coffee and took a long pull. His senses were getting into gear. The butterflies had flown beyond the horizon.

"I still don't get it. So where's the murder part?"

Worth appreciated how his friend's analytical brain approached a case.

"Dr. Hughes had a second home here and kept a boat in Silver Lake. My understanding is she was an experienced sailor, good enough to solo, day or night," Worth said. "The problem was she wasn't wearing any foul weather gear. She wasn't dressed for going out. The weather called for it. The damage to her skull looks like somebody bashed her brains out. Also, the fact that her body fell out of the boat instead of remaining in the boat is suspicious. I'm thinking she didn't intend to go out, but maybe met somebody there, or went there for some other reason." Worth let this sink in.

"Was her gear on the boat?" asked Calder. "Maybe she just hadn't put it on yet."

"You keep thinking, Butch. Her gear bag was still in her car. It looks like she planned to return to her car, either to get her gear or go home. The impending weather, time of night, low amount of fuel in the boat's tanks, all mean she wasn't going out. I did a brief exam of her body before it was sent to the M.E.'s for an autopsy. The structural damage to her head looks like she was hit twice, once from behind and once from the front."

"Any defensive wounds or bruises?"

"None. I don't think she saw this coming. What kind of psychologist was she?" asked Worth.

"Not very good, in my opinion. She was one of those 'kids-don't-lie-about-sex-abuse' therapists who in the late 80's began to see almost everyone in her practice as either a borderline personality disorder, multiple personality disorder, or satanic abuse victim. She had great credentials, as I recall, but some serious blind spots. She was also a religious fundamentalist whose zeal, combined with New Age methods, was a central part of her therapy. Later in her career, she'd been doing some forensic work, child custody cases mainly. I was never very impressed with her grasp of professional boundaries."

"Well, somebody sure crossed her boundaries and now mine," retorted Worth, whose voice had that angry growl Calder had heard many times before.

"I'll be back home tonight," Worth continued. "I'm gonna stop by the Coast Guard station to look at her boat, go see the sheriff again, and then go over to her house at Oyster Creek before I leave and see what I can find. What say we have dinner at your house and you tell me some more about her? I'll bring the beer and you cook us some steaks."

"I'm glad you're still the shy, retiring type, Detective. What kind of meat would you like?"

"New York, medium rare. Caesar salad, with extra anchovies. No potatoes. I gotta keep my girlish figure. 8 o'clock good?"

"Good for me," responded Calder. "I'll introduce you to a new Boss, aka Springsteen, CD that will prove white guys invented rap."

"Now you gone and proved dumb," Worth said. "Maybe all white psychologists go around getting hit on the head. One other thing, Doc," Worth added. "When her body was fished from the drink, the sheriff found what looks like part of a child's drawing in the back of her mouth, at the top of her throat."

Calder interrupted his sip of coffee and squinted his eyes. "What do you mean, part of a child's drawing?"

"A piece of paper was folded in her mouth and it looks like a child's drawing," Worth said. "That may not be what it is, but that's what it looks like. I'll bring a photo of it with me. The original's got to go off to the lab in Raleigh, but I'm gonna look at it before it goes. I'll trace it or sketch it if I can."

"That's too weird," said Calder. "I'll see you at eight. Bring an appetite and an open mind."

Calder spooned a can of cat food for Blackjack, poured dry food into Jonah's bowl on the floor, and replenished the water bowls for each animal. Calder snapped shut his phone, refilled his coffee, and wandered with his cup out to the screened porch off the kitchen. He let Jonah out the door. Calder paused to take in the view. A fisherman in a jon boat sat out on the lake. It was a bright blue morning. Calder took in a deep breath of the sweet air. What Worth had told him was upsetting. He sank into his favorite reading chair and recalled his previous encounters with Mildred Hughes. He had met her through the state psychological association and had seen her at professional conferences. He remembered, too, he had a case several years back in which she'd been involved as the therapist for his client's children. She could be abrasive and not always competent, but who would want to kill her?

Chapter 4

Up a Creek

After hanging up with Calder, Worth stopped by to see Captain Nash, who commanded Ocracoke's Coast Guard station. Nash agreed with Worth that all the signs indicated an experienced sailor like Dr. Hughes was not going out. Although the forecasted storm missed the island, he emphasized no seaman ever bets on that. Her boat also didn't have enough fuel in the tanks for her to risk venturing out, and the island's two nautical fuel stations closed at 5 PM. The Captain was certain going to sea had not been in Dr. Hughes' plans on the night she died.

Nash had towed her boat to a secure berth near his office and roped it off. At the sheriff's suggestion, Nash's men had covered her vessel as best they could with a plastic sheet. With Captain Nash watching, Worth put on some surgeon's booties and gloves and inspected the boat. He took digital pictures as he went and noted the boat's particulars: type, manufacturer's serial number, and identification number. He checked its hours. He searched the dash and storage compartments but saw nothing out of the ordinary. Worth noted what Garrish had said about the height and design of the boat's gunwales. They were tall and sloped enough to prevent a person from falling out. Because of what Garrish had said, the location of the blood splatter, inside the boat, low on the left gunwale, near the stern, set an idea swirling in Worth's head, but he'd wait on the autopsy results. Worth and Captain Nash re-covered the boat with the plastic.

On his way to see Garrish again, Worth stopped by the Ocracoke Coffee Company, a locally owned café, and picked up a couple of coffees and some bagels. Worth was dedicated to changing the public stereotype that on-duty cops only ate doughnuts. The Ocracoke sheriff's station was located at the south end of the village next to the island's only recycling center. Garrish saw Worth walk into the station and signaled him into his small office that looked and smelled like a combination of a cop's lair and a bait shop. Leather and chum with a hint of pipe tobacco. Garrish had more fishing rods than guns on the wall-mounted gun rack off to the right of his desk. A sign over his desk displayed a fish skeleton that read "Bad to the Bone."

"Come on in," Garrish said, motioning Worth towards a chair.

"Bill. Sorry to bother you." Worth indicated the coffee and bagels and set them on the desk between them.

"Yer not bothering me. Got all day. Thanks fer the treats," he said, taking a bagel and coffee from the bag.

"How are things going with your end of things?" asked Worth.

"Some progress. With the 'elp of some locals and the doctor's colleagues in Wilmington, I spoke with 'er son who's in med school in California. "E was pretty upset. The M.E.'s gonna do a full autopsy as quickly as 'e can, and I got word two SBI agents are on their way 'ere. You probably want to see that drawing?"

"Yeah, that, and ask you a few more questions."

Garrish spun around in his chair and opened the evidence safe behind his desk, from which he produced a plastic bag. He then offered Worth a pair of disposable surgery gloves.

Before getting down to work, Worth set the gloves aside for the moment and removed the lid on his coffee. Both men munched on the bagels and drank some coffee.

Nodding at the baggie containing the paper found in the victim's mouth, Garrish said, "We dusted it after it dried. There're no prints, and the salt water caused a little fading, but it's still pretty all right. See what yew make of it. What's on yer mind? Did ya get to see 'er boat?"

Polishing off his bagel, Worth set his coffee aside, and tossed the empty bagel bag in the round file to create space for the drawing. "Yeah, I examined her boat and I agree with you about the location of the blood."

He then washed and dried his hands carefully in the sheriff's private lavatory. He worked the gloves over his powerful hands and slid open the plastic baggie and laid the paper on the sheriff's desk. It was about 3 inches by 4 inches and had rough edges, making it difficult at first glance to discern if it had been torn or cut in a careless, hurried manner. As Worth carefully studied the paper, he said, "A few things about the doctor. Do you know how long she'd lived here?"

Garrish said, "I asked my deputy, and he said Mildred 'ughes bought the Oyster Creek property in the mid-90's and built that 'ouse o' 'ers about 10 years ago."

Worth took a pad of tracing paper out of his brief case and tore off a sheet. He carefully placed a sheet over the drawing and, with a marker, so as not to cause any indentation on the original, gently copied the crude sketch and the outlines of the drawing's edges. He then wrote the word 'red' in the margin of his copy.

"What do yew think that is, Worth?"

Worth studied the piece of evidence on the sheriff's desk. "I see what you mean. It looks like a child's drawing of a child, maybe a baby, except the baby's head ain't connected to its body. The red, of course, could be blood."

"It didn't end up in the doctor's mouth by no accident," Garrish offered.

Refolding the drawing as it was when he got it, he put it back in the baggie and returned it to the sheriff. "No, it sure didn't," Worth responded. He removed the gloves and sipped on his coffee. The comfort of the onion bagel settled in his stomach. The caffeine brought Worth's homicide detective skills front and center.

Worth eased back into his chair and said, "Whoever put it there maybe hoped the sea wouldn't wash it out, assuming her body was meant to be in the water and not on the boat. Or, maybe our killer didn't care if the drawing was found or not. What we don't know is whether our killer wanted the body to be found or hoped it would be taken by the tide out to sea. Then there's the possibility the body ended up falling out of the boat by accident or by the momentum of the killing blow to her head, but the blood evidence says otherwise. Given the way the drawing was folded and stuffed, we can rule out that the killer made her put it in her mouth. I think our killer bashed her head in, stuffed this into the back of her mouth and dumped her overboard. The drawing may or may not have been something our killer wanted anyone to find. It could have been a personal message to the doctor. This was a vicious attack, up close and personal. It was a nasty piece of business. Did the victim have any local enemies?" Worth asked.

"Now that's the interesting thing, Worth. She 'ad quite a few people she'd ticked off. Seems she outbid some of 'er neighbors for the lot she built 'er 'ouse on. It's a prime piece of real estate. Yew'll see what I mean when yew go over there."

"What do you mean, outbid?"

Garrish leaned back in his swivel chair and said, "Scuttlebutt was she offered the sellers several thousand more than they were askin'. It was rumored one of 'er neighbors, a colorful fellow named Johnny Santos, 'ad already agreed on a price with the sellers and 'ad all but sealed the deal, and she back-doored 'im out of it. The sellers laughed all the way to the bank and moved off the oiland, but Johnny was none too 'appy. 'Is 'ouse is next to 'ers, and I don't think 'e ever got over it. She was also active in local politics and managed to get a dock put on the sound side of 'er 'ouse, which ticked off the preservationists, and we got a lot of card-carrying, turtle-egg saving preservationists on this 'ere oiland."

"I don't suppose there are too many murdering eco-terrorists on Ocracoke," Worth responded. "This Johnny fellow get worked up enough to make her dead?"

The sheriff put the baggie with the drawing back into his safe, finished his bagel, and replied, "I'd doubt it, but 'e's a 'othead. New Jersey Greek-Italian. I've 'ad 'im as my guest 'ere in jail a few times, mostly for being drunk and disorderly. 'E's a regular at 'Oward's Pub. I don't think 'e'd be stupid enough to kill 'er, if it turns out she was murdered, but there was no love lost between 'em. The drawing doesn't make much sense to me, if it was Johnny. Johnny's got a mean-ass temper, though. If 'e mixes 'is daily consumption of beer with some shots o' liquor, 'e can get out of control. I thought you might ask." Handing Worth a computer print-out, Garrish said, between sips of coffee, "'Ere's his rap sheet. One prior for assault on a female in 1988. I did some checking and it was 'is wife, or ex-wife I should say. Seems our boy used to get into 'is cups and smack 'is wife around. She got tired of it, left with their son, and filed for divorce, got full custody, and left New Jersey. Johnny retired and move to our oiland 'ere in 1990."

Worth placed the copy of Johnny Santos' rap sheet in his briefcase and asked, "How'd he make his retirement money?"

"Can't say I roitly know," the sheriff stated. "'E's told people 'e sold a manufacturing business. 'Is divorce records could shed some light on that. I've already asked the cops in Newark to send me those."

"Bill, you're too damn good a detective to be here," Worth declared.

Garrish adjusted the blotter and pens on his desk and chuckled. "Don't go puttin' down my life 'ere. I get paid to keep peoples' 'ouses from fallin' down with my carpentry work, fish pretty near every day, and protect the citizens of this fine oiland. And in that order. My real talent was gettin' yew 'ere. 'Sides," said Garrish good naturedly, "Yew and I both know yew chose New Bern over a lot of other more exotic places." Garrish then stood up and said, "Come on. I'll lead yew to the doc's 'ouse. My deputy and I have already dusted for prints and secured it, and he tells me Johnny's 'ome. If 'e's gonna talk, it'd be best if only I talk with 'im, at least at first."

"And why's that?" Worth queried, taking a last swig of coffee and tossing his empty cup into the bin. "The man got racial issues?"

Garrish chuckled at Worth's on target question. "Yeah, yew moight say that."

Oyster Creek was a small, relatively new residential area of the island about a mile as the gull flies from Silver Lake and the village of Ocracoke. Street names included Cutting Sage, Fish Camp, and Harbor Cove. Worth eased his ride into Dr. Hughes' driveway behind Garrish's Ford Expedition. Four-wheel SUVs that could handle any terrain were a necessity for cops on Ocracoke. Nice house, Worth thought. Two-story cedar shake on 16-foot pilings, high enough to store her boat underneath and to let the ocean flow through, as it did from time to time, with an unobstructed view of Pamlico sound to the right. As he walked from his car, Worth pulled on a fresh pair of surgical gloves and followed the sheriff up the front stairs where they were met by Deputy Blake, who informed his boss everything was like they'd left it. Worth noted no alarm system on the house.

The victim's house was tastefully decorated in muted browns and sandy creams. The foyer opened to a large living room with a cathedral ceiling that looked out to the northern bay over a small dock with no boats. There was no TV visible, so Worth concluded she probably didn't have the girls over for Sunday football, beer, and nachos. The kitchen to the right indicated a meticulous woman who liked to cook. It boasted a full complement of alphabetized spices, Sabatier knives and Calphalon cookware. The dishes, from what was probably her last meal, were washed and in the drain rack. One plate, one glass, and one set of silverware. Worth pushed the message button on the digital answering machine. Nothing. No message pad by the phone. What doctor didn't keep paper and pen by the phone? Doors to the back deck were locked from the inside. The windows were secured, and there were no signs of forced entry.

Worth climbed the carpeted stairs to the second floor. Her bedroom on the left overlooked the creek, and her office was across the hall. Even though it was not her main office, the doctor had made it fully operational, with a satellite-feed wireless desktop computer system, printer, fax, and copy machine. The windows high in the ceiling were made out of stained glass, which gave the room a dazzling display of the late morning light. Southern Baptist motif, Worth thought, except the figures in the stained glass appeared to be hooded female figures, dragons, and faeries. Southern Baptist does the mists of Avalon, Worth chuckled to himself. Every room, including her office, had candles of all sizes and shapes, as well as small ceramic bowls containing fine white sand, holding burned sticks of incense. Framed, high quality reproductions of seascapes by Homer, Courbet, and Chase adorned the walls.

Worth punched the keypad on her desk top, and it sprang to life, opening the main screen. She had closed out all running programs before she left but kept her computer on. He then opened the filing cabinet and thumbed through some of the files. Mostly personal finances, home decorating, and travel. She probably kept her professional files in Wilmington, where her therapy office was located.

Worth stood back and looked at her office desk. Nothing seemed out of order. He had examined her pocketbook after the sheriff had looked through it. He began asking himself some questions. What was missing? What was still in it? She had a reason to leave her house, late at night, to go to her boat. What was it? Who or what lured her out? She had no message on her answering machine. No message pad. No note in her pocketbook or car. Maybe she had voice mail at her Wilmington office she checked from here. Worth knew he'd have to check her e-mail, too. No one had been able to find a cell phone anywhere. Of course, it could have been lost when she fell overboard, but maybe not. Maybe she had a Blackberry. Do they even work out here, he wondered.

Worth went outside and walked around the house, looking at the sand and dirt near the foundation. No signs of obvious footprints or ladder leg indentations. When Worth turned at last to leave her house, he found Garrish and the deputy standing in the front yard with a small crowd of people. The three cop cars had drawn a curious audience. Word of Mildred Hughes' possible murder had spread across the island. Garrish was talking with one fellow, a deeply tanned, beefy man about 60 with salt and pepper hair and beard to match. Worth figured him for Johnny Santos. Worth took off his gloves as he approached the crowd.

Sheriff Garrish then said, "Detective Brown, meet Mr. Santos."

Worth looked at Santos. He was about 6 feet 2 and, despite his protruding belly, his muscle definition indicated he was once an athlete. His dark eyes were full of rage and bitterness. Despite his tan, his nose was a mixture of purple and red cirrhotic tones. Worth could smell the aroma of beer and cigarettes that wafted off Johnny's body. Johnny's glare at Worth immediately confirmed Garrish's admonition about Santos. The look he gave Worth suggested his issues might not just be with women. He had that look Worth knew all too well. A white guy who didn't think black folk should be in his neighborhood. Or maybe Johnny was a white guy who didn't like even sharing air with black folk.

Worth held out his hand. "Mr. Santos."

Johnny didn't respond to the offered hand. He turned away from Worth and said to Garrish loudly enough for all to hear, "I ain't done shit, Sheriff."

Garrish looked Johnny straight in the eyes and said in a soft, firm manner, "Then, you won't need to get excited."

He then said to Worth, "Mr. Santos has agreed to an interview with just me in the comfort of 'is own 'ome, 'aven't yew, Johnny?" Turning to his deputy, the sheriff said, "Blake, please get everyone's name and address and see if anyone might 'ave seen or 'eard anything of interest recently, particularly last night, then git 'em to go 'ome. If Worth is finished looking over the doc's 'ouse, then lock up and re-secure the perimeter of 'er 'ouse. No one is to set foot on 'er property without my okay."

Santos spit out a question: "You arresting me, Sheriff?"

"No, Johnny, I'm not," Garrish said. "Yew are but one of many possible witnesses to a possible murder. Yer importance to our investigation should not be underestimated. Let's go chat fer a spell."

Worth watched Santos try to process what the sheriff meant as Garrish and Santos turned to walk towards Santos' house next door. Johnny's little gray cells probably were rusted from his daily ethanol consumption. Worth admired the intelligence and skill he had just witnessed in Bill Garrish. He thought again about how far Sheriff Garrish might have gone in the law enforcement world. Then again, he thought, inhaling the warm, salty air of Ocracoke, maybe Garrish was the smart one.

Worth looked at his watch and knew he still had enough time to make the 12:30 PM ferry from Ocracoke to Cedar Island on the mainland. He'd be in New Bern by 4:30. He also wanted to get a look at the ferry logs to see if they could offer some clues. He viewed the doctor's house once more from the outside and realized why Santos could be a player in this case. Her property butted against the national seashore, so there were no houses to its right, and there never would be. Its location alone probably made it worth twice that of any of its neighbors'. Maybe Johnny Santos had been squeezing the doctor in some way. Maybe the sleaze had been squeezing her in several ways. It was easy to connect means and motive to Santos, but would Doctor Hughes meet him alone at night at her boat, assuming she was alone? Given what little Worth now knew about their history with one another, he doubted it. Besides, Worth would have to connect Santos to the drawing in some way. Right now, he had no idea about how to do that.

As Worth put his car in reverse, he caught Santos taking a glance over his shoulder in Worth's direction. Yeah, maybe Mr. Santos and I need to get to know each other a little better, thought Worth.

Chapter 5

Ruthless

Ruth McPherson was startled out of her sleep by a vivid dream of Mildred Hughes falling backwards into water, reaching her arms and hands out, as if begging for Ruth. Her friend's mouth was open, as if framing a scream, but made no sound. The desperation in her face terrified Ruth. She lay there in the dark, realizing how fast her heart was beating. It was 3 AM. Five hours later her eldest daughter, Colleen, who was off at college, had called to say a news story in the Chapel Hill and Raleigh papers was reporting Mildred's body had been found in the ocean off Ocracoke and she might have been murdered.

Ruth was shaken to her core by her daughter's call. Even though she asked her daughter to repeat several times the horrible truth she had just learned, Ruth was not shocked by the coincidence of her dream and her friend's death. Mildred had visited her in the dream to say goodbye. They had been close for years, like sisters. It made sense that dear Mildred's spirit would run to her in her moment of peril.

After talking with Colleen, Ruth didn't want to know any other details about Mildred's death. That would have been too painful. *Have to put some distance between me and that,* she'd say to herself. Over the years, Ruth had developed an inability to emotionally screen out or discriminate everything life threw at her. Events outside of her self assaulted all her senses and overwhelmed her. She had learned the deadliness of detail, the kind of detail that could haunt a person for life. She didn't want to live the murder of Mildred. The dream was enough. Mildred's look of terror, her outstretched arms, and muted scream were all Ruth needed to know.

Because she knew how her momma could be, Colleen had offered to break the news to Colleen's younger sister, but Ruth knew she had to be the one to do it. Starr was still asleep, and Ruth needed some time to get ready.

Ruth knew without question who held enough dark hatred to kill Mildred. She had firsthand experience with the drunken rages. *That sonofabitch is going to burn for eternity,* she'd mutter to herself.

When Starr awoke and shuffled sleepily out of her tiny bedroom into the kitchen, she knew instantly that some shit had gone down because Momma was building another one of her impenetrable prayer walls. Her momma had moved the crude, wooden altar into the middle of the room. A demon barrier. Ruth was kneeling in the middle of the floor, her Bible between her praying hands. Her eyes were shut tight, and she swayed a little, as if the power of the words she was muttering passionately were a great weight. She had lit some candles, a powerful, healing ritual she had learned years ago from Mildred. Ruth was startled from her reverie when she heard Starr enter the kitchen, and the Bible dropped to the linoleum.

"What's wrong, Momma?"

Ruth tilted her head, looked at her daughter and spread her arms and hands towards Starr, like Mildred had done in the dream.

Starr was too scared to respond to the invitation of an embrace. She shouted her question this time. "What's wrong, Momma!"

Ruth had practiced the gentle way she would tell her youngest daughter, but great emotion had built up from her prayers and had overcome her. Controlling her emotional expressions was not one of Ruth's strengths. She blurted instead, "Somebody's murdered Mildred! Some Godless, sick bastard has snuffed out the life of that dear woman. May Sweet Jesus bless her loving soul. May the Satan who took her life rot forever in the pits of Hell. Amen."

Starr didn't move. She was immobilized, like Daphne, who in the wonton clutches of Apollo, was transformed into a laurel tree by the mercy of Zeus.

Chapter 6

Dr. Hughes

In addition to buying the steaks, Calder figured he'd better go by his office. He was pretty certain he still had a copy of Dr. Hughes' resume in one of his case files. Maybe something in it would help Worth. Calder had interviewed her as a collateral witness in a high-conflict custody case several years back. The mother's attorney had sent Calder Dr. Hughes' resume. She had been the children's therapist. Calder thought she'd screwed the pooch on that one.

Calder fired up his 2002 Jaguar XKR coupe and cranked up Top Tracks on his satellite radio. He adjusted his baseball cap over his longish dark hair. One of about a hundred caps he owned, this one had on the front two large letters "CB," for Crested Butte. He rolled the windows down, to test the station's boast with his car's eight speakers that its music was the best way known to blow a set of speakers. Calder had a rock and roll heart, and his head was filled with rock and roll trivia. He knew the words to a lot of songs. In the past two years, he had taken up playing the electric bass. He and Worth, a sax man, jammed locally with a few friends from time to time. Calder didn't play his radio loudly in town or at a traffic light next to somebody.

He thought that habit was just one more sign civilization was going to hell in a hand basket with subwoofers, but when he stretched his Jag out on a country road, he let it rip.

As he drove to White's Meat Market just outside town to get the steaks, 'Can't You Hear Me Knocking?' by the Stones came on. Calder considered this maybe the best rock song ever, so he took a longer route than usual to get to the store. The song is over seven minutes long and the Keyes' saxophone solo alone put this song and Calder into orbit. He sang all the way, playing the Wyman bass riffs in his mind.

The Whites run a classic butcher shop that has the best meat and seafood around. Calder selected two prime New Yorks and some fresh shrimp for appetizers. Mrs. White bagged a bit of ice to keep the wrapped food fresh until he got home. Calder had the salad makings already. Worth wasn't getting a Caesar. Knowing Worth, he'd accuse Calder of serving an iceberg Brutus.

Calder took the short route from the store to his office in downtown New Bern. His office was a loft in an old cannery overlooking the junction of the Trent and Neuse rivers. It had red brick walls and twenty-foot high windows on the river side that could open to let in the breezes, and Calder had divided some of the space into smaller, soundproof rooms for therapy cases and interviews. But it was the natural light bouncing off the river, and the indescribable smell of a river moving towards the sea, that made his heart sing every time he entered the place. The compelling nature of his forensic work, plus the aesthetics of his office, helped assuage the pain of the tragic loss of his wife.

Once the building went condo, Calder had bought the space, and it was appreciating nicely. He had also negotiated three private parking spaces and some storage space in the basement that was secure and waterproof, so his case files had a good home, too.

Calder had long since adopted the policy that the ethical and prudent thing to do was to keep his forensic files in perpetuity, even after the case appeared to be closed. He just never knew. Thinking about the call from Worth, Calder could not imagine what, if anything, in the case material he had might be of interest to Worth. He hoped Worth was wrong about Dr. Hughes' death being a homicide.

He thought about the drawing found in her mouth his friend described. Could she have been swallowing evidence, like in some bad spy novel? He doubted it, but he thought the drawing made murder a good bet. It was just too weird.

Calder punched the gate opener and drove into the basement. His secretary was gone as expected, since she left at 4:00. He parked his car and unlocked the storage room. It was a well-lighted room about 18 by 20 feet. He checked the hard copy of the inventory of his files and found the file box he wanted containing the case and Dr. Hughes' resume. Relocking everything, Calder put the case box in his trunk and took the elevator to his office.

He checked his voice mail for messages and shuffled through the mail. Email could wait. Calder often wondered how much time he now spent each day reading the few emails he really had time to read versus holding down the delete button. His secretary had summarized the day's phone messages.

He secured everything and returned to his car. As he drove out the basement security gate, he didn't notice he was being watched by someone in the alley across the street from his office.

In the summer, Calder lived in a tree house. Although his house sat on a bluff overlooking a lake, not much of the lake could be seen during the summer because of the foliage. It was thick. North Carolina thick. During the fall and winter, the view was spectacular, but the summer months brought a green embrace. Calder loved this place for its isolation and peace. He called it Castleheart. He had to drive six miles through the Croatan National Forest to get there. In the summer it was hot and dusty. It was tough for visitors to find it. Calder sometimes didn't want to be found. He'd spend two or three days at his house alone and not talk to anyone but his dog Jonah and Blackjack the cat, especially when he was writing a forensic psychological report in a complex case. He also liked its privacy for security reasons. Some of the folks Calder evaluated for attorneys were what Isaac Hayes would call 'bad muthafuckers'. Calder had reasoned it was best they not know where he lived, because his evaluation results were not always appreciated by everyone he evaluated. Fifteen years ago, after Calder had submitted his written report to the court, he had been threatened by the boyfriend of a woman who was suing her ex-husband for custody of the children. The boyfriend actually stabbed the children's father in the back during a visitation exchange as the little girl and boy watched.

Although Calder consulted on murder cases, the irony about forensic psychology was that the level of conflict and stress was higher in custody and visitation cases than in any other type of forensic evaluation. One criminal defense lawyer told Calder she had stopped practicing family law and started representing murder defendants because the murder cases were easier. Explaining her reasoning to Calder, she had said, "At least in murder cases, the killing's already happened." To a large extent, Calder knew she was right. He had been practicing forensic psychology for twenty years and a lot of his practice involved conducting court-appointed child custody evaluations. The level of conflict in some custody cases could reach epic proportions because the stakes were so high. The parents and their extended families often spared no expense over the possession of the child. It was also a rule of thumb among seasoned custody evaluators that when a divorced couple went to war with each other over the children, there was a high probability at least one of the parents, if not both, had a personality disorder. Personality disordered litigants often delivered an abundance of rigid, self-serving actions that made life miserable for everyone else involved.

Because of the risk associated with his work, Worth had convinced Calder to keep some firepower at his home and at his office, so Calder learned to shoot and got a concealed weapon permit. He carried a Glock 23 40 caliber handgun in his brief case that he took to his office, and he kept a Mossberg 12 gauge pump-action shotgun at his home. Worth had emphasized, "The Mossberg ain't a hunting gun. It's for home-defense." Calder knew he meant it was for close range. Calder was not a hunter and didn't find any pleasure in shooting animals, but he figured if someone came at him in a state of mind Clouseau would call "a rit of fealous jage," he'd defend himself. Worth had lined Calder up to do some range-firing of both weapons and get the training required for being able to carry a concealed weapon. The Craven County Sheriff's Department small arms instructor was tenacious about Calder's training. She made sure Calder learned a two-handed pistol grip, didn't blow his feet off, and could hit the pie plate target from various distances.

Calder took to his gun lessons like a Southerner to a fish fry. His instructor had a body worth killing for. Calder loved to watch her firing stance. When she stood with her legs apart, displaying a combination of sensuous muscle definition and more than ample curves, all poured into a police uniform in a way that should have been illegal, her profile sometimes made Calder forget to breathe. He'd find himself thinking, how do those buttons not pop? After his second lesson, when he asked her out for a drink, he quickly decided her body was like one a man could get killed for. She'd told him her girlfriend was an internationally-ranked bodybuilder. Then, to drive the point home, she added unceremoniously that her girlfriend could hit a moving squirrel from 50 yards with a handgun. After that, Calder regained a proper focus on how to shoot but retained his deeply felt awe of her unmitigated voluptuousness. Some months later, Calder told Worth over a few beers about his hit on the instructor, and Worth laughed for at least five minutes. It was two minutes into Worth's laughter when Calder looked at him and said, "You knew, didn't you?" Worth just laughed on.

After his weapons' training, Calder reconstituted his ego and felt confident he could use either weapon, but he also knew shooting another human being was almost unimaginable. Worth emphasized over and over: shooting another human, face to face, goes against human nature. Worth acknowledged he'd had to do it several times, and it never got easier.

Calder had over an hour before Worth arrived, so he thumbed through the box he'd brought home and started to look over the Hughes' resume as he poured a beer. Blackjack jumped on the table and sat in the middle of the document. He was a tall, dark, and handsome cat, and talkative. He looked Calder in the eyes and issued a command, "meow." His tone and inflection meant two things. One, you'd better pick me up 'cause I won't leave you alone until you do, and two, when I've gotten enough strokes and chin scratches from you and am satisfied, then you can feed me. All this is to be done now and in that order. Touch first, food second. Commence now. Cats rule.

Calder picked him up and draped him over his left shoulder. Blackjack shifted and put his front legs around Calder's neck, one on each side. His purr made a sound like the hum of a small electric motor. Maine Coons could be affectionate, as well as fierce, but that was another story. Calder scratched under the cat's head, around his ears and asked him how his day went. Blackjack purred and rolled his head back like Stevie Wonder at a keyboard. Calder walked around the room, scratching and stroking the master of the house until the cat had enough. Time for phase two. Calder dropped him to the floor and filled his food bowl. Jonah was outside chasing his tennis ball around the yard, so his preoccupation allowed for no cat-dog food collisions. Blackjack crunched away with not so much as a thank you.

Calder returned to his review of the Hughes resume. She had some impressive credentials, including a Ph.D. in psychology from UCLA. He thought more about his two significant professional encounters with her over the years, neither one pleasant. He had been critical of her role as the children's therapist in both cases. In one case, hired by the dad, she had recommended custody and visitation in the father's favor to the department of social services and to the court without evaluating or even speaking with the mother. Dr. Hughes' opinion carried so much weight—inappropriately Calder thought—it caused the mother's visitation with her children to be disrupted. In the second case, she had been the therapist for two girls in the early 1990's, had given the girls some extreme diagnoses and had come to some outrageous conclusions about the father as well as his extended family. Calder had interviewed Dr. Hughes years later about her involvement in the second case and thought she was wacky.

While living in California, or Mellowfornia as Worth called it, during his psychology graduate school training, Calder had watched the child sexual abuse hysteria in America roll eastward like a tsunami. He had witnessed a number of his otherwise competent colleagues lose their rudders in child abuse cases, as they accepted, often without question, outlandish abuse allegations as true. Child sexual abuse victimization suddenly became the explanation for a vast number of psychiatric ills. Calder concluded Dr. Hughes had become one of many mental health professionals who lost her objectivity when it came to child sexual abuse cases.

Jonah's bark signaled Worth's arrival, confirmed by Worth's distinctive knock on Calder's door. He delivered on the beer. Two six's. One of Guinness, one of Grolsch.

Worth fixed his eyes on the kitchen counter. "Ah, cold shrimp cocktail. White folks got taste."

Calder removed two beers and put the rest in the fridge. He placed a bowl of Heinz cocktail sauce next to the shrimp. "My special sauce," he said. "An old family recipe now available in supermarkets everywhere."

Worth hung his sport coat over the back of a chair and removed his gun and belt holster. These moves signaled off-duty comfort. He pulled up one of the bar stools and leaned his massive arms on the kitchen island. He dipped a large shrimp into the sauce and said, "Just think, if Kerry had been elected, we'd be dipping in 'first sauce.'" He popped it into his mouth and pulled out a notepad, flipping over several pages. He tossed the pad and a manila envelope on the butcher block.

Calder opened the Guinness bottled draft and poured it down the middle of an English pint glass. He loved the beer's coloration and waterfall effect. He edged his own stool closer to the counter and leaned over to look at these notes while Worth opened the envelope that contained a series of photos of the drawing and the tracing he'd done of the original. Looking at the notes and the sketch, Calder's first thought was that it looked like a child's drawing of a baby. The baby's head was not attached to the body. Scribbled lines were between the body and the head.

"Why'd you write 'red'?" Calder asked.

Worth washed down another shrimp as he finished his first beer. Handing Calder some color prints he'd made, he said, "Here are some decent shots of the actual piece of paper. The original looks like it was done in black pencil or something with a small bit of red. I thought you might have some ideas about this."

"Like what?" Calder asked.

"Like, why does a child psychologist who appears to have been bludgeoned to death and tossed overboard have a crude drawing of a decapitated baby in her mouth? Either the good doctor had some strange dietary habits or we've been given a clue. I'm going out on a limb here, but I'm guessing the latter. I'm bringing said clue to my favorite psychological detective who's about to fix me a steak." Worth popped the top off his next beer. He liked to see how loud he could make the unique Grolsch bottle tops pop. Blackjack considered the noise rude and left the room.

Calder studied the drawing some more. Then he said, "You get the iceberg wedges out of the fridge. They're soaking in some ice water. We're having those with bacon and creamy blue cheese. You get a Caesar another time. Besides, anchovies are out of season. Is this tracing the actual size of the drawing?"

"Yeah. Since she'd been in the water, it was damaged somewhat, but it looked like it was either torn or cut around the edges. The paper was kinda thick, like construction paper or something. From what Sheriff Garrish said, its position in her mouth was at the top of her throat. Unless the autopsy tells us some more, we may not know if this is where the drawing was placed, or whether it was moved by the sea water." Worth then asked, "So what's your take?"

"My first reaction is the drawing was hard to swallow. Or maybe represents something that was hard to swallow."

Worth took a long pull on his beer and said, "You talking symbolic shit now."

"Yeah, maybe."

Chapter 7

Brain Salad

October 2005

    Emma continued to value the work she was doing with Dr. Samantha Cooper. She had decided it made sense to pursue a second course of treatment with a different therapist. A new perspective was illuminating. Emma wanted to explore her mental condition now that her daddy had re-entered her life and she had started college. She was totally done with Dr. Hughes, her first therapist. After the many horrible years that corrupted her childhood and teenage years, Emma decided to take control of her own destiny. She had some sorting out to do and some decisions to make. For the time being, Emma decided not to tell anyone about her weekly therapy with Dr. Cooper, not even her mother, her sister, or her roommates, and to pay in cash. She knew Dr. Cooper would keep everything in absolute confidence, except if there ever became a question of whether or not Emma became a danger to herself or others. Emma had assured the doctor neither of those two issues would ever arise. Emma was eighteen now and was going to direct her own life. Under the circumstances, Emma knew

Dr. Cooper would come to understand why she was doing what she was doing.

Emma had done her research on Dr. Samantha Cooper. "Sam," as she was often called by her patients, had been practicing outpatient psychotherapy for thirty years in the small college town of Chapel Hill, North Carolina. Her home office was within walking distance of the UNC campus, and many of her patients were students. She had done her clinical internship at the Federal Psychiatric Hospital at Butner, North Carolina, which had housed some of the country's sickest criminally insane.

Emma smiled to herself as she recalled Dr. Cooper's face when Emma told her she had been diagnosed as a multiple personality disorder, or MPD, at age five. Emma recalled to herself how attentively Sam listened as she proudly told her that she and her former therapist had identified five "alters," the so-called alternate subpersonalities or alter egos that are the hallmark of MPD. In the beginning stage of her therapy with Sam, although Emma didn't know it, the pride, rather than the expected pain, with which she presented herself, had signaled some possible trouble to Samantha Cooper. But Sam had known there was a possibility her young patient did not have, and perhaps never did have, this rare psychiatric disorder.

Emma perceived that Sam was responding carefully to her psychiatric history. Emma was glad Dr. Cooper had the wisdom to know how delicate the first few appointments would be in working with her. During her second appointment, Sam had looked across the short distance to her patient and said those words that were forever to change Emma's life:

"Was there ever a time that you doubted the accuracy of that diagnosis, Emma?"

The question had jolted Emma so profoundly she could still feel the muscle memory of how she flinched. As skilled as she was at hiding much about herself, this question still got to her. She remembered pushing the blue and purple strands of hair from her face and looking at Dr. Cooper's kind, sky blue eyes. She had heard no judgment in the question.

Sam, too, had seen the flinch, but Emma assumed she probably wasn't yet sure of its meaning. Sam had known not to press, and she had waited for Emma to process both the probe and its impact.

Emma had tried to cover her reaction by shifting her legs so that she curled them under herself. As a general rule, men can't sit that way. Emma liked the distinction. She recalled how hard she tried to hide in the colors of the abstract oil painting that sat on an easel in Sam's office. Dr. Hughes had that stupid Van Gogh sunflower print on the wall over her chair. Emma's eyes wandered in the blues, blacks, and creams of the oils in Sam's painting. There was something desolate, yet strangely comforting in its brushstrokes. Emma found courage in that painting. She remembered how hard it had been to whisper her response to Sam's question:

"Sometimes."

Emma recalled with satisfaction that she had been clever enough to notice Dr. Cooper's almost inaudible sigh of relief. Or maybe she had imagined it. It didn't matter. Sam later told her, as the therapy entered a deeper stage, that she had, at that moment, interpreted Emma's whispered "sometimes" as a message from Emma's best self and that Sam knew it was vitally important for her to connect with Emma's movement towards authenticity. Emma totally loved the concept. Awesome. She could kiss Sam for giving her that. The best self speaking and moving towards authenticity. Hallelujah. Sam had sat very still so as not to disturb the moment, and smiled only with her eyes. She somehow sent that smile into Emma's eyes and followed it with another one of her potent zingers:

"Emma, can you tell me about the first time you had such a doubt?"

Emma remembered that question too and she had closed her eyes. She was either going to trust this woman or bullshit her like she did everyone else. She adjusted herself. She time traveled and thought to herself about another of the early therapy appointments with Dr. Hughes thirteen years ago when she was five.

"Hello, Emma," Dr Hughes had said. "Your momma said you were being quiet. Why don't you and your momma come back to my office and we'll talk a little bit. I have all those wonderful toys and dolls you can play with. Would you like to draw again?"

Clinging to her mother, Emma remembered whimpering and reluctantly following her mother and the doctor down the hall. She had looked around Dr. Hughes' office again and saw some things she hadn't noticed before: more dolls and doll houses, buckets of crayons and pencils, paper, and a small table. There were big peoples' chairs too.

"Let's sit down here for a while," Dr. Hughes had said. "You want to sit on your momma's lap? That's fine." The only sound Emma remembered she had made was the almost inaudible cry in the waiting room.

She remembered her momma spoke up quickly. "She's been like this since she came back from her daddy's last weekend. Not talking. I just know something happened," her momma said. "Sonny's always been weird. Sex was always so important to him. He's perverted, you know. I just know he's done something with Emma. He always wants to hold her. Treats her like a baby doll. I saw him once kiss her on the mouth."

Emma slid out of her momma's lap and went to a doll house. She turned her back on the big people. Even though she didn't understand much, Emma had taken all this in. She'd heard her momma and daddy fighting yesterday in the driveway, had heard them yelling, but didn't know what it was about. Their fights had frightened her so. She'd hidden in the corner of her bedroom closet and had decided that if she closed her eyes she couldn't hear them. She'd tried to think nice thoughts until she heard her daddy drive off. This time, though, her momma had seemed really upset. Emma hadn't understood why her momma and grandma had made her show them her pee-pee and bottom that afternoon. She hadn't understood all the questions. What she had understood was that her momma and grandma were really mad at her daddy.

Dr. Hughes had replied softly to her momma, "How long have you been separated?"

"Five months, but we stopped having sex a year before that," her momma had said.

"What caused the break-up?"

Pretending she was playing with the big doll house, Emma remembered that she listened with all her might. She was angry her daddy had left so suddenly. She knew it was her fault. Otherwise, he would have taken her with him. She knew her daddy loved her. I want my daddy, she said to herself.

Dr. Hughes had smiled warmly at her momma and said, "How about you let Emma and me talk for a bit?" She then turned in Emma's direction and said, "Emma, your momma will be right out in the waiting room. We can go get her if we need to, okay?"

Standing and opening her office door, Dr. Hughes gently had ushered her momma out, and had patted her momma on the arm. "Don't worry," she had said. "I've seen many situations like this before. Emma will be just fine."

By this time, Emma had found the dolls' kitchen. She remembered she had carefully arranged the tea set on the small table. Everything had to be in order. Dr. Hughes had pulled up a chair beside her. The doctor had smelled funny, like the clothes in her grandma's closet. She'd heard her grandma once say that smell kept the moths at bay. Emma hadn't yet decided if she liked Dr. Hughes, but she knew for sure no moth did.

"Emma, I want to show you some special dolls."

Emma had reached for one of the dolls in the doll house, but Dr. Hughes had said, "No, not those. These in here," as she opened a cabinet behind one of the big chairs. She had placed four dolls on the small table near the doll house. There were two large dolls and two smaller ones. Dr. Hughes had picked up the small female doll and showed Emma what made these dolls special. Undoing one of the buttons on the doll's dress, Dr. Hughes had whispered in a sing-song fashion, "See Emma, these dolls are special because you can take their clothes off and they have all their privates."

Emma remembered taking the girl doll from Dr. Hughes and eyeing it curiously. She'd never seen anything like this doll before. Emma remembered that she put it down and picked up the small boy doll. Dr. Hughes then asked, "What makes boys and girls different, Emma?"

Emma knew boys were different from girls because she'd seen her two boy cousins in the tub. They'd been younger than her. She knew they had wee-wees and girls had ginas. She knew mommies had boobies and daddies had hair. Emma remembered she had thrown the boy doll on the floor in Dr. Hughes' office and had growled like her dog Max. Both Max and her daddy had left her. She had known Max was mad.

Emma thought her growl had startled Dr. Hughes.

Dr. Hughes then asked, "Has something happened to you that makes you mad?"

Sensing that Max's growl had had an impact, Emma turned to Dr. Hughes and uttered "Grrrrrr," even louder at her. She wanted Dr. Hughes to know she was mad. Everybody in her family had been mad at each other.

Dr. Hughes had then asked, "What are you, Emma? Are you an animal?"

Emma remembered she decided she'd done enough. She'd made enough noise. She had turned back again to the doll house kitchen. Satisfied that it was in order, she had gone to the nursery. She arranged all the furniture so it was just right.

"Do you want to play with the special dolls some more?" Dr. Hughes had asked. Emma remembered she had thought this was a stupid question. Dr. Hughes then asked, "Can you show me with the dolls if something happened at your daddy's?"

Emma remembered she had sat in silence. She recalled the worried look on the doctor's face.

"Come on, Emma. Let's go see your momma. We've talked enough for today."

Emma had blinked her eyes and looked into Dr. Cooper's eyes. Sam Cooper had waited out the silence, not knowing what was going on in the mind of this eighteen year old. Emma had seen acceptance and caring in Sam's eyes. She'd never seen these two things with her previous therapist.

Emma remembered regaining her composure and deciding she could roll the dice with Samantha Cooper.

"Quite honestly, Doctor," she had said in a very mature voice, "I had my doubts from the very first day." Now, Emma thought to herself, with this doctor's help, I am ready to perform my own retrospective analysis of how I was treated as a child.

Chapter 8

Rock, Paper, Scissors

August 2006

Over the years, Calder had learned there were certain things Worth loved about being a cop. One of them was his car. Worth had a serious appreciation for the muscle machine issued by the city of New Bern. A black, totally tricked-out 2004 Dodge Intrepid SXT. Worth chuckled when he talked about his car because he said it reminded him of the scene in the Blues Brothers when Elwood described the car to Jake as they drove away from Joliet Prison: "It's a cop car. It's got a supercharged cop engine. It's got cop tires, cop seats and cop brakes." As much as he loved the Dodge, Worth loved the computer that not only allowed him to get instant information on any person's driving record or criminal record from almost anywhere in the world but also came equipped with a sweet GPS and commander's software program on laptop that could practically tell him the color of the building he was trying to find. His computer connected him with almost every law enforcement data base in the world. He also dug the amount of fire power his car offered, including the Mossberg shotgun in the trunk and the Colt Python under the seat. Even though he didn't make traffic stops, it came equipped with an in-the-grill video camera. The car also had several blue and red lights tucked here and there Worth sometimes turned on just to get people out of his way.

Worth turned onto Salisbury Street in Raleigh and found the office building that housed the State Medical Examiner's office. Sheriff Garrish and Worth had agreed it made sense to send Dr. Hughes' body to Raleigh for examination not only because of the lab's sophistication but also because of the forensic medical skills of the Chief M. E., Dr. Edwin O'Neill. O'Neill had called Worth's office a few days later and told him he thought Worth would want to come in person to discuss the autopsy and other forensic results. His message didn't say what he had found, but Worth knew it must be something important or else he would have just sent a written report.

Worth placed a portable blue light on his dash for the benefit of any meter maids and parked his ride in a no parking zone. He entered the building, ID'ed himself to the security guard, and checked his Glock before he went through the metal detectors. The M. E.'s office was on the third floor. Worth grinned when he heard Marvin Gaye coming out of the elevator's speakers, and he made a note to tell Calder at least one state office had class.

Dr. O'Neill was probably in his early 60's but he looked about 80. His skin had an odd yellow-brownish color undoubtedly caused by a combination of the cigarettes he chain smoked and the formaldehyde that permeated the air. Smoked and pickled. He looked up when he saw Worth.

"Kenilworth, how are ya?" extending his hand as he spoke.

"I'm good, Edwin." Worth said, shaking O'Neill's hand. "Good to see you. You keepin' it between the ditches?"

Dr. O'Neill brushed off some ashes from his lab coat, and said, "I am, but I may be the only one who has that opinion of myself. The bodies keep piling up in the basement, and our State Legislature, in its infinite wisdom, continues to cut funding, so we, like other state agencies, live in a perpetual state of disarray with increasing work and decreasing staff. If the citizens of our fair state would stop killing each other with such frequency, things might be a little better. But, of course, no one listens to me, and America is fond of homicide."

Worth always liked O'Neill's straightforward appraisal of things. He knew, too, that he should get right to the point.

"I understand you may have some more information about the body from Ocracoke?"

Dr. O'Neill said, "I think I do. Curiouser and curiouser. Let's go back to my desk. Would you care for a cup of coffee?"

"No, thanks," Worth said.

Worth knew one of the reasons they were moving back to O'Neill's office was because O'Neill liked to smoke back there, even though it was illegal for anybody to smoke anywhere in any state building. Edwin O'Neill's office looked like a grenade had gone off in it. In the center of it was a desk about the size of an aircraft carrier, except you couldn't see any surface because of the piles of files, books, scattered papers and at least two ashtrays overflowing with old butts. Three of the walls were covered in floor-to-ceiling bookshelves stuffed with the same disarray of books, papers and files. One shelf, however, had a human skull sitting on a block of wood. *Memento mori.*

Once at his desk, O'Neill pulled a pack of smokes out of the drawer and lit one with his lighter, exhaling the smoke up into the ceiling fan.

"You know the drawing that was found in the decedent's throat? That was intriguing to me. Maybe I've been watching too many of these CSI TV shows, but I took the liberty of sending a portion of the drawing over to the SBI lab for analysis. They have a gal over there who could tell you what time of day Eve tempted Adam if she had a chance to run the apple through her lab analysis."

Worth chuckled to himself at the thought of a medical examiner watching crime scene television shows for entertainment. "What's your favorite show, doc?"

"Reruns of 'Quincy.' But I also like 'Bones' and 'NCIS'."

"That figures," said Worth. "So what did you find out?"

"The paper the drawing was made on was a heavy bond type I thought might be unique, so I asked Susan, the wizard at the SBI lab, to see if she could figure out what it might be. The results are in."

Dr. O'Neill handed Worth an e-mail from Susan Goldstein, evidence analyst, that read "Spectromatograph analysis of the paper sample number 427831, case #978, reveals that paper fiber is 30 weight, cotton bond, manufactured in Wheaton, Massachusetts, by the A. L. Dunn Company between 1985 and 1990. This type of paper was most often used in the type of gummed artist tablets sold in specialty art stores. The A. L. Dunn Company went out of business in 1990. Chemical analysis of the particulates of the drawing revealed wax substance, i.e., crayon. Forensic inference: sample #427831 is part of a crayon drawing, possibly done by a child, maybe done in the late 80's or early 90's. Let me know if further information is needed. And stop smoking."

Worth set the e-mail down on O'Neill's desk and said, "I'll be damned. Is she that good?"

O'Neill said, "If we want her to, she could probably tell us the age and gender of the artist and whether the person was right or left handed, but I figured this was enough to get you going."

"Did she re-check for prints?" Worth asked.

"Yep. None found," said O'Neill.

"Anything else you can tell me about the victim?"

The M.E. continued, "Her postmortem exam revealed she was in relatively good shape, well-nourished, good muscle tone, no fibers, skin, or foreign substances under her fingernails. She'd had dinner about an hour before she died. Blood toxicology indicated she'd had a glass of red wine with dinner. No other drugs or toxins in her system. She hadn't been in the water long, maybe six hours. That puts her time of death between 10 PM to midnight. The skull trauma though, was definitely caused by a blunt object. Her skull was crushed in two places. The killing blow was probably the first assault to her skull that came from behind to the back right of the parietal region, near the lambdoidal suture. The impact and location on the skull suggests her killer is right handed, like she was hit with the force of a full swing of a baseball bat and the killer was swinging for the fence. She was hit with a tremendous amount of force. The skull fracture didn't have the kind of creasing that you might expect if she'd hit her head on the sharp edge of the side of the boat, as I gather was what some officials at the crime scene first thought. The trauma to the left temporal region and sphenoid bone and the pattern and flow of the internal hemorrhaging suggests her body was then propped up, facing her killer, and hit again. The small amount of water in her lungs suggests she was dead before her body went into the water. She died of her brain hemorrhaging in two places. There's also a recent contusion on the back of her left knee that probably happened when her leg scraped against the boat as her body went over the side. There's no trauma to her fingers, hands, or forearms to suggest she tried to defend herself. There was no indication of any sexual assault. So far, we've found no foreign fibers from her clothing. I'd say she never saw it coming."

"Like maybe she knew the person who killed her?" said Worth.

"Or the person surprised her" responded Dr. O'Neill. "Although it's our loved ones who most often kill us, it's also possible, given the nature of her death and sequence of the blows - she might have been completely taken by surprise and never saw her assailant."

Worth mused about this, and responded, "It's also possible, isn't it, that she knew the person, they met on the boat, and she had her back turned, like maybe she was looking at something or had casually turned away for a moment during a conversation?"

"That's also possible," O'Neill said. "The second blow to the head only occurred after the killer moved the victim's body, turned it around, and hit her again. I would venture to say it was after this second *coup de grace* that her killer shoved the drawing into the oral cavity. There is no evidence of any other foreign matter, except remnants of her dinner, or any other human matter not belonging to the victim in her mouth, throat or stomach. I'd say our killer was wearing gloves."

"I'd say our killer was also really angry at the doctor," Worth added. "How certain are you the murder weapon was a baseball bat?"

"Not terribly certain, but I've had cases before where we knew that was what was used to crush the victim's skull, so that would be my preliminary impression. I could find no traces of wood in either the skull or brain tissue, so it might even have been an aluminum bat."

Worth then showed O'Neill the photos of the location and blood pattern on the boat's left rear gunwale. Pointing to several photos, he asked, "Might the blood evidence, especially its location and flow pattern suggest the killer propped her up against the inside of the boat?"

The M.E. studied the photos. "That makes sense. The killer hit her very hard from behind, causing the fracture on the back right side of the skull, then probably turned the victim around in a sitting position, leaned her against the side of the boat, and delivered another blow to the left temporal region. The trauma locations may suggest our slugger was right-handed. I'll get my report typed up and sent to you as soon as I can. You still teaming up with that forensic psychologist, Dr. Miro, from time to time? This might be a good case for him to look into too?"

"Yeah, Calder's in. I'm having dinner with him tonight."

"Please give him my best."

As he drove away from the M.E.'s office building, Worth punched the memory dial on his cell phone and called Calder's cell. Calder was sitting at his office desktop computer when his phone played a few bars of Mancini's theme "The Pink Panther," that he had assigned to Worth. He was working on a child custody evaluation that was particularly difficult and was glad for the interruption.

"Hey, man. What's up?"

"You busy?" asked Worth.

"Not for you. What's going on?"

"Dr. O'Neill and some forensic genius have dug up some important information. It seems they've run the drawing that was found in the doctor's throat through some kind of analysis, kind of like carbon dating, and figured the paper was a heavy bond, artistic paper probably manufactured in the late 80's or early 90's and the material used to make the drawing was probably a crayon. The drawing may have been done by a child. There are other details the M.E.'s put together, but we can discuss those over dinner.

"Where are you now?" asked Calder.

"I'm just leaving Raleigh. I'll be in New Bern in about two hours. I've got a few more things to follow up. Let's meet for dinner and discuss this thing further."

Calder smiled at this. "Be glad to, my man. You know, of course, what this means?"

"Yeah," said Worth. "I'm buying. Where are we gonna eat?"

Calder knew what he wanted to do. "Let's meet at Captain Ratty's at 7:30. I'll make the reservations. We can get a booth and it'll be private. Let's meet at the bar."

"So you've heard about the new bartender, too?" said Worth.

"Well, if she's half as smokin' as everybody says she is, we might just eat at the bar."

"Now you're thinking. I'll see you at 7:30." Worth put his black Dodge into warp speed.

Calder returned his attention to the custody evaluation report, but this new piece of information about the drawing had gotten him thinking. If it was a child's crayon drawing, why would a child draw a baby with its head cut off? Why would somebody, presumably the murderer, put a child's crayon drawing of a baby with its head cut off in a child psychologist's throat? This case was getting heavy. He decided to call it a day. He didn't want to work on this custody report anyway. It was one of those all-too-familiar situations in which both parents had significant personality disorders, denied they had any personal problems themselves, and were more interested in beating each other into a pulp than thinking about their children's welfare. So coming up with a reasonable set of recommendations for the court was not easy. Besides, Calder decided going for a long run and thinking about the new bartender at Captain Ratty's might be a better plan.

Chapter 9

Diggin' in the Dirt

As Worth drove to New Bern, he glanced at his investigation notes, in his small, flip-style pad in which he wrote new, important information, ideas, to-dos, and questions to be answered. He held it up next to the steering wheel and read as he put Raleigh behind him. He had written 'check cell phone, voice mail, email, ferry records. Get Santos divorce papers. Santos ex-wife. Murder weapon? Hughes family? Money? Shoe marks on the boat?'

There were three terminals on the North Carolina mainland from which a person could get a ferry to Ocracoke. Worth first called the Cedar Island office, then Swan Quarter, and lastly the Hatteras office. They all said the same thing. If a person boards a ferry on foot or with a bicycle, they're not required to register by name. Only travelers with cars, trucks or motorcycles have to pay and thus get logged in. Even then, it's only the person making the reservation who gets entered into the log by name. The Hatteras ferry was free, so it had no fee payment records. Until he had a name to go on, the ferry logs were not going to be much use. There was always the possibility a ferry employee had noticed something unusual about one of the passengers.

Worth then called his office and talked with Officer Baker, a smart, reliable cop who enjoyed helping Worth in his investigations and would some day make detective. He asked her to get Dr. Hughes' personal phone records - both cell and land line - and see if she had any voice mails. For starters, Worth wanted a look at her incoming and outgoing calls for the past twelve months. Baker said she'd get right on it and get back to him when she had something. Worth also asked her to track down all of the names of Dr. Hughes' business partners. He knew she was in a group practice in Wilmington. They just might know something. Maybe one of them wanted to reduce the size of their practice. Maybe she was treating a dangerous patient. Worth also asked Baker to get Dr. Hughes' bank statements. Though this angle might take a court order, his experience had taught him the smell of money to a person could be like blood in the water to a hungry shark. He'd seen some sick killing frenzies over a few grand.

He then called Sheriff Garrish, who surprisingly was fishing, but took Worth's call anyway, and asked him if he might be able to locate the name and telephone number of Santos' ex-wife. Worth wondered what she might have to say about Santos' dark side. According to Garrish, Santos believed she had cheated him out of any type of relationship with his son and Hughes had cheated him out of the house deal. Worth wondered to himself, did our boy Santos ever try to kill his ex?

The drawing seemed to eliminate Santos as a serious suspect. There just wasn't any obvious tie between the drawing and Santos, but Worth couldn't just dismiss him because of that. Santos could have used some kind of ruse to get Mildred Hughes to her boat, and he certainly looked like the kind of guy who'd swung a bat or two. If he had done it, would Santos be stupid enough to put the bat back under his car seat or hide it in his house?

Worth had his cruiser on auto-pilot and rolled down the highway at a respectable 75 mph. He adjusted his big frame in the seat and settled back. He did some of his best thinking when driving. The Neville Brothers harmonized through his car's eight-speaker system. They, too, were theorizing about what made the world such a mess: fear, hate, envy, jealousy. Sing it, brothers, Worth said to himself.

Chapter 10

Sympathy for the Devil

Calder's favorite running route was a seven mile loop on an unpaved fire trail that ran through the Croatan National Forest along the Neuse River. The trail surface was soft and the air smelled of pine trees and sea. Depending on the time of day, he rarely encountered any other humans there, but the area was populated by great blue herons, bald eagles, egrets, muskrats, seagulls, and an occasional snake. After changing into his running gear and stretching, Calder whistled for Jonah and left his house at a pretty good pace. Jonah was a Nova Scotia Duck Tolling Retriever, a breed that loves water and the outdoors. He kept stride with Calder, but occasionally ran off in pursuit of a squirrel or rabbit. Calder had learned just to let him go and keep running, since it was his primary task to keep Calder, a duck he was taking for a run, always in sight.

Calder couldn't stop thinking about Hughes. Long distance running always proved a good time to think. As he ran, he wondered who might have hated her enough to murder her. Calder could easily come up with two people, both custody litigants, whose relationships with their children had been seriously compromised by her zealous professional actions. It was too much of a reach, though, to think either one could kill her. Still, he figured he'd better tell Worth. Calder also realized there was a whole lot about her, both professionally and personally, that he did not know. The child's drawing, if that's what it was, suggested a professional angle. She was, after all, a child psychologist.

The particular forensic case Calder had several years back, in which he'd had some difficult contact with Dr. Hughes, was a real doozy. He had been contacted in 2000 by a family law attorney representing a member of one of North Carolina's richest families. It was a case as complicated as any in which Calder had ever been involved, and he had interviewed Hughes as a collateral witness. It was the first and last time Calder realized just how histrionic she truly was. Histrionic was a term that had replaced hysteria to describe individuals who could be superficial, self-centered, extremely naïve, and prone to over-dramatizing everything. It fit Mildred Hughes like white on rice.

John Andrews, a family law attorney who practiced in New Bern, had retained Calder to evaluate his client, Sonny McPherson, the middle son of Griff McPherson, who owned about half of eastern North Carolina. Griff controlled McPherson Enterprises, and he and his family lived on a plantation along the Trent River called Loren Farms, which was roughly the size of Rhode Island. Griff was a staunch Republican who often entertained politicians there. *Newsweek* had once run a story on Griff's life, and Calder remembered seeing pictures of the first President Bush and Billy Graham at the McPherson Farm. Bush had gone on to carry every county in eastern North Carolina. Griff had juice.

When John Andrews first called Calder, he had explained to Calder that ten years earlier, his client, Sonny, had been accused of sexually molesting his two daughters and had not seen them since. Not only that, there had been allegations of satanic ritual abuse and child pornography that engulfed not only Sonny but many family members as well, including Griff. Andrews told Calder the children and their mother made allegations that a child pornography ring was operating out of Loren Farms. Sonny, under the advice of his previous attorney, had given up contact with his children to avoid a public scandal. Andrews had explained to Calder that Sonny had decided, now, ten years later, he wanted to clear his name and get his kids back.

Calder's evaluation had been in two parts. He had completed a comprehensive forensic psychological evaluation of Sonny, including a psychosexual assessment, which thoroughly evaluated Sonny's knowledge and attitudes about sex, the sexual behavior he engaged in with himself and other people, and his fantasies about sex. A psychosexual assessment was an intrusive, but sometimes necessary part of a forensic psychological evaluation. Sonny had basically come up clean. Calder had also taken an assessment of the child sexual abuse allegations as far back as a trail ten years old could take him. Modesty aside, Calder thought he did a reasonably good retrospective analysis of the case.

Dr. Hughes had been the therapist for the two McPherson children; and it was her therapeutic efforts, in combination with the children's mother's suspicions, in Calder's opinion, that had created the tragedy that ultimately engulfed the McPherson family. He had submitted a written summary of his findings to John Andrews that eventually found its way to Sonny's ex-wife, Ruth, and her attorney. In his report, Calder had concluded that a preponderance of the data strongly suggested the children had never been sexually molested by their father, or by anyone, and that suggestive and leading interviewing had probably created the outlandish allegations. The worst part was that Calder had concluded Dr. Hughes had provided what was probably "iatrogenic therapy" to the children, meaning that the treatment caused, not cured, the illness. It was his opinion that her efforts had established harmful misdiagnoses of both girls and instilled in her young patients the false beliefs that they had been horribly victimized. The file data that was still available provided limited evidence of what the children actually described to their mother, their maternal grandmother, or to Dr. Hughes. During his interview with Dr. Hughes, she admitted she had taped over many of the video recordings of her interviews of the children.

Jonah was now herding Calder back to the deck of the house where Calder filled his water bowl. Calder was more winded than Jonah. Calder's canine master emptied his bowl in loud gulps as Calder stretched. Jonah's own post-run routine was to return to the concrete floor of the basement where, in a belly flop position, he cooled down. After stretching, Calder retrieved a cold Guinness and thought some more about the McPherson case. He began to wonder if he had missed something about Sonny, who had re-established contact with his children after Calder's report went in. Had his rage about Dr. Hughes been simmering for the past few years? The satanic ritual abuse and child pornography allegations had also named other perpetrators, but as far as Calder knew, no one else's life had been harmed like Sonny's.

Calder went inside his house and found his file copy of the McPherson report from the box he'd gotten at his office. As he thumbed through its pages, he recalled his evaluation of Sonny McPherson.

Sonny McPherson called Calder's secretary a couple of days after Calder's conversation with John Andrews and had scheduled an all-day evaluation. In addition to putting an individual through a battery of psychological tests and measures, including a mental status exam and an extensive clinical interview, Calder had learned over the years that spending 7 or 8 hours with a person over the course of one day usually provided extremely useful information as well. People tend to settle in and become more of who they truly are over the course of a full day. Being decent and respectful with individuals while you put them through a carefully designed forensic evaluation often leads them to relax and tell you things that sometimes are not only surprising but also self-incriminating. It is a well-known principle that the interrogations that yield the most accurate information happen under conditions where the questioners are kind and decent and respectful to prisoners; not harsh and torturing. It was just too bad, Calder thought, so much of the world hadn't caught on to that piece of wisdom concerning human nature.

Calder recalled his initial meeting with Sonny in 2001. Sonny McPherson had arrived early for his appointment. He had come into the office with a three-foot cloud of cigarette smoke surrounding him, wearing a Lacoste lavender polo shirt with blue pleated slacks and tan Nubuck shoes. He had the kind of perfect tan someone could only get and maintain if he played more than he worked. Calder suspected tennis or golf. Maybe sailing. Turned out Sonny was, apparently, quite a croquet player and toured a national circuit. He was pacing around the waiting room when Calder came out to greet him.

"Mr. McPherson?" Calder held out his hand and received a reasonably firm handshake. "It's very nice to meet you. Please come on back." Gesturing with his hand, Calder said, "We'll be in the room through the first door on the left down the hall."

Calder followed Sonny McPherson into his testing room where he had a table that was about 8 by 4 feet and two comfortably padded leather swivel chairs in which two people might not mind spending a long hard day. The room was adequately lighted and ventilated, and on the walls hung some artwork done by various artist friends of Calder. On the table sat a small desk lamp, a box of tissues, and a high-quality micro-cassette tape recorder which Calder used to record all his forensic interviews.

As Calder sat down across from him, Sonny said, "Nice office."

"Thank you very much. Let me tell you what we're going to do today so you'll know what to expect, although I'm sure your attorney, Mr. Andrews has already filled you in somewhat."

Sonny responded, "He just told me you were the best at what you do; and if I had any chance of clearing my name and getting my kids back, we had to get you on board."

"Well, I want to talk about the reasons you're here, Mr. McPherson, but first I want to explain a few things. I'm going to record my interview with you, and the tapes will be made into a verbatim transcript so I will have an objective record of what you and I say. If it turns out your attorney wants me to write a written report, then I will use the transcript to quote you accurately. Do you understand?"

"Yeah," he said.

Calder turned on the tape recorder and ran a brief test to make sure it was working properly. He then rewound it and stated the day's date and that it was 'in the matter of Sonny McPherson'. He then said to Mr. McPherson, *"I have explained to you that I will be tape recording my interview with you today, and you have agreed to that, and you are aware you are being tape recorded now?"*

"Yes," said Sonny McPherson. "I'm a little nervous though. I've never seen a shrink."

"It's quite natural to be nervous," Calder responded. "Subjecting yourself to the type of evaluation I'm doing is difficult. I will be asking you a lot of detailed and personal questions, but the degree to which you choose to be open and honest will strengthen the validity and reliability of my evaluation."

"I understand," Sonny said quickly. "I'm going to be straight up with you, Doc. I just want to get my kids back and undo what the bitch did to me. I've waited 10 years for this. I ain't gonna blow it. I got screwed. I don't know my children. They don't know me. They probably think I'm some kind of pervert. I'm going to tell you whatever you need to know."

"Let me be very clear with you, Mr. McPherson, about something. A little while ago you said you and your attorney wanted to get me 'on board'. I want to emphasize that even though you and your attorney are paying my fee, I'm going to do an objective analysis and evaluation of you and the case circumstances, and—"

Sonny McPherson cut Calder off, "I know, I know, that's all we want. A thorough, objective analysis. I didn't mean to suggest…"

Calder cut Sonny off. "I'm not trying to be critical, Mr. McPherson. What I'm emphasizing is that the data in this case will take me and my conclusions in whatever direction the data go. Despite the fact that I have done work with your attorney before on other cases, he knows I call them as I see them. I can promise you that you will get an evaluation that puts the good, the bad and the ugly in as clear and honest a light as possible. I will not take a case in which I agree ahead of time to render the opinion that is expected of me."

"Yeah, that's what John said you'd say. I know what happened. I know I got screwed. My previous attorney told me I had to give up my kids or do time. I can't believe I followed his advice, but I did. It's water under the dam."

The water under the dam slip was interesting. Calder wondered what that meant.

"Who was your former attorney?"

"Henry Driscoll."

"I know Mr. Driscoll. At some point I'll probably want to talk with him if you'll give me your permission."

"Yeah, no problem. He's got a file that might have some helpful things in it."

"In fact, this form I'm showing you right now is a consent for release of information. I'd like you to read it, sign it and date it with today's date, and I will use it to talk with various people and obtain information that will be relevant to my evaluation. This form also emphasizes that the evaluation you are doing with me is not confidential, and by signing it, you are acknowledging you understand that I will release the results of this evaluation, either orally or written or both, to your attorney, John Andrews." Calder slid the form over to Sonny and watched as he read it and signed and dated it as instructed. Calder then wrote his own name on the witness signature line.

"Before I begin my testing of you, I want to return to the point I made earlier which is to encourage you to be as open and honest as you can be. Let me illustrate my point. People who come in for a forensic psychological evaluation approach the evaluation in ways that are dependent on their particular situation, their context if you will. For example, I do a lot of court-appointed custody evaluations and custody litigants almost always answer the many questions and questionnaires and tests in a way that says they do not have any problems. Most custody litigants deny they've ever had any psychological difficulties and usually end up answering questions that make them more saintly than Mother Theresa."

Sonny nervously laughed.

Calder continued: *"On the other end of the spectrum, I do a lot of criminal evaluations for defense attorneys. I might go to a prison to evaluate a defendant who's been charged with murder. I give him many of the very same questions and tests that I do a custody litigant, but he decides to answer the questions in a way that indicates he has every psychological problem ever known and takes the position that he's the craziest human being on the planet. Neither of these ways of responding is accurate. So what I'm saying, Mr. McPherson, is that the degree to which you can be as honest and open as possible during this evaluation, will be helpful to me in providing you and your attorney with an evaluation that means something. Does that make sense?"*

"Yeah, I get where you're coming from, Doc. I got nothing to hide. I ain't no saint, but I never abused anybody either. I'm gonna open myself up, and you can talk to whoever you want to. I want to lay it all out."

"Okay. That sounds good," said Calder. *"One other point I wish to emphasize, Mr. McPherson, is that I am not providing any counseling*

or treatment of you or your children as part of my professional services, either now or in the future. The only hat I am wearing is that of a forensic psychologist who is conducting an evaluation of you for your attorney. I may conclude you need treatment once I have completed my evaluation, but, if that turns out to be the case, I will not be the one who provides you treatment."

Calder remembered picking up the mental status exam recording form from the table and beginning the formal forensic psychological evaluation of Sonny McPherson that, on that day, was to last nine hours. That had been three years ago. Sonny had a lot to say, stemming out of ten years of pent up rage, agony and grief. Calder remembered thinking his story was stranger than fiction. Had Sonny had enough rage to kill Dr. Hughes? Had Calder's assessment missed this potential in this man?

Calder pondered this notion some more and pulled off his sweaty clothes, threw them into the laundry room off the kitchen, and headed naked upstairs to get a shower. A fringe benefit of living deep in the woods was he could wander around in the all together without being seen. Castleheart had four stories with windows on all sides. Only a few windows had shades. One of the best features of his house was a four person hot tub on the back deck overlooking the lake. Bathing suits were not required.

Calder dressed quickly. He wanted to beat Worth to the bar to get his own face time with the new gal in town someone had dubbed the Irish Princess.

Chapter 11

Multiples

November 2005

During their fourth or fifth appointment, Dr. Cooper had wasted no time in pursuing Emma's doubts about the multiple personality disorder, or MPD, diagnosis. She looked at her eighteen-year-old patient and asked as gently as possible, "Emma, please tell me, if you will, what you remember about your doctor's treatment of you, especially about the question of multiple personalities?"

Dr. Cooper had also been thinking about the issue of her professional duty to consider contacting Emma's previous therapist who might be under the impression Emma was still her patient. Emma refused to give Dr. Cooper the name of that therapist. She said she wanted to let sleeping dogs lie. Dr. Cooper had not insisted, but she did encourage Emma to formally end her therapy with this therapist. Emma said she'd take care of it. Dr. Cooper made a conscious decision to accept, for now, Emma's position on this matter. Dr. Cooper was convinced Emma, for all practical purposes, had ended her therapy with her previous doctor, or perhaps fled her therapy, and, if that assumption was correct, Emma was in need of some serious healing. Dr. Cooper decided to trust Emma and not press this issue for now. Sam Cooper was operating on a hypothesis that Emma's first therapist may have been incompetent and done some damage clinically. Emma clearly had some concerns about her previous therapy. Besides, Emma was resisting the idea of such contact, and Dr. Cooper didn't want her new patient to run.

Emma, too, had minor concerns within herself about this issue. Some people might call these pangs of conscience, but that wasn't what was going on in Emma. Being dishonest with Sam, and withholding information, was necessary. Fundamental, she told herself. Emma kept telling herself to keep her eye on the ball.

Prior to finishing high school, Emma had begun reading what she could on multiple personality disorder, repressed memories and satanic ritual abuse, especially from Internet sites, but also from books she could find. She'd found the best source for psychology and psychiatry books was the medical school at East Carolina University, a forty-five minute drive from New Bern. Since beginning her freshman year, she had continued her own research in the UNC psychology library. She had learned that MPD now had a fancy name—Dissociative Identity Disorder, or DID. Emma thought the acronym was a stitch. D.I.D. "DID what?" she'd say to herself. Emma had learned that MPD or DID was considered to be a defensive effort by the psyche that fragmented the identity into various parts called 'alters.' In the late 80's and early 90's, she'd learned the prevailing popular theory among therapists was that MPD was directly related to sexual trauma. Its proponents claimed that when the sexual trauma so overwhelmed the personality, the personal identity shattered, and the individual developed two or more identities. Emma had read with fascination that as more and more victims reported their abuse, thanks to the nationwide attention sexual victimization was finally getting, the number of MPD's in professionals' clinical practices in the United States had exploded. Emma had learned from her momma that Dr. Hughes had known of one famous psychiatrist who had reported at a conference that he had at least twenty MPD's in his caseload. He claimed one patient alone had sixty personalities or 'alters.'

According to what Emma had learned from her momma, once she had begun treating Emma and her sister, Dr. Hughes had sought clinical consultation with this psychiatrist and she was convinced the cure for the sexual trauma experienced by her patients lay in the reintegration of the shattered selves. She saw it as her mission to identify the children's alters. Emma had framed this in her mind as a fairytale metaphor: *you couldn't put Humpty Dumpty back together again until you knew how many broken pieces there were to assemble.*

Emma's research into the history and diagnosis of MPD also led her to discover a body of research in which some skeptical people questioned the legitimacy of the causal connection between MPD or DID and child sexual abuse. She also learned the issues surrounding the legitimacy of satanic ritual abuse—or SRA as some called it— were very controversial.

Responding to Sam's question, Emma told Sam that her former therapist used to probe in a repetitive and seemingly endless manner.

Dr. Cooper looked at Emma and asked, "Can you recall an example of this kind of treatment?"

Emma closed her eyes and dredged her memories to the surface. She described for Dr. Cooper what she'd been through. She recalled a painful appointment as a child:

"I had fought with Momma about going to see the doctor that day. I didn't want to go. Me and my sister were still seeing Daddy. Daddy had been grilling me about whether or not Momma had taken me to see a doctor. I had clammed up, but Daddy got mad. You have to tell me, he'd say. He'd scream, 'Your momma has no right to take you to see anyone without my approval.' I got confused. I didn't know what he meant. He got even madder. He told me to not say anything. About what? I'd ask. Momma told me I had to go. She told me to tell everything. About what? I'd ask. I told Momma I didn't want to go. I threw a fit. I told her Daddy said I didn't have to. That made Momma mad. 'You have to go. It's important. If your daddy did something, you have to tell.' About what? I'd say. She'd scream, 'If your daddy's hurt you, you have to tell. If he's hurt you or your sister, the doctor will help you. She's good with kids, she's a God-fearing Christian woman, she knows. You have to go. Now stop crying and go get ready.' My momma was spitting nails, so we went."

"All three of us. Me, my sister, and Momma. Pointing her finger at me, Momma had said right off, 'She's been crying, Doctor. She didn't want to come. Her daddy told her not to come. I'm afraid to send her back there this weekend. It's his time for visitation, but I'm afraid to send them back. If he's hurting them, well, I have to protect them, no matter what. Even if it means violating the court order. Please help me.' Momma was pleading with my therapist. Momma could be very persuasive."

"My therapist then smiled at Momma, like she was in on a joke that nobody else knew about. She knew what she was doing. She knew she had a big fish on the line. I remember her saying calmly to my momma, 'Let me talk with Emma. I'll see what I can do.' My momma pleaded, 'Please help us, Doctor. Please. You're our only hope. He has lots of money and powerful rich attorneys. You're our only line of defense. Don't let him hurt my children anymore.' I can still see Momma crying buckets."

Sam noticed that Emma was describing all this in a factual, emotion-free manner—almost surgical. Her patient appeared cut-off from her feelings about what she was describing. Sam also thought it was odd for a an eighteen year old to have such clear memories about what people had said and the words they used, like 'court order,' so many years ago.

Emma continued, "I remember going down this long hallway. I slumped onto the floor of the therapy room. I remember making a clear decision. Best be a clam today. Everybody's mad at me. Momma and Daddy can't get along because of me. The doctor switched on something I later learned was a video camera. She taped all our sessions like we were some kind of social experiment. She never told me or my sister she was taping. 'Emma, who are you today?' she had asked me. 'Can you tell me, Emma?' I shook my head. 'No.' She had said, 'Well, can you draw who you are?' The doctor gave me a piece of paper and a box of crayons. I shook my head again. My refusal apparently made her try something else. She brought out those fucking dolls again."

Sam noted this change in tone. There was a lot of anger there. Emma's emotional lability was creating some concern for Sam.

Emma went on, "She reached into her special little voodoo cabinet right beside her chair and pulled out a box. She put the box on the floor and handed me one of the four dolls from the box. I'd seen these before. This time, she gave me the daddy doll. She had said, 'These are those special dolls, remember? If you take off his clothes, you'll see what I mean.' I was curious. The doctor removed the shirt and pants from the doll. It had a floppy penis-like thing. I took hold of the penis. She then asked me, 'Do you know what that is?' I nodded my head. 'Have you ever seen one?' she asked. I'd seen my little cousin's when he was taking a bath. That's what I was thinking of. 'Yes', I said. 'Have you ever touched one?' she asked. 'No', I said. 'Whose have you seen, Emma?' I had continued to play with the doll's penis. It was odd. Why did this doll have this thing? I had wondered. She had then asked, 'Has anyone ever had you hold their penis?' I was confused. At that time, I didn't know what the word penis meant. I didn't understand what she was asking."

"The doctor then took the clothes off the next doll and handed me the little girl doll. 'What do you call that?' as she pointed to the doll's nose. 'A nose,' I said. 'And that?' A boobie?' I said. 'And that?' A gina,' I said. 'Good girl,' she had said, like I was a puppy. 'Has anyone ever touched your gina?' she then asked. Momma and Daddy had both bathed me since I had been born, Momma mostly, and Momma had showed me how to wipe myself from the front to rear, but I thought this doctor ought to know that, since she was a girl, too. 'Yes,' I said. Then she had asked, 'Has anyone touched you in a way that you didn't like?' I thought about the shower that my daddy had made me and my sister take at the beach after we had sat all day in the sand at the water's edge. My bottom, front and back, had gotten very red and sore. After I was dry, my daddy had made me put some stuff on it from a tube. It had hurt. It had stung. Answering as best I could, I had told the doctor, 'Daddy did at the beach.'"

"I remember the doctor pausing. This had obviously been an important therapeutic moment."

Sam had sensed the sarcastic bitterness in Emma's description. There was a coldness - a distance in the way Emma described her past therapy that concerned Sam. Sam had begun thinking maybe she was seeing a dissociative process in her patient at work. Or maybe some type of depersonalization. Sam had also begun considering some character disorder might be manifesting itself. Whatever it was, Sam had begun seeing a detachment in the way her patient described things that was concerning.

Emma sensed Sam was watching her closely, scanning her in a way that her momma did, but more artfully. Emma told herself to stay focused, and be careful. This woman is no fool, she admonished herself.

Emma continued, 'Did he use his hand?' the doctor had asked. I had nodded. I didn't want Momma to be mad. I so wanted to tell the truth. 'What did you say to your daddy when he did that?' she had asked. 'It hurt,' I had said. 'It stings.'"

My therapist had then asked, 'When you told your daddy it hurt, did he stop?' 'No,' I said, 'He made me rub myself. It hurt.'"

'Emma,' my doctor had said, quickly, 'Let's go out to the waiting room and see your momma and sister.' It was an abrupt ending, but I had been glad. I threw the girl doll down on top of the daddy doll. I'm sure the doctor saw me do that. She then again said, 'Let's go see your momma and sister,' like she couldn't wait to get me out of there. Instead of moving, I had sat and stared into nothingness. I just sat there on the floor for about five minutes, staring at the wall. The doctor had asked me 'Where was I?' I had had no idea what she was talking about. I hadn't moved. She had then asked me, 'Who are you?'"

Emma then looked at Sam and said, "I think it was the day she interpreted my silence and confusion as dissociation."

Sam then asked a direct, sensible question: "How do you know you weren't dissociating?"

Emma's heart raced. She knew she had to be careful here. Be cool, she told herself. "Because all it was," she stammered, "was a little girl's confusion. I had told the doctor I hadn't seen a grown-up penis, or held one, but she ignored me. I had told her the truth about how we got sore. Being speechless is different from being fragmented. I was just being a little kid and had been trying to tell the truth." Emma cried as she said this last part.

Emma then cut off her tears, looked at Dr. Cooper. She had her attention now. "I was glad to be out of her office. I remember the doctor giving my momma a brief nod as we had entered the waiting room. I had learned later it was that day my therapist telephoned the Craven County Department of Social Services and reported my daddy for suspected child sexual abuse."

"I remember what she had said to Momma, 'I have to make a telephone call. Why don't you three just wait here and I'll be back in a few minutes?' Momma had become hysterical. What the doctor had said about having to make a telephone call had set Momma off. 'Should I come with you, Doctor?' Momma had said. 'No,' the doctor had said to Momma as she left us in the waiting room. 'I have the information I need. It'll only take a few minutes.'"

"On that day, my doctor reported suspected sexual abuse of me by my father. She told the authorities my parents were separated and me and my sister were supposed to be with our father for the next weekend and both she and my mother were worried about that. She apparently added it was possible that this was a dangerous situation for both of us, although the only information she had at the present time was that I had been victimized."

Sam's analytic mind had begun to spin. She had witnessed her young patient go from a cold, detached state, to a seemingly genuine tearful state, drop quickly away from her tears, and then reveal detailed information about the allegations made against her father a child would normally not know, or have access to. Sam didn't think Emma was simply recalling memories from childhood. How had she come to know these things? Sam wondered. Sam had wanted to ask, but she decided she should wait.

Emma had continued: "I remember my momma had become a nervous wreck. Momma had begun clutching Starr and me, pressing us close to her body. Then the doctor motioned for Momma to step out into the hallway off the waiting room, and Momma bolted out the door into the hall. The door between the waiting room and hallway was left cracked open. I remember the doctor said to Momma ever so calmly, without any effort to keep me from hearing it, 'Well, Emma has made a good disclosure, and I have reported it to Child Protective Services. Someone will be out to your house this afternoon, so I suggest you and the girls just go there and wait.'"

"'What did Emma say?' Momma had then exclaimed."

"The doctor had then said, 'She disclosed that her father touched her in her privates in a way that hurt, and when she told him it hurt, he made her touch herself.'"

"'Oh my God,' my momma had said. Momma had started to cry."

"The doctor then said, 'It apparently happened at the beach. Were they at the beach together?'"

"'Yes,' my momma had said. 'Just this past weekend.'"

"The good doctor then asked, 'Did Emma ever say anything?' Momma had told her that our privates were very red and irritated when we had come home from seeing our daddy, but my daddy insisted it was from our being in wet bathing suits all day. She told the doctor she hadn't known what to believe but had said she put some Desenex on us, and we seemed okay."

Emma had taken a deep breath and said, "I remember very well the doctor saying the next thing to my momma, 'Well, I'm afraid it may have been more than a wet bathing suit.'"

"I can remember the look Momma had on her face when she came to get us to go home. I had learned what Momma looked like when the worry creeped in and the lava began to flow. Something was wrong, I had screamed inside myself. What have I done this time? I had wondered. I quit talking for three weeks. I never saw my daddy or my dog again for ten years."

Samantha Cooper had been very moved by this story. She had continued to be struck by the fact that her patient had not cried, especially at the very end of her story about not seeing her father or her dog for the next ten years. In fact, except for that brief moment a few minutes earlier, Emma hadn't shown much emotion at all. To borrow Emma's own description of her mother, Sam had concluded Emma had her own lava flow, except it remained magma that flowed beneath the surface.

Although the hour was almost up, Sam ventured the question she had held onto earlier: "Emma, how did you come to learn about the details of the report of suspected child abuse your therapist made to Craven County DSS?"

Emma hadn't seen this coming, but she was practiced at the art of deception. "Momma learned these things over time, and as I got older, she filled me in. I may have learned some of these things from my therapist. I'm not exactly sure. How come you wanna know?" Emma was feeling wary.

Sam had then said, "It sounded like you learned more than a kid would typically know about these things. I was just curious, that's all. We can talk about it some more if you wish. I guess we'd better stop for today. Our time is up."

Emma had walked out of Sam's office feeling worried. Threatened. She was mad at herself for being careless. She had known she needed to go think things through. Her new therapy had to be seamless and flawless. Stupid bitch, she said to herself.

Sam was disquieted by her appointment that day with Emma. It wasn't just the distance from her emotions that concerned Sam. That was a common problem for many clinical patients. Sam had developed a gut feeling Emma was holding something back, something important. Sam had become worried that her patient was maybe being dishonest with her, maybe manipulating her. Were there legitimate borderline issues at work here? Sam knew Emma had struggled with not accidentally revealing the name of her previous therapist, but Sam had accepted that this issue would resolve itself over time. What was gnawing at Sam was the sense that Emma was being too careful, was choosing her words too judiciously. Knowing how to respond to patients' manipulations was part of a therapist's job. She finished her last note and dropped Emma McPherson's file on her desk. What's Emma up to? Sam wondered.

Her appointment with Emma had been her last for the day, and as she sat writing her notes and sipping her hot tea, she had decided it might be good to talk with another colleague about her concerns. Ethically, she could consult without revealing any confidential material. Sam thought about who, among her colleagues, was experienced with child custody conflict, sexual abuse, MPD, and the child abuse reporting law, from both a clinical and forensic perspective. She scrolled through her rolodex and found Calder Miro's office telephone number. She called him and left a voice mail message requesting a return call.

Emma had walked from Sam's office to Franklin Street to the Carolina Coffee Shop and was sitting by herself in a booth. She was making notes in her journal. She was agitated. Two of her classmates walked by and saw her. "Hi, Colleen," one of them said."

"Hi," she said back, but she didn't look up. Her friends moved on, sensing she was busy and didn't want to be disturbed.

As they left the restaurant, one friend said to the other, "What's up with that?"

The other girl said, "Colleen is, like, one of the brightest girls I know, but she can be weird as shit. Sometimes she'll be real friendly and nice, and other times, she can be a bitch. She's hard to figure out. All the guys I know are, like, totally hot for her, though. That body of hers is da bomb."

Chapter 12

Dial a Colleague

November 2005

Calder checked his email with his laptop and saw that his secretary told him he'd had a voice mail message left the day before from Samantha Cooper, a fellow psychologist in Chapel Hill whom he had met several years ago at a continuing education seminar. Her message said she was calling to ask about a possible consult with him. Calder didn't know her well, but he'd heard from others that she was an above-average clinician. She'd left some times in her message he'd be likely to reach her.

With his two homeboys—Blackjack and Jonah—exercised, loved, and fed, Calder poured himself a short Woodford over ice and wandered to his favorite chair on the porch overlooking the lake. He reached Sam Cooper with his cell on the third ring.

"Hello, this is Dr. Cooper," she answered.

"Dr. Cooper, this Calder Miro returning your call. Is this still a good time for you to speak?"

"Yes, it is. Thanks for calling me back. And, please call me Samantha or Sam, whichever you prefer. May I call you Calder?"

"Calder's good, Sam. How's life in Chapel Hill?"

"Life's full and busy. My family and my practice keep me hopping. How's New Bern treating you?"

Calder decided it was not time for him to talk about his wife's death. He said, "Life's pretty full, but good." He changed directions and silently sipped the Woodford. "What's the nature of the consult you're looking for?"

"Well, it's about a clinical case I have with one of my patients who's a student at Carolina. There are some historical legal and forensic overtones in the case I'd like to consult about. I want to do this straight up and pay you for a professional, confidential consultation."

"I normally charge colleagues the same highest rate they get paid," Calder responded. "If this is a clinical consult, then my fee would be what you get paid hourly by your best paying customer; if this is a forensic consult, my fee is what you would charge for a forensic consult or court appearance. Sound fair?"

"Very fair," Sam said. "I make $150 per hour for my clinical work and I don't do any forensic work and fight like hell to stay out of court, so I have no established forensic fee. I've called you because of your clinical and forensic expertise, so quote me a combo rate. I'll supersize my clinical rate a bit."

"How's $200 sound?"

"Deal."

Sam then sketched out for Calder her concerns and questions. She told him about the bind her patient had put her in by not giving Sam the name of the patient's first therapist who Sam had suspected had done some clinical harm to her patient through misdiagnoses and bad treatment. Sam worked hard to disguise her patient's identity. Calder agreed with Sam's reasoning behind not pushing this issue too hard. Sam's descriptions of her patient's clinical history led Calder and her to talk about her patient's MPD or DID history. Sam said the thing that was bothering her is that her patient seemed to have a lot of information about her parents' divorce and details from the child protection records.

Sam then said, "I've always had the impression those records are highly confidential. Is that true?"

"Yes and no. Under normal circumstances, they are very difficult to gain access to and it takes a court order, and even then a lot of judges will review them in camera before deciding whether or not to release them. On the other hand, if a judge is convinced by, say a court-appointed custody evaluator, that he or she needs to review the child protection file, then the evaluator usually gets it because the judge orders it, but even then the records aren't released to anyone else. Did your patient ever go through a divorce or custody fight?"

"Yes, as a child. My patient's knowledge of things, though, seemed like something my patient would have had to learn when my patient was much older."

"Unfortunately, Sam, sometimes warring parents, as I'm sure you know, tell their children all kinds of inappropriate things, show them the divorce pleadings in which the parents say horrible things about each other, discuss child support issues, and do other things that keep the children stuck in the middle of their parents' hostilities. These are the kinds of parental actions that sow the seeds of alienation."

"How would a child caught in a high-conflict divorce learn details from child protection records?" Sam asked. "Parents don't get access to these records, do they?"

"No, parents don't usually get to see them. Were there allegations of child abuse or neglect in your patient's parents' divorce?"

"Yeah, apparently pretty bad ones, especially child sexual abuse that led to the MPD diagnosis. Because of the allegations, my patient said she lost contact with one parent for over a decade."

This detail made Calder catch his breath. Suddenly, Calder was struck with the realization Sam's patient could possibly be one of the McPherson daughters.

"Sam," Calder said.

"Yes?" Sam queried.

"I might know this case. In fact, I might know a lot about this case. What you've told me is ringing some bells. If it's your goal to guarantee your patient is not known to me, maybe we'd better stop and call it a day."

Sam thought about this. "Okay," she said. Then she asked, "Hypothetically, you could have been involved in my patient's life somehow, maybe in a forensic capacity, and the sketch I've given you thus far makes you concerned you might know who I'm treating?"

"Yeah, that sums it up."

"Okay, then, let's stop. I'm not sure what to make of what this means. It could be coincidental, but no harm done, because you're not going to tell anyone, or it may turn out to be a good thing, because if the person in your case is the person in my case, that could be helpful."

"Let's both think about it. The confidentiality issues run both ways. You can't talk about my hypothetical involvement either, because subjects of my evaluations have a right to privacy, too, although often far less so if things enter the public record."

"Got it," Sam said. "I'll be in touch. Do you have my address so you can send me a bill?"

"Yes, I have it, but I'm not going to bill you. This has been a short call and I'm conflicted out possibly, so no harm, no foul," responded Calder. "Nice hearing from you. Keep me posted on your thinking. Bye."

"Bye," said Sam.

"Wow," Sam thought to herself.

"Damn," Calder muttered out loud. He drained his Woodford.

Chapter 13

The Red Bottom Weekend

September 2006

Calder's phone rang as he was pouring his first cup of coffee, after he had served, of course, his feline and canine companions.

"What's for breakfast?" Worth asked.

"I was planning on cereal and fruit."

"Way too healthy, white boy. You got any eggs and bacon?"

"Yeah," Calder said, "as long as you can accept turkey bacon."

"Making turkeys into bacon just ain't right," snorted Worth. "Something unnatural about that. Put pigs out of business."

"Flex a little. It'll expand your intellectual horizons and improve your diet."

"Okay, but I know I ain't gonna like it," responded Worth. "I need to talk some more about Dr. Hughes and her patients. You got any biscuits to go with that turkey?"

"I got seven grain toast or English muffins."

"I might have to arrest you for perpetrating a breakfast fraud. I'm turning onto your road now. See you in a few."

Calder hung up the phone and put a frying pan on the gas stove with some high heat. Calder pulled the eggs and turkey bacon from the refrigerator and wished he hadn't told Worth about the turkey so he could have seen his face after the first bite. As Calder turned down the burner and added the bacon to the pan, Worth came in the back door. He was dressed to the nines: a custom-made, Italian three-piece suit with a pale blue shirt with a French collar and a Ben Silver silk tie in yellow and blue stripes.

Calder whistled and eyed his friend from head to toe. "Man, you're looking studly. Why are you so dressed up?"

"Got to testify this afternoon in another murder trial. Turns out, juries like well-dressed, handsome black men. Judges don't mind it either." Looking at the pan, Worth said, "Is that the suspect bacon?"

"Yep. You're gonna love it. What did you decide about the bread? Toast or muffins?"

"Toast will be fine." Opening the refrigerator door, Worth said, "If you tell me you don't have any real butter, I'm gonna have to shoot you."

"I've got butter." Calder decided he'd better be careful and not let Worth see he was going to cook the eggs in olive oil. Calder then asked, "So where are you with your investigation?"

Pouring himself a cup of coffee, Worth straddled one of the stools next to the butcher block counter in the kitchen and opened his brief case. He pulled out some files and his note pad.

"My chief and the D.A. have agreed you can officially consult with me on this case and see the evidence," he said. "The D.A.'s gonna find you some consulting funds so you can maintain your lavish lifestyle. Here's what I'm thinking. Using the approximate date of 1990, give or take a few years, which is when the lab analysis puts the manufacture of the paper that was found in Dr. Hughes' mouth, I got a court order and went through Dr. Hughes' files at her office. I made a list of Dr. Hughes' cases she worked on around 1990. She saw mostly children for therapy and obviously used drawings, often crayon drawings, as one of her methods." Worth then slid a fat manila file across the counter towards Calder, and said, "Check this out."

The file was frayed and a bit yellow from age and was held together with a big rubber band. Calder pulled the rubber band off and opened the file. It appeared to contain some hand-written notes, many children's drawings, as well as various pieces of correspondence. Many of these letters were on letterheads from various law firms. The tab on the file said McPherson. The file also contained a manila envelope addressed to Dr. Hughes with Calder's return address on it. Calder knew right away what was inside the envelope. After he had submitted his written report on the evaluation of Sonny McPherson and the child sex abuse allegations in 2001, Sonny and Ruth's attorneys had, by agreement, instructed Calder to send a copy of his report to Dr. Hughes.

Worth looked at Calder and said, "I think we got ourselves an amazing coincidence here. You weren't very complimentary of Dr. Hughes in that report. If you turned up dead, she'd be a suspect. You ain't gonna burn that turkey, are you?"

Adjusting the bacon with a fork, Calder said, "No, I wasn't a big fan of hers nor was she of me, but I'm assuming I'm not a suspect. You know, my report basically stated there was good reason to believe her methods were iatrogenic, that her therapy was biased in support of the allegations, incompetent and destructive, not only to the father-daughter relationships, but to the girls' psyches as well. Although the way she conducted her therapy was pretty commonplace during the 80's and early 90's, it still did a lot of damage. The thing that really got me was when I interviewed her, it was as if she was stuck in a time warp and was incapable of considering that she and the children's mother may have contributed to any of the chaos in the McPherson family. She was quite defensive. She appeared to have no awareness of the impact of the parental conflict on the children, showed no inclination there was any possibility that any of my critique had any merit, nor did she appear to have any understanding of the alienation issues in the case. I know she and the mom wrote me off as a hired gun."

Worth poured himself another cup of coffee and added, "I suspect they and the mother's attorney saw you as a high-priced whore, Doctor." Worth then asked, "What do you mean, stuck in a time warp?"

Calder laid the bacon pieces on a paper towel and Worth snatched one up with a deft move. He chewed slowly. Calder could see the bacon evaluation wheels turning.

"Turkey passes, but it ain't bacon. Next time, I'll bring my own. It ain't natural to cook something called bacon and not have any grease left in the pan."

"You won't have any grease left in your arteries, either, my friend," Calder retorted. "Dr. Hughes, like a lot of therapists, myself included, used methods and made assumptions that have turned out to be harmful, misguided, and just plain wrong. Until the mid-1990's, the mental health and child protection world, including law enforcement, knew little about how to interview children who might have endured some type of trauma, and it was common practice to lead children, unintentionally, to certain conclusions. These methods were very damaging in cases of suspected child sexual abuse because the interviewing techniques sometimes led to false positives. Some of the more infamous day care cases in America got their start from inept interviewing of the suspected child victims."

"Meaning perps got identified who maybe weren't perps?"

"Exactly," Calder said. "In research language, such a thing is called a false positive. Over time, thanks to the work of people like Stephen Ceci and others, we came to realize there are techniques and methods that help children during interviews tell the truth without being negatively or inadvertently influenced by the interviewer's bias."

"So..."

Calder interrupted Worth's interruption, and started waving his fork in the air. "In addition to using poor interviewing methods, therapists and child interviewers had inaccurate models of how children remember things. Further, there was a blind acceptance of some fantastic, outrageous elements in children's accounts of abuse. Wrongly believing that children don't lie or make things up, combined with a naïve view or blindness about our own contributions to the mess, therapists accepted outlandish stories as gospel. And, to make matters worse, a simple notion swept across this great land of ours that child abuse, particularly child sexual abuse, was at the heart of most mental health and behavioral problems. So, if a child was acting out at home or school, or if an adult patient had depression or anxiety as her presenting problems, the therapist, following the prevailing theory at the time, rooted around the patient's psyche looking for evidence of abuse. Cases weren't approached with the idea of 'maybe there's an abuse history here,' but with the assumption 'there's abuse here, I just have to bring it to the surface.'" Calder finally paused.

Worth looked at Calder and said wryly, "Why don't you tell me what you really think, Professor?"

Calder heard his tone and said, "Yeah, okay, I'm pissed. I was no angel. I made some of these mistakes too. I think most therapists got excited about the possibility that one cause could explain many psychiatric conditions. All therapists did, but things got out of hand, and I witnessed many of my colleagues, who were bright and well-trained therapists, lose their objectivity and their sense of skepticism. It seemed almost overnight everyone was focused on abuse as the cause of most mental illness. The thing that really got to me was how so many of my colleagues during the mid to late 80's began reporting that their practices were full of multiple personality and borderline patients. It was like an invasion had happened overnight. I was stunned at how many people I knew who were suddenly treating MPD's. Repressed sexually traumatic memories were flying to the surface under this new popular regime of therapy. Multiple personality disorder and borderline personality disorder got linked in rather unscientific ways to horrible abuse histories. Many otherwise reasonable therapists and child protection investigators accepted without question their patients' or clients' tales of satanic abuse. Post traumatic stress disorder or PTSD became the diagnosis *du jour.* Dr. Hughes was one of these therapists. The problem was, when I examined the McPherson case, not only had she appeared to approach the case in a highly biased manner, she showed no flexibility in her thinking ten years later."

"What woke you up to all this?" asked Worth. "You gonna get to them eggs or do I hafta cook?"

"I'm on the eggs. Over easy." Calder continued. "While there was certainly a possibility Sonny McPherson and his family had molested his daughters, the way he described how he lost contact with his daughters and what happened to them and him was not only plausible, but also, in a historical sense, had a familiar ring to it. Sonny's account of the events led his children to accuse him of child sexual abuse and, over time, to accuse his family of satanic ritual abuse and child pornography had all the elements of a certain type of child sexual abuse case that I had come to call the 'red bottom weekend.' I didn't think of myself as especially enlightened or anything, but just by paying attention to common sense and the emerging research, it became clear to me that some of the more bizarre claims of some of the children in the more famous day care cases were hard to swallow.

"There's that phrase again."

Calder realized what he had just said. "Yeah, interesting, huh? I said that without thinking."

"Kinda like a Freudian slip."

"Nah," Calder responded. "More like a Jungian t-shirt."

"You hilarious, white bread."

Calder positioned himself between Worth and the stove, so he could pour the olive oil in the pan without Worth seeing it. He cracked six eggs into the pan, turned the gas down low and placed a glass lid on the pan. The secret to cooking good eggs was to let the steam cook the yolks.

Worth then asked, "What's the 'red bottom weekend' thing?"

"As I shifted my practice more and more into forensic psychology, I began to take on an increasing number of court-appointed evaluations in child custody cases. Many of these cases had allegations of child sexual abuse embedded in them, and over time I began to see a pattern. These were cases in which one parent, usually the mom, was the primary custodian of young children. She gets the kids back from a weekend with their father, a daddy-come-lately, because before the separation, he had little to no experience in the care of his children's toileting needs, especially little girls. The kids would return from visitation and have some vaginal or anal irritation or urinary tract infection. Mom would ask the kids what happened, they would say, 'daddy touched me,' and mom would go nuts, thinking the worst about a man she used to be in love with and married to. Out of defensive fear, Daddy would deny he ever touched the girls, even though he probably had made some clumsy efforts at helping his daughters' toileting or bathing needs, and the case would explode."

"Sonny had taken the girls to the beach and Disney World on one of his weekends and they had essentially lived in wet bathing suits for two days. The dampness and sand had irritated both girls' bottoms and Sonny had done a lousy job of some basic caretaking. He had applied some Desitin ointment to both children, but, as the accusations started to fly, he stupidly denied he had ever touched them."

Worth got two plates out of the cabinet, lathered butter on his toast, and layered on a thick layer of strawberry preserves. "Your analysis was the McPherson case had its roots as a red bottom weekend?"

"Yeah," Calder said. "In a small percentage of divorced families, the conflict and animosity between the parents reaches epic proportions before the children are even born. Sonny and Ruth, the children's mother, were one such couple. They fought with each other from day one. Their first baby, Colleen, was born out of passion, but with little or no love for each other. The second child, Starr was conceived in a similar manner. They thought having a second baby might save their marriage. In these types of cases, the marital conflict becomes a caldron that contains most of the baser human emotions that simmer to toxic levels. These are couples who, during a forensic interview, cannot recall or articulate any positive attributes—past or present—about one another. One or both of them has some serious psychopathology."

Pouring himself some more coffee, Calder continued, "When the girls came home from the visitation weekend with Sonny and complained to their mother of vaginal irritation, the climate between Sonny and Ruth was strained to the point that Ruth impulsively assumed Sonny had molested both girls. She was already mad as hell at him for a bunch of things. The children were put through a series of leading, suggestive interviews by their mother, grandmother, social workers, and Dr. Hughes confirmed sexual victimization. Under Dr. Hughes' therapy, the girls were diagnosed with some serious mental illnesses, including borderline personality, multiple personality disorder and post traumatic stress disorder. Both girls eventually described being victims of horrible sadistic abuse that had elements of Satanism and being the objects of child pornography."

Calder slid the eggs onto their plates. He noticed Worth already had eaten two pieces of bacon and toast. Worth worked one of the eggs onto another piece of toast and ate half of it in one bite. He reached over and pulled a paper towel off the roll and wiped his mouth, followed with a big gulp of coffee, and then said,

"So what I don't get is, if they're not true, where do these satanic ideas come from?"

Calder sampled his eggs and was satisfied with the quality. "Man, that's a great question, and I'm not sure anyone really knows, but it appears that fantastic images described as being real can arise out of a child's response to adults' questions, and they arise out of adults' simplistic assumptions something evil has to be at work, because it's evil that causes humans to molest children. The co-mingling of adult and child images of evil—the devil and his agents—with biased and suggestive questions, a child's desire to please adults, and a hysterical, prosecutorial, non-skeptical drive to get to the root of the evil, all combine to create a modern-day equivalent of Dante's *Inferno*. And that can sometimes lead to a witch hunt. Throw in a heavy dose of Christian fundamentalism and New Age therapy, as was true in the McPherson case, and you have yourself a bona fide crusade."

"So what made you so sure Sonny wasn't a pervert?"

"I was never 100% certain," Calder responded, "but his story was plausible, my psychological testing of him suggested nothing really concerning, and my analysis of the collateral information and my interviews tended to corroborate Sonny's side of things." Calder ate some more of his eggs and bacon, then continued.

"One of the more telling moments during my evaluation was when I called one of your colleagues, Detective Mark Smith, whose name had shown up in the file as having investigated the sex abuse allegations. I had known him from several previous cases. When I called him and explained my involvement with the McPherson case, there was a long pause at the other end of the line—I thought maybe we'd been disconnected. Then he said the most amazing thing, 'You know, Dr. Miro, I keep a small stack of files on my desk that I just know I'll hear something about again.' To which I said, 'Do you mean you've had the McPherson file on your desk for ten years?' And he said 'Yeah.' I said, 'Well, this is the call.' It was like he had a stack of cold child sexual abuse cases, and the McPherson case had remained in that stack.

"Then Smith went on to tell me he thought the mother was loony tunes and the kids' accounts of things kept getting more and more bizarre. He said the kids' accounts never quite squared with what the mother and grandmother told him the kids said to them. He said he had conducted a forensic analysis of the alleged satanic ritual sites, including the McPherson plantation, and had found zero evidence. The kids said they were forced to watch men in devil masks and goat suits dance through fire, saw people cut up babies on an altar, dance around naked, and film the whole thing. They said their grandfather was the cameraman. Before it was all over, Detective Smith said the girls and their mother had named about 15 perpetrators. Detective Smith said, 'I, quite frankly, believed it was a load of hogwash and I told that to the D.A.'"

Calder continued, "As the case developed after I submitted my report, I had my own interview with Dr. Hughes. I interviewed her at her office and she told me she had destroyed all her records of the children's therapy after seven years, which is the length of time required by North Carolina law for hanging onto records."

Worth looked at the folder sitting on the kitchen counter and made a stabbing gesture with his fork. "So the doc was lying to you, huh?"

"Looks that way," Calder said. "I think she knew enough to know she needed to be careful with me and the girls' father, but she had no qualms about the fact that she had given two small children diagnoses of MPD and she had no question or skepticism about the satanic ritual abuse, or SRA as she kept calling it. Here we were at the beginning of the twenty-first century and she had a mindset like an inquisitor at the Salem witch trials. She had never met or spoken with Sonny McPherson and believed he was Lucifer himself. I left her office that day thinking she was a dangerous zealot."

Worth then said, "Well, you're gonna find a reading of her file interesting. Her billing records indicate she continued to see both children periodically throughout their childhood and adolescence. She apparently videotaped a lot, maybe all, of her appointments with each child, but I didn't find any tapes, and her file contains almost no notes about her treatment of the girls. She saw both children after your report. According to her notes, that appear to have been made during appointments and telephone calls with the girls' mother, both children had an abiding hatred and fear of their father—coupled with an unquestioned devotion to their mother. Colleen agreed to see her father after your report came out, if he paid her way to college, which he did apparently. Hughes' last appointment with Colleen appears to have been just as Colleen was accepted to UNC. I would guess Starr is still, I mean, until the doctor's death, the dead doctor was still treating Starr."

Calder picked up the photos of the drawing and the sketch Worth had made, and said, "So if the murderer put the drawing in her mouth, who might want to make such a point?"

Between munches of toast, Worth replied, "According to your report, there's a host of possibilities. Daddy's number one, but the kids also named a bunch of satanic perps, any one of whom might be pissed. And then there's this fellow, Johnny Santos, who lived next to the doctor on Ocracoke. Last, but not least, there are the girls themselves."

"Who's this Santos guy?"

"He's a neighbor Dr. Hughes screwed out of a sweet property deal."

"Not likely he'd have access to any drawings, is it?"

"No," Worth replied, "but he may be cagey. He's still on my early list of possibles. Santos is a sleaze. What say you and I go to Ocracoke for a little detecting and fishing? We could interview him, check out the doctor's house again, interview some neighbors, and catch us some blues. You need to get that jeep dirty."

"When you want to leave?" asked Calder.

"Tomorrow. Tonight we got to see which one of us is hotter."

"You mean…?"

"Maggie, the bartender," Worth mused. "If she got taste, she'll go for hot chocolate. If she lonely and blind, she might fall for skim milk."

Calder grinned. He was certain neither one of them had scored big points with her yet, but persistence might pay off. "In terms of tomorrow, I need to check my calendar. We'll come back Sunday afternoon?"

"Yeah, that'll work for me." Worth sopped up the last bit of yolk with his fourth piece of toast. "One more thing," he said.

"What's that?"

"The olive oil tasted good."

Chapter 14

Blues Brothers

Part of Ocracoke's allure to travelers is that it is so damn hard to get to. Even after making it to the ferry landing at Cedar Island, it is still a good two and a quarter hour ride across Pamlico Sound. Worth had booked a couple of rooms at Oscar's B&B. The owner, Ann, is a native North Carolinian with what people would call an old soul. In addition to running a successful B&B, she is a first class photographer, massage therapist, shamanistic healer, and a minister. She loves gathering her guests around the table and swapping stories. Ann is known for serving the best breakfast on the island, which naturally elevates her to goddess status in Worth's eyes. Calder hoped her shamanistic self might incline her towards turkey bacon.

Worth had already called ahead to Garrish, so the ferrymen were waiting to load Calder's jeep in a prime spot. Garrish had also cleared it so they could have a little eyeball to eyeball with Santos and inspect the doctor's house again.

The drive from Morehead City to Cedar Island always seemed to these old friends one of the most beautiful drives in the world. Departing the port of Morehead City over a vast bridge span, the journey opened into a magical world of unobstructed spaces and muted colors of grays and browns only sea air and salt marshes can create. The road ran right along the edge of the water. To Calder it felt a little like being on a race track built on top of an ocean marsh.

Calder picked up Worth at 5:30 AM on the nose. He had cleared his calendar and his secretary had agreed to hold the wolves at bay. Calder had the important stuff. Warm clothes, rain gear, cooler, sunscreen, fishing rod and tackle. They planned to see Santos and inspect Dr. Hughes' house by lunch and be on the south end of the beach by high tide, or "hoiy toide" as the locals say.

Worth got in and Calder handed him a thermos cup of Peet's coffee. Calder had become a devotee of Peet's when he lived in the San Francisco area and thought it was, bar none, the world's best.

Worth took a sip and said, "So, I been thinking."

"Easy there, it's still early," Calder jabbed.

Worth ignored him, "If Sonny was such an innocent lamb, why'd he roll over without a fight and give up his children? Seems to me if he'd fought the allegations, he'd have won. Maybe he'd even have gotten custody if Momma really was yanking everybody's chain."

"That might be true," said Calder, "if the allegations and circumstances were to happen today. But in the political and social climate of the '80's and '90's, he was a hair's breadth from having criminal charges filed against him. I interviewed his former attorney during my evaluation, and he confirmed he'd advised Sonny to walk away from his children rather than run the risk of going to prison."

"Yeah, but you said Detective Smith decided the allegations were bullshit and recommended a no-file to the D.A."

"That's true. But that wasn't true, or hadn't been decided yet, at the time when Sonny's lawyer gave him that advice. The newspapers at that time were full of stories of people going to prison because of convictions of child sexual abuse. Successfully defending against sexual abuse allegations was mission impossible. Given the way things were at the time, I think Sonny's attorney probably gave him sage advice."

"But there was a bigger reason he walked away from his children. I only briefly alluded to this in my evaluation report, but I think Ruth McPherson used the sex abuse allegations to parlay a rather large alimony payment for herself in exchange for backing off the allegations. Sonny is wealthy, but the real money, and I mean big money, is held by his parents. Sonny's father, the girls' grand-dad, is the famous Griff McPherson, maker of kings and presidents. Sonny sounded pretty bitter when he told me he fell on his sword for the family to avoid a public scandal. If the child sex abuse allegations had reached a level of public disclosure, the McPherson empire would have taken some serious pounding. It would have been a PR nightmare. Corporations don't like being associated with satanic ritual abuse and kiddie porn. It hurts the stock. I think Ruth leveraged a pretty sweet deal for herself. I have no doubt she believed and probably still believes Sonny molested her daughters, but money made the more public side of the issues fall off the table. The McPhersons basically bought Ruth's silence."

"Do the McPherson girls know that?"

"I hope not," Calder replied firmly. "I put a strongly worded caveat in the report no one was to share any of the report with the children, but I've learned that once I send a report in the mail, it's out of my control."

Worth's question about how much the girls knew made him recall his brief consult last year with Sam Cooper, whose primary concern about her patient had been how much the patient appeared to know about case details. If Calder's hunch had been accurate about who her patient was, the details could have come from Calder's report. He needed to think about the relevance of the consult to the Hughes' murder, especially if it confirmed that Colleen had read his report.

Worth responded, "What if Ruth's squirreling away money each month was a secret she not only kept from her children but also from Dr. Hughes? What if, when Dr. Hughes learned that piece of history, when she read your report, at some point, she got in Ruth's face, and that got her killed?"

"That's possible, although if that's true, that's probably just a piece of it. Remember, Dr. Hughes had read my report in 2001 before I interviewed her, so why would Ruth wait three years to kill her? Still, as the children's advocate, Dr. Hughes may have gotten angry at Ruth for depriving the children, and one thing led to another that got her brains bashed in."

Worth added, "Yeah, maybe our victim found out Ruth had more money than she'd admitted to Dr. Hughes, and the doctor got pissed because she had been treating the children for years at a reduced fee? She might have confronted Ruth about depriving the children and herself."

"That's an interesting angle, man. Ruth would be somebody Hughes would go out to meet, although the time of night is an odd time to agree to meet anybody. If they'd been having a conflict about finances, it'd be unlikely Hughes would invite Ruth to Ocracoke. If Ruth's the murderer, it's more likely she sneaked onto the island and created a ruse to get Hughes to the boat and surprised her. And, the drawing fragment may have been something one of the kids did at home, or brought home. Also, we don't know for sure if the drawing fragment was actually done by a child or by a clever adult trying to make it child-like. If Ruth's a suspect, the drawing didn't have to come from Hughes' files."

Calder and Worth arrived in time for the 7:30 AM ferry and were guided on. The boat captain met and welcomed them aboard. Worth headed upstairs with the captain to get a view from the bridge and chat with the crew. He wanted to see if, by chance, anyone had noticed something unusual about any of the passengers around the time of the doctor's murder. Although he still didn't know who he was looking for, he'd learned if he could just turn over enough rocks, a snake might eventually crawl out.

Calder settled himself into a comfortable lounge seat for some studying and sleeping. Calder had brought along some electric bass chord books, so he was using this opportunity to study some progressions. He was digging walkin' blues and reggae riffs. He was in hot pursuit of the twelve bar blues. Worth was pretty mean with a sax himself, so who knew where it might all lead? Calder and Worth had fantasies of doing some gigs at the Grand Escape bar in the Sheraton in New Bern. They'd found a decent drummer and a rhythm guitar man and had begun some weekly practices.

Once the ferry docked, Worth decided, as Calder had predicted to himself, having spent years as a hostage to Worth's bottomless well of a stomach, they should eat first. Besides, they were both recovering from bruised egos and an unsuccessful conquest at the bar the previous night. The bartendress, Maggie, was indeed beautiful, but she wasn't buying their two-on-one maneuver. Calder thought she was amused. Still, those green eyes and red hair. Calder knew he wasn't down for the count. He'd forgotten to ask her if she could sing blues-rock.

Worth cut his eyes at Calder and said, "Snap out of it, boy. You'll get over her. Rejection by the Irish princess got to you, didn't it? If I had been on my own last night, you'd be fishin' solo today."

Calder chortled, "Yeah, Casanova, I hear ya. I was definitely in your way last night. Why, I bet she musta talked to you a whole two minutes. Some sort of record, I bet."

"It wasn't what we said or how long it took," Worth quipped. "It was our future foretold in her eyes. I'm a trained detective, and I could see those emerald eyes signaling, 'Come back when you're by yourself.'"

"Well, now I'm deeply hurt. Rejected by the Irish princess and now backstabbed by my African buddy. I guess I'll drown my sorrows in some coffee and throw myself into a seafood omelet at the Pony Island. We've missed the window of opportunity for breakfast at Oscar's. You probably feel guilty enough to pay for breakfast, right?"

"Wouldn't bet on it."

After their meal, Worth and Calder decided first to pay their visit to Santos. Sheriff Garrish was sitting in front of Santos' house when they pulled up. He climbed out of his SUV and smiled as he greeted Worth. Worth hooked his thumb at Calder and said, "Bill, you remember my friend, Dr. Calder Miro, who some claim is a reasonably talented forensic psychologist."

"Nice to see you again, Sheriff," said Calder. "It's been a while."

"Good to see yew again, Doctor. Santos is inside. I'll say a couple o' things and leave yew boys alone. Santos is in a foul mood and the blues and Spanish mack are 'ittin' on the point. Yew'll probably find me there unless somebody disturbs my peace. 'Ere's a key to the doctor's 'ouse. Yew can drop it off later. He then handed Worth a sheaf of papers. "Also, 'ere are the computer print-outs of the ferry logs for the time period before and after the murder. They may not be much 'elp, but yew never know. Also, 'ere's a copy of the Santos divorce papers we were able to get through the public record. As yew'll see, at one point, 'e was put under a restraining order after assaulting 'is wife."

"How serious an assault?" asked Calder.

"Doesn't say, but 'ere's 'is ex-wife's name and telephone number in California. Don't know if she'll talk with either of yew, but it's worth a shot."

"Also, the SBI guys went over 'er boat and found no evidence of shoe marks or anything out of the ordinary. There is the possibility that if we find the murderer's shoes, we might get lucky and find some traces of the doctor's blood."

"Bill, I appreciate your doing all this. I'll call Santos' ex, or go out there to see her if necessary. And those logs might help, Bill. Thanks for getting those too. If we can tie a name of a passenger to someone who knew Dr. Hughes, that would help," said Worth.

"You're welcome, Worth," said the sheriff, who was getting that gleam peculiar to a seasoned fisherman when the blues are running. Worth and Calder knew that look well, and both of them were fighting their own urges, but they had work to do.

"Thanks, Bill," said Worth. "Leave some fish for us."

As they approached the Santos house, Calder could see a crack in the blinds of one of the upstairs windows. The crack disappeared as they approached the house. Worth rang the bell and stepped back.

Santos opened the door, and although it was noon, he looked and smelled like he'd been drinking for days.

"Mr. Santos, I'm Detective Brown. We met once before. And this is Dr. Miro, a forensic psychologist from New Bern. We're here to talk with you and then look at Dr. Hughes' house. We appreciate your willingness to speak with us."

Santos opened the door to let them in, saying, "I ain't got much choice in the matter. Garrish made it clear to me I'd better cooperate with you two. Besides, I ain't done shit, so I ain't got nothin' to hide. I'm a victim of small town Southern bullshit justice. Garrish runs this island like he's that dumbass sheriff *In the Heat of the Night*."

Worth stepped up and got within inches of Santos' face. "You're sure dating yourself, man. I guess that makes me Sidney Poitier," and stepped past him into Santos' living room. Santos followed right behind, ignoring Calder. Santos' house smelled of beer and cigarettes, the way a bar smells after years of smoke clouds have leeched into the wood, fabric, and pores of everything, animate and inanimate alike. About six ashtrays were visible all over the room. He did have the back door open, letting in some sea air, but nothing was gonna cleanse this room.

Before Worth could begin, Santos said, "I ain't done nothing, and I did not kill her. She was a sneaky, arrogant, self-righteous bitch who screwed me out of a deal I had with my neighbors. She got that land by back-doorin' the deal I had with the owners. I was ready to close the deal, and it turned out they were blowing smoke up my ass, but she's the one that blew the deal up. I didn't like 'er, but I ain't killed nobody."

"You sound really sorry she's dead," Worth quipped.

"Fuck no, I ain't sorry, but I didn't have nothin' to do with it. I ain't never even been in her friggin' house."

"Never?" said Worth.

"Never. I ain't said jack shit to her for a long time. I seen her come and go in that fancy Mercedes of hers, but I didn't give her the time o'day."

Calder kept wandering around Santos' house, trying to figure out what kind of man he was from his living environment. One thing was true. Besides his being addicted to alcohol and nicotine, he was a serious computer geek. Calder counted three CPU's and six flat panel monitors in his den. By the looks of things, Santos was a serious surfer.

Worth then asked, "So who gets her estate, now that she's deceased?"

"How the fuck would I know?" retorted Santos. "You think I forced her to change her will and leave me what's rightfully mine to begin with? That's a dumb fuckin' idea. No one could force that Baptist bitch to do anything."

Worth baited Johnny: "Mr. Santos, I didn't say that was my idea, or anybody else's. It's a good question though, and I deduce from your pithy answer that you don't know. I'm assuming you probably would like to know the answer to that question though."

Santos was now following Calder's movements and had placed himself so he could watch Calder and keep his eye on Worth. Pointing at Calder, he said, "Where you going, doctor asshole? You a shrink, too? You got no right to go snooping around my house."

"You're correct, Mr. Santos," Calder said as he turned to look at Santos, "And I apologize if you think I was snooping. I was admiring your computer set-up. I admire someone as skilled with computer technology as you clearly are."

Santos' hostile demeanor left his face. So flattery's the key to his dark heart, thought Calder.

"Yeah, well, I'm a bit of a 'net nut," he boasted.

Calder's quick look into Santos' office suggested he was more than an average surfer. What he saw were three out of six flat screen monitors side by side, allowing him to view several sources at once, and beside his desk he had a rack mount box labeled with the words 'DELL Edge Blade Server'. Because the lighting in that room was so dim, Calder wasn't sure, but he also thought he saw a CISCO router and switch box. It looked like their boy was into some serious hacking or cracking.

Worth looked at Santos and asked, "So I assume, Mr. Santos, you have an alibi for the night your neighbor was whacked?"

Santos stopped following Calder and said with a smile, "Yeah, I got a fuckin' alibi. I had my ass parked on my friggin' stool at Howard's, knockin' back neat. I figure I got about 8-10 witnesses. I was there til about 1 AM."

Ten bucks says his witnesses are all named Jim Beam, smirked Calder to himself.

"We'll check that out. So what's Dr. Hughes' house like inside?" asked Worth.

"Don't try that shit on me, Detective. I said I ain't been in there, and besides, you have, so you know more about it than me. Why don't you two get the hell out of my house?"

Worth stared at Santos and decided to push him a little bit more. He then said, "Back when you used to knock your ex-wife around, did you get off on that? Make you feel manly?"

The rage that filled Santos flew out of his eyes right at Worth, but he kept his cool. Worth had braced himself for Santos' reaction, but it didn't come. Not for now anyway.

Santos glared at Worth for a few more moments and then bellowed, "Get the fuck out of my house! The only way you're talking to me again is when my attorney's present, so get the fuck out of here!"

Worth smiled. Calder followed Worth as he headed for the front door. Calder noticed that Worth picked up one of Santos' cigarette butts from the ashtray and put it in his pocket. Santos was too busy bulling his way to the front door to notice.

"Thanks for the chat, Mr. Santos. We'll be in touch."

"Go fuck yourself," snarled Santos.

Worth and Calder walked next door to Dr. Hughes' house and watched as Santos watched them from his porch. When Santos was sure they were looking his way, he gave them the international hand signal of no affection and closed his door.

"Nice chap," Calder said.

"Yeah, a graduate of somebody's charm school for sure. I wanna read his divorce papers carefully and talk with his ex-wife. He's got a temper he barely manages to keep under wraps."

Calder responded, "He strikes me as a raging paranoid-narcissistic alcoholic."

To which Worth chuckled and said, "Yeah, he's one messed-up motherfucker."

Worth and Calder ducked under the yellow tape surrounding Mildred Hughes' house and let themselves in the front door. Calder was impressed with her use of subtle color in the décor, and the view from the living room and kitchen was spectacular.

"Wow," he said.

Worth said, "Not too shabby. Several things stood out for me when I was here the day after her murder. One, she had no cell phone in her pocketbook or on her boat or here in the house. Two, there was no message pad by the telephone. I checked the answering machine and there were no messages. If she did get a call from somebody who left a message, she either erased it or somebody else did. She could have taken the message pad with her, but most people would tear off the relevant sheet and leave the rest. Her telephone records may tell us something. I had one of her colleagues check her voice mail at her Wilmington office, and there were no new or saved messages. Her colleague also gave me her cell phone number, but the phone has never turned up. The dishes in the drain indicated that she ate alone and cleaned up before she left. There were no signs she left in a hurry. The doors and windows to the back deck were locked from the inside. Her computer in her office upstairs was on, but no open programs."

"Computer could link her to Santos," Calder offered.

"Yeah, I know. Maybe they were having virtual sex."

"Lovely mental image. Thanks. Or maybe Johnny boy was hacking her computer," Calder said. "My bet is he knows how."

"Why don't you go look at her office upstairs and see what you find. Everything's been dusted, so don't worry about touching things. I wanna look around some more in her kitchen and storage room. I don't know what I'm looking for, but we'll know it when we find it."

Calder climbed the stairs to the second floor. Dr. Hughes' home office was comfortable and well equipped. Calder knew Worth was working on getting access to her computer files, but Calder had a friend in Charlotte who used the code name Tekatak, and computers were his thing. He was a child of the 60's and had no respect for authority. Firewalls to his mind were simply minor hindrances. From his lab and fortress, Tekatak could access almost any system, from banking and government institutions to military and corporate satellite feeds. Every time Calder watched the television show "24," the character Edgar Stiles reminded him of Tekatak.

Calder switched on Dr. Hughes' CPU. He called Tekatak on his cell and surveyed her office.

"Computers R Us," a familiar voice said.

"Tek, this is Calder. How ya doing, man?"

"Groovy as always, dude. What's happening?"

"I need a favor. Actually, a big favor. Can you hack into a computer for me and get the pass code so I can read some files?"

"Does Pinocchio have wooden balls, man? How illegal is this?"

"Not illegal, not legal. The owner's dead. Been murdered it looks like, and I'm here on Ocracoke with the homicide detective. I'm standing at the computer and I need to read her files ASAP. Can you do it now?"

"Is the system on? And do you know her e-mail address and mailing address?"

Calder read out the information from Dr. Hughes' business card. "See if this works."

Tek ran Calder through a couple of quick key strokes to access her operating system info. He then said, "This will take a few minutes, unless there's something sophisticated. Let me call you back."

"Thanks, man."

"No problemo, dude." While Calder waited, he looked through her desk drawers and filing cabinets. There were several photos on the walls of a boy and then a young man Calder took to be her son, who looked to be about 20.

Tek rang Calder a few minutes later, "Okay, I'm in. Her password is '?empathy65.' That's question mark, e, m, p, a, t, h, y, 6, 5. No spaces. What else you need? Murder, huh? That's heavy shit, man. You doing okay?"

Calder could hear his friend's smoky exhale. With Tek, you never knew if it was Kools or weed. "Yeah," Calder said. "I'm fine. For right now, that's what I need from here, but if you don't mind, I'd like you to scan her system to see if anybody else besides me and you have hacked into her system."

"What timeframe?"

"Past several years. I just wanna know if anyone's been tapping into her data, and if so, what data?"

"Okay, man. Call me, dude. I'm not going anywhere. I'm married to my lab. Got three new contracts and I'm building websites at lightning speed. Gotta go. Stay in touch, man. I'll let you know if I find anything. Leave her system on. Later."

Talking with Tek was like watching a squirrel on speed climb a tree, but he was a genius. Calder used the pass code Tek had given him and made his way into her e-mail. He went under old mail and found the activity for several weeks preceding her death. He turned her printer on and opened each e-mail and printed a copy. It all seemed professionally related. There was one e-mail exchange between her and her son a couple of days before her murder caught his eye. He read it and called down to Worth.

"Worth, can you hear me?"

"Yeah," he yelled, "What's up?"

"I may have found something."

Worth bounded up the stairs rather quickly, given his size. "We needin' a break. What you got, Sherlock?"

Calder showed him the e-mail. On the day before she was murdered, she told her son, Matthew, she was meeting an old friend on Ocracoke. No other identifier but 'old friend.'

"Unless they patched things up, that probably eliminates the Soprano wanna-be next door," said Worth.

"True," Calder said, "but there's nothing here that directly ties this visitor to the murder."

"Nothing except the timing. Satisfies one prong of the 'means, motive, and opportunity' triangle. Being on the island satisfies opportunity. Being an old friend doesn't eliminate motive. Now we look for names in the ferry reservation log to see if we can connect a name to this old friend. How'd you get into this computer?"

"I got means, motive, and opportunity. I dialed a friend."

"Okay, don't tell me. I'm impressed, Doc. Good piece o' detecting. You get two gold stars. Now we get to the real point of this trip—the South Point—and catch us some fish."

"Copy that, Detective. I got some great fishing music. You heard of the Commitments?"

"Yeah," said Worth. "They white Irishmen who think they sound black. What a sad world."

"They do sound black."

"Eminem sounds black too, but he's whiter than yo mama's derriere. We'll compromise and put on some Wilson Pickett. The fish be dancin' right up on the beach once they hear 'In the Midnight Hour.' They'll think we having a revival."

They locked up the house and called Garrish as they drove to the point. Garrish told them he'd already been in touch with Dr. Hughes' son, who was coming to North Carolina from California to identify and claim his mother's body.

"Good 'unting," he said. "The blues biting mullet and the Spanish biting anything. I caught my limit already and packed it in. I'll probably see yew when yew drop 'er key by."

A quick stop at the Tradewinds for some essentials—beer, ice, munchies, and they scored some bait fish. Calder shifted into 4WD and headed down the point road. The two friends put the murder behind them for a while. The Blues Brothers were loose.

The only way to the south point on Ocracoke was the last right turn on the edge of town towards Cape Hatteras taking a windy, sandy road that sometimes was almost impassable because of the conditions. It might be three to four feet deep in sand. It might be washed out, with no road at all. Sometimes it was partially covered in water. The weather on this part of Ocracoke was always more extreme than anywhere on the rest of the island.

The end of the entrance road opened up to the beach, where the sand grew even deeper. On previous trips, Calder had gotten other 4-wheel drive vehicles stuck at least twice in his life, but so far, not this particular jeep. The beach access road goes left or right and both directions lead onto a national seashore. People are allowed to walk or bike or run or drive on the beach. There are no houses. Calder turned right towards the south point, or simply "the point." That was a particular place on the island where the ocean was on the left and the sound was on the right not more than 200 yards apart, so fishing could be done right where the ocean and the sound joined. The fishing, as a rule, was good, because fish of all varieties tended to make the turn at the island's end, either coming into the sound or coming out of the sound into the ocean.

Worth was completely Zen when it came to fishing. He seemed to have an uncanny knack for communicating with fish. Mincing few words when he prepared his rod and tackle, he'd pronounce, "She blowin' purty hard," or "Doc, I'd use a 4-weight if I were you. I don't believe we can hold anythin' lighter than that." Then Worth would load up his double blue rig with some mullet, which he had unselfishly cut into bait-size pieces for both of them. He then took his rod and reel and hurled the weighted rig and bait about 200 yards, it seemed, out into the water, cranked a few spins on his reel, pulled in the slack, and turned around and faced away from the ocean, looking toward the sound. It wasn't how normal people fished, but it worked. Worth would put his fingertips on the line, feeling, somehow, the faint, miniscule bump only blue fish could make when sniffing at the bait, and then *boom*, Worth would whip his rod at the right velocity to set the hook and crank in his line. Grinning, he'd settle into the thrill of hauling in his catch. Sometimes he'd even snag two blue fish at the same time.

After this ritual happened a few times, Worth would take a break. He'd put his rod in one of the rod holders he had shoved into the sand at the water's edge and saunter back to the jeep to dig through his special stash of peanut butter crackers, or 'nabs' as Southerners called them. Then, he'd get himself a cold one from the cooler, and stroll back into the surf, with the waves breaking just below his knees. He'd gaze out at the ocean, contemplatively munching his favorite snack. He even ate a 'nab' in a Zen-like fashion.

At the end of the day, it was possible that Worth had caught the limit, all of keeping size. He'd pack them in the cooler along with Calder's meager catch for filleting back at the B&B.

On this particular day, Worth had decided to school Calder about some of the inadequacies of white rock and roll. The Wilson Pickett tunes that blasted from the jeep's stereo had stimulated Worth's brain. He turned to Calder at one point and said, "You know, sometimes white rock and rollers don't make any sense."

Calder thought about it and replied, "Yeah, I suppose that's true. But you're gonna tell me all rappers got sense?"

"No, I wouldn't say that, but, take Steve Miller for example. One phrase in 'The Joker' has never made any sense at all."

"What phrase is that?"

"'And they speak of the pompatus of love.' Just what," implored Worth, "Just what is the *pompatus* of love? And how do you even *spell* pompatus?"

"Now, my friend," Calder said without hesitation, "I'm afraid you're showing your lack of education. The pompatus of love, or the *pompata* in the Latin plural, is the pinnacle, the zenith of love. It is the *heart* of rock and roll."

"I knew you wouldn't know," snorted Worth. "I bet Miller was high as a damn kite when he wrote that."

Chapter 15

Suffer the Little Children

May 2004

Ruth and her two girls lived in a modest three-bedroom home outside the city limits of New Bern. The house was down a road that was a composition of crushed rock and asphalt, and a county crew sometimes sprayed oil on the surface during the summer to keep the dust down. They had no neighbors to speak of, and their small lot was surrounded by farmland and large, isolated stands of trees. Except for the ten foot high wooden cross standing in the front yard, there was nothing unusual about the place.

The interior of the house was decorated in Spartan comfort and was spotless. The girls long ago learned that dirt was not tolerated. Their momma told them their daddy didn't pay any child support, which was why they had to live the way they did. Your daddy is rich and evil, and that's a bad combination, she'd always say. The girls had grown up not having a lot of the material things that other kids had.

Ruth McPherson was raised in Havelock, North Carolina. Her maiden name was Purdy, but for reasons known only to her, she had kept Sonny's last name. She was the only child of a man that some said was the meanest Marine drill instructor ever to wear a uniform. Her mother found deep refuge from her husband's drunken, abusive rages in a local Pentecostal church that interpreted the gospel through twice weekly prayer meetings at the church and tent revivals at least once a month. During her teens, Ruth's father found salvation, gave up drinking and molesting Ruth, and became a locally famous itinerant, full-gospel preacher known as Reverend Roy. His sermons were famous for their exuberance and drama. Although he reportedly survived several previous bites, thus ensuring his reputation as a man who could throw down Satan, the story was that Ruth's daddy lost a serious fight with the devil one Sabbath night when he was viciously bitten by a large rattlesnake he was handling during a revival and died on the spot of a heart attack. They said Reverend Roy's wife didn't shed a tear at her husband's funeral.

Ruth Purdy was fifteen when her father met his maker. She wasn't too sad about it either. His almost nightly visits to her room had stopped a few years back, but the smell of whisky on a man's breath still made her nauseated. Ruth never told anybody about what her father had done and buried herself in her school work. Although she graduated near the top of her high school class, she never pursued college because she felt obligated to stay home and take care of her aging mother who became sickly after Reverend Roy's death. Ruth's mother died from lung cancer on Ruth's nineteenth birthday. Her parents had left her no inheritance to speak of. Things might have been different if she hadn't gone to a party with a friend and met a rich kid named Sonny McPherson. She claimed it was the only time she strayed from the true path and got drunk. Colleen was conceived on that night of impassioned intoxication. Ruth denied any willingness or voluntary participation with Sonny that night. Over time, the full force of her hatred for her father's sick actions hit Sonny as rape allegations in her divorce pleadings.

Colleen and Starr usually rode a bus to and from school, but Colleen had gotten a ride home with her cousin Woody in his redecorated hearse. She'd told her momma she'd had something school-related after school, but she'd spent the afternoon with Woody getting high off some new weed that had come in from Atlanta. Her momma was in the kitchen, chain smoking and fixing dinner. A static-filled AM station was playing hymns. Colleen dropped her backpack in the hall, yelled hi to her momma, and decided to avoid any possible collisions with Momma's lava flow. A few weeks earlier, their momma had received a report from some psychologist hired by their daddy, and their momma hadn't been right since. Whatever had come in that envelope had churned their Momma up something awful.

Starr had gotten home earlier. Colleen found her sitting on the side porch swing staring into space. Colleen looked at her little sister who seemed more depressed than normal. It's a shitty deal when depression is all you know, thought Colleen. Starr always looked like a train wreck, but that day she looked especially wrecked. Starr had on a skirt that looked like a Bedouin camel blanket, a tight-fitting black, long-sleeved torn t-shirt with "Pain is weakness leaving the body" printed across the front, and no shoes. It looked like she had added some more pierced loops to her ears, if that was possible. Colleen long ago had given up trying to keep Starr from her on-going body piercing project. Colleen sat on the stoop at Starr's feet and lit her fifth cigarette of the day.

Blowing a perfect smoke ring, she said, "You've read it, haven't you?"

Starr hadn't moved or looked at her sister. She stared out into space. Colleen noticed that the typical heavy black eye liner Starr used looked a bit washed out, as if she'd been crying.

"Come on. Talk to me. If you've read it, tell me. I read it too."

Starr shot a glance at Colleen to see if her sister was lying. She looked away and focused on the red dirt tunnels that were forever stuck to the front porch columns. She'd always appreciated how the mud dobber's nests escaped her momma's cleansing and stayed there all year round.

"It's like total bullshit, you know," Starr said. "He's an asshole."

Colleen had been thinking about the implications of the report that her mother's attorney had sent her mother. Colleen found it on the kitchen table. *Her fucking father had gotten some hired gun expert to nose around in their family's past and had somehow concluded that Sonny had never molested them. The report also said their mother cut a deal with their daddy's family and had taken money in exchange for not pressing charges. Un-fucking-believable.*

"Who's an asshole—daddy or this guy Miro?" Colleen asked.

"Both of 'em, but I meant like this Miro guy. What a dumb fuckin' name, rhymes with queer-o. He said he thought Dr. Hughes might have screwed us up. That's not, like, possible. She's helped us. She got to the truth. She's, like, healed us. She's been our friend. She didn't do anything wrong. She's had Jesus' guidance. She and Momma stood by us. She's been the only one who, like, understands what we went through!"

The tears had begun to run down Starr's face. She looked at Colleen in wild wonderment. The pain in Starr's eyes was replaced with rage.

"I'd like to stick pins in both of his eyeballs. All his balls," muttered Starr.

Colleen had been thinking hard all week about Dr. Miro's report. The thing she noticed the most was how much more nervous her mother had gotten since it arrived in the mail. It was her mother's worsening condition that tipped Colleen something significant had happened. Colleen noticed her momma was retreating to her room either to pray or to talk on the phone. She had been bitchy as hell. Once Colleen found the report, she knew it was no accident her momma had left it on the counter. The asshole doctor who wrote it had written into the conclusions that the report should not be given to or read by the children. *What an asshole. Momma knew best.*

Colleen wasn't surprised Starr had read it too. Nor was she surprised at Starr's reaction. The two of them had been through hell. Daddy was a sick son-of-a bitch. Miro's report, though, shifted a lot of the sickness to Momma and Mildred.

"What'd ya think's gonna, like, happen now?" asked Starr, as she wiped her eyes and nose on her shirt.

"I dunno," responded Colleen. She looked out over the fields surrounding their tiny home and thought about what all this might mean. Colleen was sixteen, but her mind was much older. She saw numerous possibilities. Some she liked and made her smile. Some were dark and smelled of sulphur. She thought it best to keep these possibilities to herself. "I dunno, sweetie. I'll figure something out.

You know I always do. Best thing for you is not to worry. Momma's doing enough worrying and praying for all three of us. For right now, let's keep it a secret between me and you that we read the asshole report. No need for Momma or anyone to know that. Not yet, anyways."

Colleen stood up and flipped her cigarette butt into the yard and motioned for Starr to move over a bit in the swing so they could sit together. Starr put her head on her big sister's shoulder and sighed. Colleen always had a plan, she thought. That was comforting. The two sisters sat and rocked together until darkness began to fall over the whole situation. Starr then said through clenched teeth to no one in particular, "Somebody's gotta pay!"

Chapter 16

The Smell of Money

November 2006

Deep Throat, the covert source for Woodward and Bernstein during the Nixon Watergate scandal, kept telling those young investigative reporters to follow the money. Worth believed that was sage advice.

Calder continued some of his own investigation. His reading of the Santos divorce pleadings led him to conclude that they were classic 'he-said-she-said' documents. Even the restraining order offered little in the way of objective evidence, although Santos' ex-wife did allege that he pushed her, choked her, and slapped her across the face. His man, Tekatak, had turned up a number of things in his search of Dr. Hughes' computer. One, he confirmed Santos had hacked into his neighbor's computer, but he wasn't doing it from the outside. Tek insisted Santos had gained access to her computer from inside her house. When Calder told Tek there was no evidence that he had ever been inside, Tek declared, "Well, he has, I can tell you that!" It turned out he was right. At some point, Santos had loaded a clever piece of spyware into her hard drive that allowed him to wander about and look in her files and see what she was doing. To do that, Tek insisted, the best way was from the inside. Santos had discovered that Dr. Hughes did a lot of her banking online, so, not too surprisingly, Tek found out Santos was spending a lot of time combing the doctor's financial files. So far, Tek said it didn't appear he had done anything but look. He was a peeping hacker.

Worth, in the meantime, needed to interview Sonny McPherson, but had decided first to interview Griff McPherson, Sonny's father. Griff had his own attorney present, Roscoe Byron Ornish, III, who was on permanent retainer and worked only for Griff. Roscoe Ornish was a polished, old-school Southern lawyer of the Sam Ervin variety. Ornish wore handsomely tailored lightweight, British, three-piece suits in the fall and winter and seersucker suits in the summer, and always sported a bowtie. Ornish was Griff's *consigliere* in the best sense of that office and sat at Griff's right hand for most business activities. Griff confirmed that his estate paid Ruth a monthly stipend for "support of the children's welfare," but insisted its amount and conditions were confidential. Worth hadn't pressed that point, but it definitely confirmed that Ruth was hiding things from her children. The impoverished lifestyle imposed on herself and her children was yet to be understood.

Ornish emphasized that he had represented the McPherson family and had negotiated the settlement directly with Ruth McPherson's former attorney. Ornish also emphasized, without being asked, that there was no connection between the financial arrangements and the investigation of the child sex abuse allegations. Griff pointed out, and Ornish concurred, that the allegations went away because the authorities concluded there was no substance to them. They were not substantiated by social services and there were no criminal charges. Griff added that Ruth McPherson was a very disturbed woman and that, were it not for the fact she was the mother of his grandchildren, she would not remain affiliated in any way with his family.

Worth went to see Ruth McPherson at her home when the children were not there. Before he had a chance to knock, she had greeted him at the door holding a worn Bible. She was dressed in plain, simple clothes without make-up or jewelry. Her hair was pulled back in a bun. They sat in the living room that was tidy and functional, but neither inviting nor comfortable. There was a simple, wooden altar pushed against the wall of what was once the breakfast nook. Worth noticed the altar had casters on it, so it could be rolled. Several times during the time he was there, Worth had wondered, if she's been socking away money she leveraged from the McPherson's, where is it? During her interview, Ruth's righteousness faded and she couldn't say enough negative things about Sonny. Worth later told Calder that he could see Ruth's growing tension by the grip and twist of her hands on the Good Book. There was no question in her mind that her ex-husband killed Mildred. She kept describing Sonny as the Devil's right hand and said the Miro report gave Sonny time to build the courage he needed to murder Mildred. The fact that Calder's report had come out several years earlier didn't bother Ruth's logic. When Worth pressed her for any evidence she might have to support her belief, she stopped her tirade, looked Worth right in the eyes, and whispered with words coated in rage and venom, 'Because he is the son of Lucifer, Detective.'

Worth also later told Calder that Ruth wasn't too complimentary of Calder either. She was convinced that he had a black soul. Although Worth knew what she meant, he told Calder he had chuckled to himself, thinking, "If she only knew his taste in music."

Worth left Ruth's house with the impression that she struggled during his interview to contain her rage and bitterness. Her personality had a kind of instability to it Worth had seen before in others, something Calder had helped Worth come to understand as a hallmark of the borderline personality disorder. Under her façade of righteousness, lived maybe some murderous impulses. As he backed out of her driveway, he wondered what kind of person would erect a ten foot cross in her front yard. Worth was also struck again by how sparse and unadorned the house was, inside and out. Where did the money go? Ruth definitely didn't spend it on her house or its furnishings. He made a mental note to talk with Calder about that.

A few days later, Worth also separately interviewed Colleen and Starr. They confirmed what their mother had told him: that neither child had seen Dr. Hughes for over a year prior to her death. At their mother's insistence, they had gone back to see her a few times right after their daddy began his efforts to see them. Although they said they knew a psychologist had done an evaluation of their daddy, neither gave Worth any indication they had seen Calder's report. In response to his question to each girl if either had ever seen another therapist, Colleen had volunteered that she had begun seeing one in her freshman year at UNC, but she didn't want to give Worth a name. Her withholding of this information made Worth curious, but he didn't press the point. Starr asserted that she would never see another therapist again. Worth came away from those interviews with several conclusions. Starr was physically and psychologically in shambles. She looked like a caricature of adolescent rebellion, with body piercings everywhere. She would have been funny, but she was so pitiful. Worth couldn't help feeling sorry for her. He thought her expressed feelings about the doctor's death seemed genuine, but he couldn't tell for sure. Her emotions went up and down like an out of control roller coaster. Her fury aimed at her daddy and at Calder mirrored her mother's rage. He didn't detect any rage at Mildred Hughes, but it was possible she was covering this up. She also had this odd mannerism of blinking her eyes, like she was changing channels or something. Something else to talk about with Calder.

Colleen was also a mess, although a complicated one. She dressed like a typical college student—multi-layered top that showed some midriff and jeans. Blue and red streaks of hair. Worth thought there were layers and layers to her personality that made her a bit inscrutable, and that made Worth suspicious. Worth noted that she didn't spew venom towards other people like her mother or sister. Unlike her sister, as Worth learned from the McPhersons, Colleen had spent a considerable amount of time in recent years with her father and occasionally with her grandfather, including trips abroad. In response to Worth's question about her not attending Dr. Hughes' funeral, Colleen had offered simply that it was just too painful to go.

Both girls claimed they had never been to Ocracoke and none of the ferry personnel had ID'ed either one of the girls, or Ruth or Sonny from the photos Garrish showed them after he got them from Worth.

With a court order, Worth's investigation had given him access to Dr. Hughes' clinical files, and he met with one of her business partners in Wilmington whom she had named to handle her files in the event of her death. Turned out such professional anticipation and planning was encouraged within the professional ethics of psychology, and such a transfer of control was nothing out of the ordinary. Worth and one of her business partners, Dr. Anderson, agreed to divide up her files into active and closed files. Without explaining himself to her colleague, Worth agreed to the logic that, if any of her patients were connected to her murder, it would make sense to start with examining her closed files. The evidence so far pointed back to the early 1990's. Dr. Anderson was in the process of transferring her current cases to other clinicians. Worth was keeping the fact about the sketch fragment in her mouth to himself, and this detail, so far, had been kept out of the news accounts. If the murderer had forced the drawing into the doctor's mouth, the killer was the only person outside of the people involved with the investigation who knew about that.

None of Hughes' business partners or her ex-husband, Robert Stein, had any ideas about who might have murdered Mildred Hughes. She'd been divorced for almost 15 years and had taken back her maiden name following the divorce. Worth could find no hint of a motive that her ex-husband might be a suspect. There were no money issues between them, and their divorce, by all accounts, was amicable. Worth confirmed Robert Stein had been in Asia on a business trip at the time of his ex's murder, and there did not seem to be any rancor between the two. Stein said he didn't know much about the issues between Mildred and her neighbor, Johnny Santos, because he and Mildred just didn't discuss things at a personal level anymore. All he knew was they had some sort of run-in with one another, but he didn't know what it was about.

Worth also interviewed Dr. Hughes' son, Matthew Stein, a junior in pre-med at Stanford. He had agreed to stay a few extra days after his mother's funeral. Matthew also had an airtight alibi the night of his mother's death. He was in Cozumel with twenty other pre-meds, taking one of their infrequent breaks from the rigors of pre-med life. Matthew had been shooting tequila and eating worms with several beautiful Air Mexico flight attendants the night his mother was killed. Worth found him to be a bright, engaging young man grief stricken by his mother's murder. He gave Worth no indication of any troubles between his mother and father, and seemed genuinely angry when Worth pursued that particular line of questioning. Like everyone else who knew his mother's habits, Matthew did not find it odd that she was at the Ocracoke house alone. She liked to go there often to get away. He confirmed she was a skilled and careful mariner. He also agreed with Worth's assessment that his mother would have been fully prepared and her boat tanks topped if she were going out in the boat that night. He said matter-of-factly that, given what he knew about the time and circumstances of her death, she was on the boat for some other reason. Matthew said he used to spend a lot of time at his mother's beach house when he was younger, but school and other interests in recent years made his visits less frequent. He knew his mother had some sort of financial conflict with her neighbor, Mr. Santos, but he never heard his mother say anything negative about Mr. Santos and never saw anything happen between them that concerned him. Matthew did say Santos was well-known on the island as a regular at Howard's Pub and offered the opinion that he thought Santos was like a certain type of person who retreated to an island. He was bitter about something before he got there and his treatment was to sit on a bar stool at Howard's and stare into a whiskey glass as his liver corroded.

Worth then asked Matthew about the email his mom had sent him about an old friend coming to visit her. Matthew had forgotten about that. He grew concerned when he thought about its timing in terms of when she was killed, but he had no idea who she was referring to and he hadn't asked. He said, thinking back on it, that it sounded like someone was coming to Ocracoke his mom hadn't seen in a while, but that was about it. He was now worried he'd maybe missed something important by not asking for more information, by being self-absorbed. He wanted to know if the police investigation had turned up anything about who might have killed his mom. He spoke with Worth in the slow, measured pace used by people in deep grief and shock. Worth had seen a lot of people die during his life, on a personal and professional level. In his job, he often had to tell the living about the dead. He was familiar with the many faces of grief. It had a thousand faces and thousands of stages, not the sequential four that modern psychology fostered. He felt deeply for this young man.

"I am very sorry for your loss, Matthew. I truly am. Thank you for taking the time to talk with me. I know this wasn't easy."

"Thank you, Detective," he said in a most gracious tone. "Please find the person who did this. Please do that for me."

Worth closed his notebook. "I will, son. I will."

Worth got a chicken salad sandwich and coffee from the Handy Mart and returned to his office. The food and coffee helped him shake the images of Matthew's palpable grief out of his mind. Worth turned his attention back to the big picture of his investigation. His mind wrapped around a common subject in homicide. Money. Worth sat at his desk and drew a diagram that had the word "money" in the center of the paper with a circle drawn around it. Then, outside this central circle, out near the edge of the paper he wrote "Sonny." He then wrote "Ruth" in another place on the paper, then "Colleen," then "Starr," then "Griff," then "Santos," then "Hughes," then "?" He thought about all the possible suspects some more. He then added "other alleged perps." This was an angle he hadn't considered, but, maybe, just maybe, Mildred Hughes had tried to blackmail the McPherson family. It had paid once to keep Ruth silent. Why not again? All of these names and the question mark were drawn like spokes of a wheel equidistant from the central circle that contained what he thought was one of the possible central motives.

Worth figured the money angle was a good bet because Ruth had secured a pay-off from Griff and yet, inexplicably, lived a modest life. Where did Ruth put her money? Was there a connection between the pay-off and Dr. Hughes? Santos also had lost a lot of money due to Mildred Hughes' actions. Did Sonny kill Hughes because of money? It was his family's money that paid for the children's therapy. If either of the girls found out about their mother hiding money from them and forcing them to be deprived of so much, could either one of them have killed Dr. Hughes? He then drew a circle around each name and connected each circle to the one in the center. His drawing looked like a small solar system, except to Worth it was a murder investigation system.

Worth had long ago concluded that money has a certain smell. If you hold a dollar bill up to your nose, there's a certain faint smell. If you hold a $100 bill up to your nose, the smell is stronger. A $1 bill and a $100 bill smell differently. If there were such a thing, a $500 dollar bill would smell differently than the $100. If you hold a million dollars to your nose, that's got its own unique smell. Put that in the plural and imagine what millions must smell like. There was the possibility he'd caught a hint of the aroma of billions, but he wasn't sure. Even though he didn't know what millions or billions smelled like, he knew he'd had a whiff of that when he interviewed Griff and Ornish.

Worth looked some more at his drawing. Santos may have killed Hughes because of money. From what had turned up, money was what motivated Hughes to backstab Santos.

According to Sonny's statements to Calder and Calder's report, Griff's position, first and foremost, was to protect his name and considerable wealth. If Griff had Hughes killed, it was probably for reasons other than money, unless she was trying to blackmail him, and so far there was no evidence of that, but it remained on the table.

Colleen and Starr stood to inherit a whole lot of money. Forbes estimated McPherson Enterprises was worth approximately nine billion dollars. It was possible that one of them killed her therapist because she felt cheated out of all that she could have had from her daddy and grandpa during her childhood. The McPhersons were world famous for their lavish trips to India, Africa, and Russia.

Ruth stood the most to lose by getting cut off from the McPhersons. She'd never dropped their name as her own. Worth liked her for the money angle, but he couldn't figure out how to tie her into the murder of Mildred Hughes. Everyone described Ruth and Mildred as two peas in a pod. They were both born again evangelical fanatics who saw Satan's handiwork everywhere. Calder thought they had teamed up and done a number on Sonny. Maybe Ruth killed Mildred because of some disagreement they had about the way things were going with the girls and their father. Ruth was none too happy Sonny had managed to worm his way back into the girls' lives. If this motive were viable, then Calder might be in danger. Worth thought Calder was way too casual about this possibility, but at least he was armed. Maybe Ruth felt Dr. Hughes hadn't done enough to convince the girls of their father's sickness. Maybe Ruth thought Mildred hadn't stood up to Lucifer's son, Sonny, or to Lucifer's agent, Calder.

Chapter 17

Change in Circumstances

May 2004

After Sonny McPherson read Dr. Miro's forensic psychological evaluation report, his attorney could hardly contain Sonny's reactions. Sonny felt vindicated, and became filled with optimism and revenge. The report put him on his own path of righteousness and he wanted to gather an army to rescue his children from the sick clutches of their crazy mother. He wanted to file multiple ethics complaints against Hughes and sue her for malpractice. He wanted to force his ex-wife to apologize for all the pain she had brought him. He wanted to see his children right away. He wanted his pound of flesh. He wanted it all now.

John Andrews had been practicing domestic law long enough to know that sometimes you just had to let your clients vent. You had to let them charge around the office and spew out revenge scenarios. Especially rich people. Clients whose families no longer had titles but whose view of themselves was founded on entitlement. John saw himself as an attorney and counselor at law, and his expensively printed business cards and letterhead said so. He didn't mind getting paid

$400 an hour for his clients to rant and rave, as long as they didn't go busting up his office, insulting him or his staff, or running off unleashed to execute one of these vengeance schemes.

Andrews was good at listening to the many ways his clients had been victimized by their ex's. He'd sometimes think to himself: I've heard it all, but then a new case would walk in and the client would unfold a story that couldn't be made up. The landscape of domestic law was littered with tragic stories that prove real life can become twisted and bizarre beyond description. The McPherson case had been such a case, and Andrews knew Sonny, once he felt vindicated by Miro's evaluation, needed a good helping of firm, legal guidance and more than a dash of reason.

A good family lawyer's knowledge of family law and the capacity to give their clients reasonable, thoughtful advice was what was needed most by people who couldn't settle their divorce and custodial issues themselves. Otherwise, litigants who decided to pursue any method for extracting their pound of flesh from the ex-wife or ex-husband might fly off and do something stupid.

"Sonny," Andrews said softly.

Sonny didn't hear him. Sonny was practicing law now. He was telling Andrews his next legal strategy should be to scorch the earth around Ruth and rescue the children. Sonny was seeing blood in the water and smelling charred flesh.

"Dammit, John, I want you to get this report before a judge today. A good judge. One that'll listen, and get one of them, what you call 'em, ex parte orders, and get my children released from the prison their mother has them in. I want her to feel what it's like to have your children ripped away from you. I want—"

"Sonny, I want you to shut up."

Only Griff talked to Sonny that way. Andrews knew that, which is why he did it. Sonny needed a father and a lawyer right now. "You don't know this, but you pay me $400 an hour to tell you sometimes to shut up. I'm doing that right now. I want you to sit down and listen to me. No, better yet, go outside, smoke a cigarette, collect your thoughts, and come back. We need to formulate an effective plan, not a SWAT operation. I have some ideas, but I need you to listen to me. I want you to let me be your lawyer right now."

Sonny nodded his head and picked up his cigarettes from the desk and turned toward the door. He needed the last word, as he always did with his father. "Okay, but she's gotta pay."

"We'll make Ruth pay, Sonny. Have a smoke, get some coffee, and come on back. We've got some strategizing to do." Andrews buzzed his secretary and said, "Let Sonny come back to my office when he returns from his smoke break."

A section in the North Carolina General Statutes allows a court order for child support or custody to be "modified or vacated at any time, upon motion in the cause and a showing of changed circumstances by either party or anyone interested subject to certain statutory limitations."

Andrews' plan all along, once he agreed to take Sonny's case, had been to retain a forensic psychologist like Dr. Miro, and to give him free reign to examine his client and the merits of the case from a forensic psychological point of view. Andrews needed unimpeachable evidence to show Sonny was not a child molester. Once the Miro analysis and report came back, Andrews believed Sonny had a good chance of getting his visitation re-instated. The Miro report would allow him to argue on his client's behalf that the foundation of the Miro report supported the "changes of circumstances" basis for a lawsuit against Ruth McPherson and a motion in the cause to get visitation started between Sonny and his children.

Andrews figured, correctly it turned out, Ruth's attorney would figure that out too, and rather than fight, the two attorneys would use what leverage each had with their clients to broker a deal to avoid a public courtroom battle.

Sonny had returned to Andrew's office and, as usual, propelled a cloud of acrid smoke across the room.

"Okay, I'm calm. I'm good to go. What's the plan, Mein Herr?"

Andrews ignored Sonny's passive-aggressive stab at his authority. He knew Sonny had suffered a lot from powerful people telling him what to do and how to be.

"Sonny, if you'll let me, here's what I think we should do." He then handed Sonny a single sheet of paper labeled "CONFIDENTIAL MEMORANDUM" that had a number of bulleted points.

Andrews read them out loud from his own copy to his client:

"Number one, I draft a Motion for Visitation based on the Miro report and the obvious change in circumstances, and we send it to Jennifer Ledford, Ruth's attorney. This gets everyone's attention."

"I like that," said Sonny.

"Then we set up a meeting with Ledford, Miro, and me."

"I wanna be there for that one," added Sonny. "I wanna see Ledford's face when we tell her how we're gonna kick her ass."

"You can't be there for that one, Sonny. That meeting will just be for the attorneys and our expert to establish some common understanding."

"The only thing Ruth needs to understand is that I'm coming to get my children back!"

"The meeting with Miro and me will accomplish getting that message across. You can be sure Ledford will tell her. I also want to see if Ledford and Ruth will agree to have the children evaluated by Miro."

"Somebody competent needs to," chimed Sonny. "People tell me they're pretty messed up," he added quietly.

Andrews continued: "Whether they agree or not about Miro evaluating the children, Miro still meets with Hughes."

"I don't get that. What does he need to do that for?"

"I think it will help keep things calm. Also, he may be able to learn additional information about the girls' therapy. Besides, Miro has already asked me if he could do this, and I've agreed."

Sonny scowled, but settled down a bit.

"Then, we use the recommendations from the Miro report about a "reconciliation therapist" to forge a legal agreement to get such a therapist on board." Andrews could see Sonny was stewing about something. He figured it was the next item on his list. He read it to Sonny and waited for the reaction. "We get you started in your own individual therapy."

"I don't need any fucking therapy."

Andrews had thought about how to respond to this. "You may not need it, Sonny, but it will look good to the court if you're engaged in some type of treatment. It will also speed up your seeing your kids."

"Shit, John, this kinda crap will take months! I wanna see my kids now! I don't wanna have to wait for all this legal bullshit. She ain't gonna agree to shit. She's evil, John. You don't know 'er. And Dr. Hughes is a quack and a witch. And I don't need any therapy."

Andrews decided to leave this last point alone for a bit. If anybody needed to see a therapist, it was Sonny McPherson. He had so much rage and pain bottled up, he was a walking, talking Chernobyl just waiting to happen.

"Sonny, I understand your wish to see your children right away, but that's not realistic. Even if Ruth were to agree you could come see them today, they have their own individual hearts and minds about you. In normal families on a good day, parents can't force fourteen and sixteen year olds to clean up their rooms or even smile. You cannot expect to walk right into your children's lives and give them a hug and have them welcome you back. I would hope for the sakes of both you and your children this is what happens, but we don't know who they are, what they think about you, or how damaged they may be. You and Dr. Miro have convinced me that they were not sexually molested by you, or probably not by anybody, but if they still think they were, and that you did it, a well-written report and a court order aren't going to change their minds. They may think you are Satan himself, Sonny."

"It would do your relationship with them more harm than good for you to force something on them they don't want. That may be what they continue to think you've already done. You know I'm right. I need for you to be a little more patient. You've come a long way, and it's been hell, but if we do this right, I think you've got a reasonable chance of seeing your kids. The best we can hope for, given their ages, is that we set up a situation where they meet you and can form their own opinions about you. Dr. Miro has emphasized that their mother needs to agree to the initial meetings, and I think I can leverage that agreement, and with a professional everyone agrees is safe."

"It ain't gonna be that bitch, Hughes," snarled Sonny. "She fucked my kids up."

"No, we won't agree to Dr. Hughes. Dr. Miro has suggested several names of people in Charlotte or Chapel Hill. There are some good people out there who he thinks can understand all the issues in this case and help you and your children meet and decide what kind of relationship between you is possible, given all that has happened. First, however, we have to play our strongest legal hand, which we've already started by sending Ledford the Miro report. Jennifer Ledford is a good attorney and she's already anticipating what our next move is. I've received some calls from some of my legal colleagues. She's been making discreet calls about Dr. Miro to find out if our expert is credible."

"There's no problem, is there? You told me he was the best."

"He is the best, Sonny, and Jennifer can dig all she wants. Calder Miro was the perfect choice for the job because he does have the expertise and can hold up to scrutiny. His report is a good one because it is balanced and puts the good, the bad, and the ugly out there about everybody, including you. Jennifer is learning that a Miro analysis in Craven County is something the judges will listen to, especially the judge in our case. The Miro report has given us the leverage we need."

"How you figure that?" Sonny had his business hat on now. He'd cut his teeth on brokering deals because he grew up at the feet of Griff McPherson who brokered deals like a drunkard drank.

"Jennifer will convince Ruth to deal because she will see the negative implications of a law suit for her client and the children."

"What'd you mean, negative implications?" Andrews had Sonny's attention.

Andrews adjusted the pencil holder next to the blotter on his desk. He then squared the edges of his IBM Thinkpad in line with the blotter. He liked order. "Besides the children, what's the one thing that ties Ruth to you and your family?"

"That's easy," said Sonny, smiling that big grin of his. "Cash. Cold, hard cash. She's as greedy as she is evil."

"So, you see where I'm going with this? Ruth will not cut and run, not even in light of the Miro report, because of the money. If you were a blue collar worker making boat parts at the Hatteras Yachts' plant, you couldn't have hired me, or gotten an expert's opinion like Miro, or meant squat to your ex. No, Sonny, you're exactly right. Even if Ruth's intentions have been as pure as the driven snow, the fact you and your family are worth billions cements her feet. She will not want to jeopardize her children's future."

"Not to mention the fact we've been paying her a yearly stipend since 1990," added Sonny.

"And that is my point exactly," Andrews said. "Ruth knows that. Her current attorney knows that, because even if she didn't before, Miro put that historical piece in his report. Ruth and the children have been subsidized for fifteen years by the McPherson fortune. She's not stupid. She will broker something that insures her children's financial well being. The children themselves may have their own opinions, too, about you, including the fact that you're very rich."

"My money's got nothing to do with how I feel about my kids," Sonny said angrily.

"That's not what I meant, Sonny. I know that. What I'm saying is the children probably have their own view—some of it real and some of it not so real—about your life. Your family is often in the public eye. They've probably seen their granddad on television. I would venture to say, even if they have very negative feelings towards you, they are probably curious, to say the least, about you and your family's world."

"Yeah, I suppose you're right. I forget about all that shit. I try to stay out of the news. Daddy eats that stuff up."

"Your daddy is a kingmaker, Sonny. Ruth can see the possibilities for your two girls. If we parlay this right, she will see the wisdom of opening the royal doors to Colleen and Starr."

Sonny took the last word position again. He was the kind of guy who probably got sent to detention a lot in junior high school for impulsive, uncontrollable actions. "My girls can come through those doors. I got no problem with that. After Daddy dies, my estate will be considerable, and the girls can share in that. They have no idea how big that is. But, that bitch Ruth, she will not walk through those doors. She will rot in hell."

John Andrews decided not to respond, knowing his client needed some therapeutic help with that rage. He then said to Sonny, "I have a draft of a motion I will finish up, and you can read it, and if it says what we want it to say, I'll fax it to Jennifer Ledford today. After she has time to digest it and talk with Ruth, my guess is she'll agree to meet with me and Dr. Miro. Why don't you and I meet at the Chelsea for some lunch in about an hour and a half and we can go over the draft?"

Chapter 18

Head's Up

June 2004

Jennifer Ledford had a solo general law practice in New Bern that allowed her to handle a variety of cases, both criminal and civil. She made a modest living, partly because she had taken on clients like Ruth McPherson who had paid her almost nothing for years, but she always liked the independence a solo practice gave her. She managed to purchase an old, downtown Victorian before anyone realized they were going to be worth something as New Bern revitalized itself. By renting out the bottom floor to another attorney and sharing a secretary, she had been able to pay her own paralegal and make ends meet.

When she got the faxed draft of the Motion in the Cause from John Andrews the same afternoon he and Sonny had discussed its merits, she was not surprised. She had read Calder Miro's report and was amazed at what it said. Over the years, she had come to know Colleen and Starr and considered them both to be pretty messed up kids. She always accepted the truth of what their mother told her had happened to them. Miro had somehow written a reasonably cogent report that, on the one hand, admitted he had not evaluated the children and thus there were some clear limitations to his evaluation. But, on the other hand, he offered a reasonable and pretty damn convincing analysis the child sex abuse allegations may have been inaccurate—and maybe false. What made the report even stronger was his non-sugarcoated personality analysis of Sonny McPherson. Jennifer Ledford knew when she read that report, some shit was going to hit the fan.

She called several of her legal colleagues around the state who practiced family law and learned that Miro had a good reputation for fairness. He had also made some enemies in his own profession for being high and mighty about the practice of forensic psychology, but by and large, he was perceived by most to be a credible and effective expert witness. He had been doing evaluations of cases involving child sex abuse allegations for years and had been qualified as an expert witness for criminal defendants, for family law courts, for departments of social services, and for district attorneys prosecuting child molesters. Jennifer had found out that Calder Miro played all sides of the street. That's what made his opinion in the McPherson matter so significant.

After she read Andrew's motion, Jennifer Ledford called Ruth McPherson right away.

"Hello, Jennifer," said Ruth.

"Hi, Ruth. How are you?"

"I'm fine. Has something else happened? Sweet Jesus, ever since we got that report from Sonny, I've been on pins and needles. I just know you're calling me about something that's not good."

"I'll get right to the point then. Sonny's lawyer, John Andrews, has sent me a draft of a document called a Motion in the Cause, in which he lays out their intention to file for visitation between Sonny and the children. He believes he can convince a court, based on the Miro report, that a judge should order visitation between Sonny and the children."

"That sonofabitch." Ruth then checked herself. "Lord have mercy. I shouldn't say things like that. I'm sorry, Jennifer."

"Quite all right. I find it necessary to cuss once in a while myself. Ruth, I think Sonny's got a good chance of getting a favorable finding on his motion if he puts it in front of the right judge, and John Andrews knows how to make that happen. He hasn't filed the motion yet, and probably doesn't intend to, but he wants me and you to know it's an option."

"If he doesn't intend to file it, why'd he send it?" Ruth asked. "Another one of Sonny's stupid, sick games?"

"No, I don't think anyone's gaming, Ruth. The real purpose of sending it the way he did was to let us know he's holding lots of cards in his hand. What he's asking for now is in the cover letter he sent with the motion. He wants to meet with me, and he wants Dr. Miro to be at the meeting. He wants me to meet Dr. Miro. He wants to discuss his report and its recommendations."

"Sonny can't walk in here after what he's done and see these children!" Ruth's voice level was elevating. "I won't let him, and the children don't want to see him. There's no way I'm gonna let that happen. I'll hide them from him."

"I know you feel that way, Ruth. I would too. But that's not the point. Andrews has a pretty good chance legally, I think, of convincing a judge to order visitation based on what Andrews thinks is a sufficient change in circumstances, that is, the Miro report, and a judge just might order Colleen and Starr to see their daddy. If the court ordered that to happen and you didn't comply, you could be held in contempt by the court. My advice to you, if you'll permit me, is to allow me to meet with John and Dr. Miro and get a bit of a further reading on things. If I agree to meet with them, John's not going to file this motion."

"I wanna meet this Dr. Miro," Ruth hissed. "I want to look that man in the eye and see what kind of soul he has. I wanna look into his heart and see what kind of man could twist the histories of these children into the blasphemous distortions he put in those pages."

Despite having represented her for years, Jennifer was always a little shocked by the suddenness of Ruth's eruptions. She could feel the heat in Ruth's words coming over the phone line. She'd love to be present when Ruth met Miro, but Jennifer knew that wasn't what was on the table right now.

"Ruth, let's do this. If you'll let me, I'll meet with John Andrews and Miro. Sonny won't be there, and I don't think you should be either. I'll make it a condition of my agreeing to meet with them that Miro has to meet with you."

"Yes," said Ruth. "And, Miro has to meet with Mildred. She can convince him that he doesn't really have a clue about how sick and perverted Sonny really is."

"Okay, I think I can do that. That makes good sense. I'll meet with them only if Dr. Miro agrees to meet with you and go see Dr. Hughes."

Ruth returned to a calm state. "The funny thing is, Jennifer, the kids aren't gonna wanna see their daddy. They hate him. He did horrible things to them they remember vividly. Starr still has nightmares. Even if a judge orders them to, they're not gonna do it."

Knowing this was a subject of a far greater complexity than she could discuss for the moment, Jennifer said as gently as possible, "You're probably right, Ruth, but let me get them to agree to our terms and I'll go meet with them, and we'll take this one step at a time. I'll call you back and let you know if they agree to our conditions."

"Okay," said Ruth. "Call me as soon as you hear anything. God bless."

"Thanks. Bye, Ruth." All things considered, that went about as well as could be expected, Jennifer thought.

After she hung up the phone, Ruth had fallen on her knees beside the kitchen counter and began to pray fervently. She knew she needed to summon all the forces at her disposal. Ruth removed the cigar box from the counter cabinet and took two dolls out. One was labeled Sonny and the other had Miro written on its arm. She extracted two hat pins from the box and slid a pin deeply into each doll's heart. She closed her eyes, twisting and rotating the needles into the dolls' chests. Satan was on the move again. Ruth was not about to let him triumph.

Chapter 19

Cruisin'

July 2006

    The McPherson family had rented half of the luxury suites on the cruise ship *Emerald Isle* that sailed from Piraeus, the seaport of Athens, Greece. The itinerary was chosen and directed by Griff McPherson and included meandering through the Greek Isles.

    The ship was headed towards Crete. On this particular night, the McPhersons had enjoyed an evening of lobster, caviar, grape leaves, olives, and champagne. Colleen had been watching her father for several hours and had consumed enough of the Dom Perignon to feel no pain. When Sonny slipped out of the party to smoke what must have been his sixtieth cigarette of the day, Colleen followed him and spotted him leaning on his elbows on the railing of the foredeck. He'd been drinking all night too, and Colleen thought this might be to her advantage.

    As drunk as she was, she cherished the clarity of the Aegean sky. That far out into the Aegean, there were no ground lights from any civilized spot that could spoil the night sky and the radiance of the stars. It was hard not to believe in the mythical gods and goddesses under such intense celestial light.

Colleen brushed her hair back a bit with her hand and adjusted her cocktail dress. She didn't know where her shoes were, but who cared. She took one last sip from her champagne and threw the crystal flute overboard. "Fucking millionaires," she thought to herself. She walked as steadily as she could to where her father stood and leaned against the rail in the same manner as her father.

Sonny turned in surprise and said, "Well, hey, darling, having fun?" Colleen swallowed the aftertaste of the champagne and her anxiety and turned her head slowly to look at the man she grew up believing was the devil's agent. Her daddy was smiling but appeared to be as drunk as she was. She heard her daddy's question echo through her pickled gray cells but decided to stick to her guns rather than respond to him.

"Daddy, I gotta know something. Did you really mess with us? Me and Starr? Did you really do all those things Momma and Dr. Hughes said you did?"

Sonny's inebriated brain grasped for a vague memory that somebody, maybe it was Dr. Miro, well, hell, somebody had told him to expect this question and to prepare for it. About the only preparation Sonny could make was to flip his cigarette into the ocean, hold onto the railing and try to stand up straight. If shock can sober a person up quickly, Sonny was somewhat sober by the time he got his body erect enough to face his eldest daughter. He'd been working hard to re-establish his relationship with her, but he stupidly had denied or ignored the possibility she might ask him something like this.

Colleen could see that her question had hit her daddy like a ton of bricks. She smiled and wished she'd brought a bottle of champagne with her, either to drink or hit him with.

"So... what's the answer? Cat got your tongue?" As she said this, Colleen grabbed her own tongue with her thumb and forefinger, thinking what an odd phrase that was and also realizing just how much her mouth was beginning to feel like it was filled with cotton or cat fur. Sonny got his emotional sea legs under him and looked straight at Colleen and said, "No, darling, I did not. I made some big mistakes in my life. The biggest one was walking away from you and your sister, but I did not do any of the things your mother accused me of."

Colleen leaned harder against the railing and let this response swirl around in her head. "I don't believe you," she said. "Starr and I both have memories of things that you and other men did."

Sonny's mind was racing toward sobriety now and he lit another cigarette he hoped would help clear his head. Without thinking, he reached across the short distance and placed his left hand on his daughter's hand that was clinching the railing. He touched his daughter for the first time in twelve years. He almost fainted when Colleen didn't remove her hand.

He was having trouble breathing, but managed to say, "I partied more than I should've in college, and I sure ain't no psychiatrist, but I do know whatever memories you have aren't real memories. They got put in your head somehow by somebody. A fellow my lawyer hired explained it all, but I can't say it in a way that makes sense, especially given how much I've been drinking. All I can say, honey, is I swear to you on my life that I didn't do any of that stuff, and I hope you'll believe me."

Colleen squinted her eyes and focused on her father's face which was illuminated by the moonlight. She had spent a lot of years developing a bullshit detector. "Well, if you didn't do any of this shit, where have you been for 12 years? If you're so innocent, Daddy, how come I've been living in a single parent family? Answer me that. How come I've had to be momma and daddy to my little sister? How come you haven't come riding in on a big white horse and swept us up out of the garden of evil?" She growled and slurred the words of this last question.

Sonny's response was interrupted by a loud gang of his nieces and nephews dressed in bathing suits as they ran by on their way to do something wicked with other teens they'd met on the ship. Sonny removed his hand from Colleen's and flicked the ash away from his cigarette.

"Colleen, look, we've both been drinking, so this probably isn't the best time to go into all this, but if you wanna talk, let's go sit down somewhere. Hell, we need to either drink some water or some more bubbly. I kinda like this Dom, but I gotta sit down."

"Okay, Daddy. There's a place right around the corner with some deck chairs. You go there and sit down, and I'll go get us some more bubbly. I think it's time we had a heart-to-heart."

Colleen watched her daddy wobble off in the direction she had pointed. Although pretty toasted, her keen mind was getting some momentum. She stood up to her full height and filled her lungs with the Hellenic air. She chuckled and then said to herself, "Now we'll get to the bottom of things. I've waited a long time for this. Wonder if Daddy's ever played truth or dare?" She and Starr had spent years perfecting this method of total, bone-stripping honesty. "Yeah," she said to herself, "I'm gonna get to the heart of the matter. Starr's counting on me."

Colleen once again adjusted her dress and headed towards the door that would take her back to the bar, the source of limitless bubbly. *In vino veritas*. Colleen always liked that phrase. It was one of the few things she remembered from her Latin class. Colleen was excited about the possibilities. She had some scores to settle.

Chapter 20

Starr

November 2005

It was time. "Momma's not here," Starr muttered to herself. Starr pulled the velvet lined box from its secret hiding place. It was covered in some of her favorite pictures. She particularly liked the one of Ozzie biting off the head of a chicken. Alice Cooper was amazing.

The ceremony was simple. She removed the packet of razor blades and selected a new one. She pulled off her sweater and skirt, making sure to fold them just so. Momma didn't like wrinkles. She examined the scars on her arms. They were healing, but they needed more time. Starr decided she would do her legs today. But first, she took a large, leak-proof storage bag from the box and arranged it in the trash can, using clothes pins to hold it to the sides. With a practiced move, she dropped to her knees and forced herself to throw up her dinner. She'd made a decision some time ago weight would not be an issue for her. Starr regurgitated one more time and wiped her mouth. She had heard of other girls whose parents discovered their so-called eating disorder because the toilets backed up. Starr was much more careful. She discarded her mess in discreet ways, depositing the bags in various public receptacles. All she needed to do was lose five more pounds and she would be perfect.

Her bedroom was not large but was immaculate. A no-dirt zone. Her bed was perfect. If it weren't for the obvious female things on the dresser, you'd think it was a Marine barracks. Order was the rule of the day. Momma liked order and Starr outwardly complied.

Starr shuffled through her CD's and found what she was looking for. Black Sabbath. War Pigs. She loved the bodies in the fire. Ancient rock ruled. She coughed a little from the remnants of her vomit. She turned the table fan on and pumped up the music. She sat down on the floor, leaning against her bed. Turning her head so the wind from the fan wouldn't interfere, she put some of the hash in the small pipe and used her butane lighter to get it going. Hash took some effort, but it got you there. Also got rid of that god-awful vomit taste. She took a long, deep hit. She looked at her toes with their exquisitely painted black nails. The music began to sink in. The generals and Satan. She closed her eyes and saw the fire. She wondered at the goats' heads they were wearing. One had a two-foot long cock. She watched herself dance, in and around the fire. The Master himself beckoned her.

It had taken a long time for Dr. Hughes to tell her about the alters. The bitch. Hell, it took her a long time to tell Dr. Hughes about the alters. She had demanded total honesty from her mother and Dr. Hughes, so they eventually told her she had a multiple personality disorder, or MPD. That's some serious shit. Seemed to turn Dr. Hughes on though. Had a certain buzz to it. Recently, Dr. Hughes had called it a dissociative identity disorder. Psychiatric progress. She learned, too, that both she and her sister had been given a diagnosis of PTSD—post traumatic stress disorder. The jury was still out about how many alters lived inside her. "Maybe I can enter the Guinness World Book of Records," she said out loud. "Wonder if they have, like, an MPD category?"

Starr held the razor with her clenched hand and made a slight incision across her right thigh. She dropped into the abyss. The pain was warm and perfect. They were pleased. She made an identical cut into her left thigh. A brace of gratitude. She took another long hit off the pipe and let her feelings mingle. Love and pain became one.

She became her best self. She called herself Angel. She rubbed herself between her legs just under her panties, but then caught herself. "No," she said. "Stop that!" Angel didn't like being yelled at. Starr remembered when her momma first caught her masturbating. All hell broke loose. Starr knew right then sex was a no-no and had to go underground. That's why she thought of her razor and stash box as the "Velvet Underground." But the best part is that is what she called her vagina too: the velvet underground.

Starr opened her eyes for a moment and wiped her fingers across each cut. She marveled at the color of blood. It was its taste that soothed her most. She hit the pipe again, and, closing her eyes, re-entered the fires. The Master was pleased. How she loved his smile. She dabbed her new cuts with a tissue.

Starr was really angry at her sister for kissing-up to their daddy. Daddy dearest had gotten Colleen a laptop, promised her he'd pay for college, taken her on some trips, and had promised her a fucking car. Daddy hated Mildred. This made Starr smile. Starr didn't understand how Colleen could forget all that had happened to them. Angel kept whispering to Starr it was Mildred's fault. Starr said sharply to Angel, "Shut up."

Starr lined up the little dolls she had made over the years to represent the important people in her life. These were not the anatomically detailed dolls Dr. Hughes was so fond of but demonically detailed figures into which Starr periodically stuck some pins. Starr glared at her newest creation, a small doll representing Dr. Miro. It still had a long hypodermic needle sticking in its brain. She picked up the Mildred Hughes doll. Angel got excited. Angel liked it better when Starr inflicted pain on the dolls instead of her. Angel could tell Starr was having some new thoughts about Dr. Empathy. Angel had her own thoughts about Mildred and knew she had to pick just the right time to push Starr.

Starr checked the time on her clock radio and knew her momma would be coming back soon. She still had some sorting out to do about these two shrinks. She collected the dolls and all her other paraphernalia and put everything back in order into the box, and the box in turn went into its hiding place. She looked forward to tonight's rave. Billy usually had good Ecstasy. He was also a good fuck. Angel liked that. They'd sneak out after Momma was asleep.

Chapter 21

Do Unto Others

December 2006

Starr waited in the shadows of the building until she was satisfied that doctor asshole was alone. The few other occupants of the building left at 5 o'clock and she knew most shrinks worked off some dumb-ass 45 minute or 50 minute hour thing, so she timed her entry into his building so she'd be least likely to encounter anyone. She slipped on the gloves she had stolen from her gynecologist's office. She took the stairs and eased open the door, looking to see if anyone else might be there. All was quiet. She took the doll and rope from her backpack and used her small folding knife to cut a good piece of duct tape off the roll to hold the rope. She eased out the door and walked quickly to his office door. It read:

"Calder Miro, Ph.D.

Clinical & Forensic Psychology"

There was also a small sign that said "No Soliciting," and she snickered at this. *I'm bringing it, you bastard!*

With her ear to the door, she heard no movement inside. Taking the chance that he wasn't in the front office, she carefully opened the door, peeped, then stepped in. *Good.* She deftly taped the rope holding the doll to the middle of his door. Pleased that it was secure and held a prominent place, she took a moment to utter a prayer to herself and twist the pins in the doll's heart and brains. *May deep, sweet pain be upon you!*

She opened the door carefully and peeked into the hall. Ninja-like, she moved quickly down the hall and disappeared through the fire exit stairway. She waited until she saw no pedestrians or cars and slipped out of the building into the alley's shadows.

Chapter 22

Revenge

December 2006

While Worth was sniffing out the money angle, Calder was thinking about revenge as a motive. After dictating a report to his secretary, he set aside other matters that needed his attention. It was mid-afternoon, and, as he often did this time of day, he fixed a skim latte in the office kitchen and settled in at his long, curved desk in his private office, located in a back corner of his office condo. He had gotten one of the three volumes of the Oxford English Dictionary from his own library and looked up the word he'd been chewing on ever since Mildred Hughes had been killed.

There's a lot to the word 'revenge,' he thought, especially when he had to read its definitions through a magnifying glass that came with the OED. Its basic meaning is 'the act of doing hurt or harm to another in return for wrong or injury suffered; satisfaction obtained by repayment of injuries.' Among the many literary references in the OED definition, one caught his eye: it was from Percy Bysshe Shelley's *Cyclops*: 'I have taken a full revenge for your unnatural feast.'

Although the mythological meanings didn't seem useful, the word's root meaning fit Santos like a glove. He certainly felt injured by Mildred Hughes. His divorce records showed he had several domestic violence charges brought against him by his ex-wife, with one conviction, and she moved to the west coast to get away from him. Although the absence of any evidence to tie Santos to the drawing made him an unlikely suspect, he was a dirty bar fighter and clubbing somebody over the head when she didn't see it coming might just be his style.

Calder and Worth knew, too, Santos was lying. He'd been in Hughes' home office and put a program on her computer he had downloaded from a hacker site, or from what Tekatak called an 'invasion' site. Tek was judicious about his use of the word hacker, because he believed true hackers were purists and not out to do harm. They hacked for the aesthetics of it. True hacking was like skiing out of bounds when you've been told not to go there--it was for the sake of the deep and outrageous snow and the thrill of not getting caught. The purpose was the rebellion-- not to start a destructive avalanche. Santos' trail through Hughes' computer suggested he was just snooping. Revenge would have led him to plant viruses or steal her money, Calder concluded. Tek thought so too. So far, there was no indication that Santos had done anything other than invade her files and look around. A review of his divorce pleadings supported his claim he had made enough money to retire to Ocracoke by selling off a ball-bearing business he'd owned in New Jersey.

Ever since Calder had known Sonny McPherson, he'd thought that if what had happened to Sonny had happened to him, he'd feel like killing somebody. Sonny was justifiably angry at Ruth when Calder evaluated him and never once appeared to be able to consider any non-malevolent or accidental interpretation of her actions against him, but he did seem content to regain contact with his kids. He and Colleen had traveled together and he seemed proud of her. His relationship with his youngest child remained estranged. Still, he had reasons for revenge, but his rancor never seemed to center on Dr. Hughes. Calder agreed with Worth. It was possible that over time, Sonny's animosity could have become fixated on Dr. Hughes.

Another poetic reference in the OED grabbed Calder. In 1818, Lord Byron had written "Sweet is revenge—especially to women." Thinking about how politically incorrect such an utterance might seem almost two centuries later, Calder knew some women who'd take their revenge on Byron for being so chauvinistic, but that would prove his point, wouldn't it? The three primary women in this case— Ruth, Starr, and Colleen—might have a revenge motive.

Ruth and her attorney never let Calder meet or evaluate the children as part of his analysis of the case, but he did meet Ruth. Though small in stature, her interactions with Calder throughout his interview were verbally combative and challenging. The first part of the interview was characterized by Ruth deflecting Calder's questions and demanding Calder tell her personal things about himself. Calder had been clear in his letter to the attorneys for Ruth and Sonny about the structure and conditions of the interview, but Ruth tried mightily to push through the boundaries Calder established. She had refused, for example, to sit in the chair Calder directed her to, and instead pulled a footstool over in front of Calder and sat on it, at Calder's feet, looking up at him. She also refused to allow him to close the interview room door. It was a clash with a forensic examinee the likes of which Calder had never experienced. As Dr. John and the Night Trippers would say, "Refried confusion was making itself clear."

To get the terms of engagement established and boundaries set, Calder had stood up, turned the tape recorder on, told Ms. McPherson that if she did not get up and go back to the chair he wanted her to sit in and allow him to close the door and ask her the questions he had to ask her, the interview was over. He looked her straight in the eyes and said he would answer some of her questions about himself if he thought they were appropriate, but she had to sit across from him, on the other side of the table, with the tape recorder between them, and with the door closed for privacy. He told her if she could not agree to these conditions, they would stop the interview and she could go home. He would then inform both attorneys what had happened. The half minute or so of silence that followed his directives lasted a long time. Ruth had gotten up, brushed her skirt with her hands, and sat down in the designated chair. Calder had shut the door, returned to his seat, and said, "Are you ready to begin, Ms. McPherson." She had nodded.

For Ruth to have killed Dr. Hughes, she'd have to have felt betrayed and abandoned by her. The two of them had formed what Sonny described as an unholy alliance to rob him of his children. Their bond was the children and a religious fervor that saw Satan everywhere. For Ruth to have killed Mildred, she'd have to have become convinced that Mildred had gone over to the other side and become one of Lucifer's agents. Ruth's religious passion could find biblical support for vengeance if she felt she was acting as God's agent. There might be something in Ruth's background—maybe someone had victimized her as a child—that might fuel murderous rage, but Calder had scant knowledge of her history, and only from Sonny. Ruth was adamant in her refusal to talk with Calder about her personal history. Sonny had claimed that Ruth sometimes alluded to having been sexually mistreated as a girl, but she never told Sonny any details. It was possible Ruth blamed Mildred for the girls' reunification with their father, but, hell, Calder thought, he should be dead then, too. That was a sobering thought.

Both Starr and Colleen had possible reasons for revenge. Each lived her childhood and adolescence steeped in the belief that their father and his side of the family had committed horrible, unspeakable crimes against them. There was no way to reconstruct all the probing maternal and professional interviews and medical exams they had endured. The repetitive therapy, driven by its confirmatory bias against their father, had blindly worked, relentlessly, to shatter their identities. Each girl had experienced betrayal from their loved ones. Betrayed by their daddy and his family. This was the reality they had lived with the majority of their lives. Betrayed by their mother, whose own beliefs and single-minded actions set the stage for the creation of their own extensive abuse histories. And betrayed by their therapist, whose incompetence and zealousness forged mental illness into their very beings.

While Calder was willing to remain open to the possibility of evidence proving Mildred Hughes was right and had provided appropriate and thoughtful therapy to these two children, he was still convinced she had messed up these children, perhaps beyond repair. *It's one thing to be in treatment because you've suffered some trauma everyone knows you went through and there's no disagreement that you experienced it,* he thought. *But on the other hand, it's a damn crime against nature to be put through therapy, especially as a child, that aims to treat some trauma that might have happened, or, more to the point - probably didn't happen. These children were subjected to a long-term course of treatment that was itself abusive.*

One significant loose end continued to bother Calder. Other than a few drawings, there were no substantive clinical notes in the Hughes' file about the content of therapy appointments with either Starr or Colleen. This could mean she was telling Calder the truth that she destroyed her notes, but that didn't wash because her billing records showed she'd seen the children after his interview with her in 2002. Calder's guess was she kept three files, one for general records, correspondence, and billing, and two others. One for each child. Calder's thinking was that, unless she didn't make any notes about her individual sessions with her young patients, he and Worth were missing two files.

Mildred Hughes and Ruth McPherson had remained steadfast that Starr and Colleen had endured satanic, ritualistic abuse, despite no findings by social services, no physical or medical findings, and no forensic evidence by the police that supported the allegations. Calder strongly believed that society fails a child when it allows, as it did under these circumstances, a mother and a fanatical therapist to put these children through what they went through.

Calder hypothesized that each child, over time, described events that either she claimed she saw or things that happened to her. Given the fantastic nature and descriptions of these events, which went well beyond the normal life experiences of any child, Calder believed in the absence of any evidence to the contrary, the McPherson girls were interrogated until they said what their interrogators wanted to hear.

These children lived in a house with a mother who once believed and still believed their father was a child molesting Satanist. They went to therapy regularly and were in the care of a psychologist who came to share their mother's opinions and beliefs about their father, but who also brought to bear all the treatment tools and erroneous assumptions about the causes and effects of child sexual abuse that were prevalent in their day.

The McPherson children were put into therapy as scared, confused children whose parents were going through a nasty, nasty divorce. Their daddy was a clumsy, inexperienced father. Calder reasoned Colleen's and Starr's answers to questions were designed to protect themselves, or one of their parents, or to satisfy the adult asking the questions. In his training as a forensic psychologist, Calder learned that children, especially age five and younger, thought adults already knew the answer to the question they were asking them. Calder also knew repetitive questioning will lead children to give answers that have the effect of making the questioner happy. Calder believed this same process was why adult prisoners, under duress, would inevitably ask or demand, 'Tell me what you wanna know.'

Calder didn't think Mildred Hughes or anyone in the children's lives during the early part of the 1990's gave much thought as to how the separation, divorce, and conflict over visitation affected either the children or the parents. As he had explained to Worth, what probably started out as a normal reaction to parental conflict—especially over the hygiene and care of two little girls by their father--escalated into two little girls naming their father as an incest perpetrator and becoming diagnosed with post traumatic stress disorder, depression, anxiety, borderline personalities, and multiple personalities. Their therapy became a process that tore their personalities apart in the service of proving they had been brutally, sexually molested by over a dozen people.

Calder let his mind chew on that a bit. Yes, he said to himself, if either of the McPherson girls arrived at the same conclusions he had about her therapy, then one of them may have sought 'repayment for injuries suffered.' It was a stretch, but it was plausible.

Zap. Calder remembered the call he'd received from Sam Cooper, whom he had surmised was treating Colleen. He and Sam had never talked again, because Calder decided it was potentially too complicated for him to mix roles. His past role as Sonny's attorney's consulting expert made it totally inappropriate for him to consult with Colleen's therapist, assuming that was who Sam was treating. Calder made that decision before Mildred Hughes had her skull crushed. Calder let his mind wander. What if Colleen was the murderer and Sam was still treating her? If that were true, it might mean Sam was at risk and maybe didn't have a clue.

Calder decided to call it a day and go home. He wanted to think about this some more. Maybe he'd get a run in before the day was done. His secretary had been gone about two hours, so he went into the waiting room to lock the front door of his office suite and turn off the lights. Then he saw it. Hanging from a piece of rope, duct-taped to the inside of his front door, was a voodoo doll with pins in its heart and skull. His heart froze when he saw it.

Calder regained his composure and called Worth, who told him not to touch it, and he'd send a couple of detectives right over. Although neither of these two friends said anything beyond that to each other, both suspected this meant Calder was now on the murderer's radar screen, and that wasn't good.

Making sure everything was locked up until the cops arrived, Calder went to his briefcase and retrieved his Glock. He snapped the loaded clip into the gun. He thought about putting it back into his brief case, but decided he would feel better if he held onto it. He sat down at his secretary's desk, put his gun on the desk, took a deep breath, and stared at the doll, waiting for the detectives. If it was the doll's intention to scare him, it had hit its target.

Chapter 23

Sonny

The detectives had found no prints linked to any of the suspects in this case either on the doll, rope, or tape, nor in his office. No one interviewed in the building so far had seen anything. Calder called Worth and told him what he was thinking in terms of the revenge angle. Using his brain to work on the case helped Calder curb his anxiety. Worth was at his desk in the precinct office. He listened as Calder filled him in on the meanings of revenge and their relevance to this case.

"Some nut trackin' you and you lookin' up clues in a dictionary?"

Calder listened not only to how sarcastic that sounded but to how stupid it must have sounded to his friend that he had spent the better part of a day reading literary allusions to the word "revenge," while somebody was possibly stalking him and leaving him death threats.

"Well, you never know," Calder responded, trying to sound cool and not too defensive. "I learned Percy Bysshe Shelley had written about the Cyclops, so that was informative."

"And who you thinkin' is the Cyclops monster in this case? If anyone's Ulysses, it's me. That brother was da bomb."

Calder responded, "I think my point is there is a real possibility the psychological motive is revenge, and money has a whole lot less to do with it. Thinking about the revenge angle doesn't eliminate suspects unfortunately. It increases the list."

"So, your reading the OED not making my job easier?"

"Not exactly," Calder replied, getting his emotional keel upright. "But it's probably making your job a whole lot more balanced and poetic. All homicide detectives need more poetry in their lives. It keeps them from becoming jaded and cynical."

"Jaded and cynical." Worth snorted.

"Like I said, you need more poetry. I won't even charge you for this consult. This is free."

Worth felt better about Calder's state of mind as he listened to the return of his friend's humor.

"I'm feelin' better already," chimed Worth. "As much as I would like to lie back in my government issued 1980's wooden chair and obtain some more poetic therapy, I gotta go. Sonny McPherson and his lawyer are here for my interview. I shall go forth and explore the depths of Sonny's soul for vestiges of revenge."

"That's all a man can ask. Good hunting," Calder said. "Three other things though, before you go. I think we're missing two files from Dr. Hughes. It would make sense that she kept notes about her individual appointments with the McPherson children and probably had a file on each child."

Worth responded, "I'll look again and call her colleague to re-check the files, but I don't think I missed 'em. What else?"

"I think the voodoo doll on my door eliminates Sonny. For better or worse, he likes me."

"Basically, I agree with you, unless it was done to throw us off track," responded Worth.

"The inscrutable, skeptical mind," chimed Calder. "The third thing is I think I may know who Colleen's in therapy with in Chapel Hill. If Colleen's our murderer, her current therapist might be in some danger."

"Why don't you call this therapist up and tell him that?"

"It's a she. I'm thinking about it. It's complicated. I don't know for sure Colleen's her patient, and she can't tell me because of confidentiality. Plus, we don't know if Colleen killed Mildred. She's nobody's prime suspect."

"What makes you think you know who Colleen is in treatment with?" Worth asked. "She refused to tell me when I interviewed her. It might help us a lot to be able to talk with Colleen's therapist to see what might go on in that sexy little head of hers."

"Last year, I got a request for a professional consult from Dr. Samantha Cooper, a Chapel Hill psychologist. We weren't very far into the telephone consultation when, based on some things she said, I got a funny feeling she was treating Colleen and was going to ask me questions I shouldn't be answering. It was only a hunch, but we both agreed to terminate the consult and it never went any further."

"What fired off your hunch, Sherlock? Musta been something case specific?"

"It sounded like Dr. Cooper was puzzled over her patient's knowledge of details about certain child sexual abuse allegations that led her patient to lose contact for over ten years with a parent. It was the 'ten years' fact that caught my attention, plus I knew Colleen had entered UNC. But it also got me thinking that maybe Colleen had read my report. Some of the details she might have been presenting to her therapist may have come from that. At the time of my consult with Cooper, that didn't seem to be important."

"And now," said Worth, "it may be very important. Taking revenge as a central motive, if either one of these girls came to believe or accept enough of your analysis of their daddy and their therapist, maybe she took her revenge. In the meantime, I got to go interview Sonny." To Worth's mind, Sonny held enough weight in both categories—money and revenge—to make him a serious suspect.

Sonny was accompanied to his interview by Michael Burke, considered the best criminal defense lawyer in Raleigh, maybe even the whole state. Word was he billed at $600 an hour.

At Worth's request, Sonny had volunteered to be interviewed. He also had agreed to be polygraphed and he passed. Burke was there to make sure Worth conducted the interview properly and that Sonny didn't incriminate himself.

Worth led the two of them back into the interrogation room.

He turned on the tape recorder that sat in the middle of the table. Since he hadn't asked, he assumed the next thing that would happen would be Sonny's attorney yelling at him to turn it off, and then they'd have a fight about procedure, rights, and other such nonsense. Burke didn't say a thing. Good for him, thought Worth.

Worth spoke into the microphone, "This is December 2, 2006, and I am conducting an interview of Sonny McPherson in the matter of the murder of Dr. Mildred Hughes. Also present is Michael Burke, representing Mr. McPherson. I want to thank you both for coming."

"Point of clarification, Detective," said Burke. "I am here as Mr. McPherson's attorney, but since he is not under arrest, and since he is not a defendant in anything except his on-going domestic dispute, I am not representing him in any formal criminal proceedings, because this matter, as far as I know, remains at the investigation stage, correct? Sonny has passed a polygraph exam conducted by your department, correct? And Sonny is here of his own free will, voluntarily and full of a cooperative spirit, correct?"

"Mr. Burke," Worth injected, "I believe that all to be true. Your client is a suspect in a murder investigation. He is here voluntarily and is not under arrest. You or he can terminate this interview at any point you wish."

"Thank you, Detective. I think it more accurate to describe Sonny as a person of interest in your investigation."

"He certainly holds my interest, Mr. Burke."

Now that the legal niceties were out of the way for the moment, Worth turned his attention to Sonny. First thing, though, Worth noticed, was that Sonny was sweating, a condition that didn't help his claims of innocence.

Sonny produced what looked like a solid gold lighter to light the cigarette he just put to his lips. Worth looked at him and said, "No smoking."

"You gotta be kidding," blurted Sonny. "I've come down here voluntarily to be interrogated and you're telling me I can't smoke?"

Entitlement has its own reality, Worth thought. "You are hearing me correctly, Mr. McPherson. Although we are in North Carolina, which is the home of some wealthy tobacco companies that have made zillions getting people addicted to tobacco, this building is smoke-free. And, even it weren't, you couldn't smoke here, because my lungs don't like breathing cigarette smoke. I have my own rules. You can take a smoke break outside if you want, but I suggest we at least get started, because the sooner we start, the sooner we finish."

"Okay, okay, get on with it."

Worth ignored the attitude and cut a look at Michael Burke, who discreetly rolled his eyes. Burke made his living—in amounts not much less than the tobacco companies' profits—representing and coddling the entitled rich. He then said to his client, "Sonny, why don't we see what Detective Brown wants to know, and then we'll get an idea about how long this is going to take. You good with that?"

"All right, let's get this shit over with," Sonny sneered. He kept his lighter and cigarette on the table.

Worth tilted his big frame a few inches across the table in Sonny's direction and said, "Mr. McPherson, you're a prime suspect in the murder of Mildred Hughes because there are a lot of reasons you probably didn't like her very much."

"I didn't kill the bitch, if that's what you want to know. I ain't sorry she's dead though. She ruined my life and my kids' lives. Both my kids are fucked up because of her bullshit therapy. Dr. Miro nailed her in his report. You read that? He got it right! I had my lawyers look at the possibility of suing her ass for malpractice, but everybody told me it would just make it all the more difficult for me to see my kids, so I never did it, but I sure wanted to. I hated her guts, but I didn't kill her."

Worth thought about asking him if he hired somebody to kill her, but he decided to save that for later.

"Do you have an alibi for the day and evening she was killed?"

"Yeah, I got a fucking alibi," snapped Sonny. "I was in Asheville, playing croquet. I was there for five days and never left the whole time. I can get affidavits from probably twenty people, thirty if you count the hotel staff."

Worth thought to himself that Sonny probably didn't count the hotel staff as people, but if he needed 'em, they'd count.

"I'd like you to make me a list of the people you were with and the dates you were there."

Before his client could spit out some belligerent comment, attorney Burke said, "We'll be glad to, Detective. I've already prepared such a list," and he handed over to Worth a typed list on expensive bond paper. He had just made his fee worth every penny. Sonny smiled.

Worth looked at the list and recognized some of the names of the rich and famous. As witness lists go, this was first class. Worth also knew Sonny would have a huge paper trail from a week in the mountains, because his class rarely used cash. Sonny's alibi was gonna be airtight.

Burke followed his presentation of the list with a graceful challenge. "Will there be anything else, Detective?"

Worth looked at Sonny and then looked at Burke. Sonny was smiling like the Cheshire cat and had picked up his lighter and cigarette. Worth returned his gaze to Sonny and said, "Murder is a complex thing, Mr. McPherson. Your being in Asheville does not eliminate you as a suspect. It just means you might not have bashed her brains out, but you might know who did. Have a nice day, Mr. McPherson. I'll be in touch."

Worth clicked off the tape recorder, picked it up and walked out of the room, leaving Sonny and his attorney staring at his empty chair. Worth didn't like smart asses.

Chapter 24

Tight Rope

February 2007

Calder decided to call Dr. Samantha Cooper. If Colleen was the murderer and was her patient and was still in therapy with her, Sam could be in danger. Calder figured there was little to risk by calling her, and knew the two of them could have a discussion in a way that maintained appropriate confidential boundaries and didn't violate her patient's privilege.

Sam called him back on her lunch break.

"Dr. Miro," he answered.

"Hi, Calder. Sam Cooper returning your call. It's been a while."

"Hi, Sam. Yes, it has. You doing well?"

"I'm fine. And you?"

"Very busy, and that's always a mixed blessing, I guess. Have you got a few minutes to talk—hypothetically—about the case overlap we might have run into when we last talked?"

Sam had been walking around with her cordless phone, shuffling various pieces of mail, but Calder's question caused her to sit down. "I suppose… I mean, yes, I have some time, but I'm not sure what there is to discuss, or what we can discuss. I'm not aware of anything that has changed."

Calder cleared his throat and said, "From my end of things, there have been big changes. In the case I was previously involved in, I conducted a forensic psychological eval of a father and his family that involved some significant child sexual abuse allegations. I wrote a report of my findings I submitted in 2003. Last August, a colleague of ours, Dr. Mildred Hughes, who practiced in Wilmington, was bludgeoned to death while vacationing on Ocracoke. I don't know if you knew that or not?"

Sam replied, "I heard about it. It was tragic, of course, but I didn't know her, and, didn't make too much of it. Why is her death significant?"

Calder took another deep breath. "The detective investigating her murder pulled me in to help with his investigation, and we have concluded her death relates to the case I had previously evaluated." Calder let this sink in.

Calder knew Sam was thinking.

Calder asked, "May I give you a few more details that are the basis of my call to you?"

"Yes," said Sam, whose heart was pounding.

"The father in the case I evaluated had two little girls—sisters—whose parents had a bitter custody battle in Craven County. Allegations made against the father and his extended family led to the girls not seeing their father for over ten years. It was that coincidental fact in your case description that made me worry you were calling me to consult on something I already knew a lot about. Mildred Hughes was the children's therapist in that case and my analysis of the case retrospectively led me to conclude that there may never have been any abuse of the children and that the children's therapy with Dr. Hughes may have been iatrogenic. Bottom line is, Sam, obviously I don't know if you're still treating the patient you called me about, but, if you are, and she's who I think she is, she's a suspect in the murder of her former therapist."

Catching her breath, Sam said, "Are you calling to warn me?"

"I suppose I am. If the hypotheticals we've discussed aren't hypotheticals, then your patient may have entered UNC the same year the oldest child in my case also entered UNC, who Worth, the homicide detective, and I know began therapy with a new therapist in her freshman year. The suspect, who is now almost twenty-one, has never given us the name of her therapist."

"I'm a bit speechless right now," said Sam. "I'm not sure what to make of all this. Can you reveal to me the name of your suspect?"

"At this point, I probably can't, but Detective Brown could, based on the fact that he's investigating a murder. Would you talk with him? Would you talk with both of us? We could drive up to your office."

"Your request is most unusual, but I clearly see your point. I cannot reveal anything to either of you without my patient's permission, so we would need to be clear on that limitation. But I suppose I can listen."

Calder then said, "There is a point at which you don't need your patient's permission, and that is, if you think she is a danger either to herself or others."

"I'm well aware of that, but I don't feel I'm at that point. I don't yet know if the hypotheticals have dissolved into reality."

Calder then responded, "Let's say we are talking about the same case and the same person. If you were convinced of that, would it change your thinking?"

"Even if my patient's a suspect, that doesn't make her guilty. I would have to have a lot more information to break confidentiality."

Calder said, "I agree. Worth and I think the murderer is dangerous, maybe in a psychotic way, or in a psychopathic way. Could you find time to talk with us this afternoon?"

Sam looked at her calendar and knew in her heart she had to do it. "Yes," she said. "Could you be here by 4 PM?"

"Let me check with Worth and make sure, and I'll call you back as soon as I talk with him to confirm or not."

"Thanks, Calder, I think?"

"You're welcome. I'll call you right back."

"Just leave me a voice mail if I don't answer."

"Will do. So long."

"Bye," said Sam. She hung up and let the worry wash over her. She wondered to herself. *Who have I got as my patient? What have I got as a patient?*

Sam had lost her appetite but not her rational mind. She went to her computer and went to MySpace. Her clinical practice was composed of mostly university students and they had educated Sam about virtual life in Face Book and MySpace. She typed in relevant information and searched for Emma McPherson. It didn't take long to find her. There was her picture and her bio, mostly random, flirtatious descriptions and comments. Just for the hell of it, Sam searched for any other McPhersons at UNC. Another name came up. Colleen McPherson. Standing at her computer, Sam almost collapsed. Colleen's posted photo was the same as Emma's. They were the same person—at least on MySpace. Sam jotted down the contact information for Colleen's mother and her sister, Starr.

Her phone rang, but she let voice mail get it. It was Calder saying he and Detective Brown would be at her office that afternoon as scheduled.

Chapter 25

Murder Too

February 2007

Ruth had some trepidation about seeing Colleen. She had made sure Starr wasn't home for this visit with Colleen. Her oldest daughter had changed since going away to college. Ruth was happy for her, but she felt that Colleen, as she had feared, had come under the sway of Sonny's money and prestige. Sonny had given Colleen an expensive car and paid for her tuition and living expenses. They'd gone on some trips together. She was glad though that Colleen was able to go to UNC Chapel Hill. Still, she prayed and prayed Colleen would be safe. Although Ruth had agreed to the visitation that eventually occurred between Colleen and Sonny, she never let go of her belief, down in her bones, that Sonny was a sick sonofabitch and had subjected his young daughters to satanic ritual abuse. Still, the money helped.

Ruth was never sure if Colleen or Starr had read Miro's report. Ruth never asked and Colleen never said. Ruth was ambivalent about that, but she had left it on the kitchen counter for a few days. Ruth was also not certain why Colleen had stopped seeing Dr. Hughes before she was murdered but had decided it was too much to expect her to go back and forth between Wilmington and Chapel Hill. Colleen had refused to go to Dr. Hughes' funeral with her and Starr. Colleen had said it was because she wouldn't be able to stand it, seeing Dr. Hughes dead. Starr was very upset about Dr. Hughes' murder and, in some ways, had gotten worse since it happened. Ruth couldn't tell how Colleen felt about Dr. Hughes' death, but Starr had become obsessed with death. Oh, she was so confused.

Colleen arrived at Ruth's door right on time. The house looked different now. It used to be her home. But not for the past two years. *It's a shitty little place*, thought Colleen. Colleen always thought that her daddy gave her momma some money, maybe child support, or something, but Ruth obviously never put it into their living situation. The Miro report had convinced Colleen Momma was hoarding money somewhere. She parked her BMW, and, after checking the contents of her handbag, got out, and, out of habit, punched the remote lock. She walked down the cracked sidewalk toward her mother's house. She remembered playing hopscotch on this very sidewalk and was humming "Sticks and stones can break my bones" when Ruth came out to greet her.

"Hi, honey."

"Hi, Momma," and Colleen allowed her momma to hug her.

Ruth had spent years tuning her maternal intuition, and she sensed something was wrong with her oldest daughter.

"What's wrong, honey?"

Colleen gained control of her insides even more. She had forgotten how hanging out with her mother was like living with that female doctor on the Starship Enterprise who was always scanning everyone's minds and bodies for alien life forms. Her momma had no boundaries. With Dr. Cooper's help, Colleen had realized that her mother's core personality was an odd mixture of borderline and narcissistic elements. Colleen didn't know about borderline personalities until one day Dr. Cooper suggested she watch a particular episode of the *Sopranos*, in which Tony Soprano's therapist helped him understand his own mother's disturbed behavior.

Colleen never told Dr. Cooper it was her introduction to the world of the reruns of the television drama the *Sopranos* that helped Colleen understand how rage-filled and diabolical some borderlines can be. Colleen went to the UNC psychology library and read about borderlines. She discovered that when a person's personality features or traits become entrenched, inflexible, and maladaptive, those traits organize themselves into a personality disorder. Her momma had become a hybrid disorder—a combination of extraordinary self-centeredness and instability. Living with her momma had become like living on the edge of a volcano that erupted sometimes without warning and sucked you into its core. Her momma's emotions were volcanic magma and lava. They flowed like magma at an intense speed just below the surface, and when they blew, the lava they spewed out burned and overwhelmed everything in its path.

"I'm fine, Momma. I'm just tired. Too much studying. How are you?"

Colleen had long ago learned the best way to get the scanning device turned off of her was to ask her momma about herself. Ruth was a quintessential narcissistic pool.

Ruth smiled back at her daughter and said, "I'm fine, too. I'm a little nervous about seeing you after so long, but I want to hear all about school, your friends, and Chapel Hill. Have you joined a church yet?"

Well, there it was, Colleen thought to herself. That was record time. As a child, Colleen used to have a contest with herself to see if she could guess just how many minutes would go by before her mother injected religion into a conversation. They could be talking about cooking scrambled eggs, and her momma would find a way to make the discussion a journey down the road to Damascus.

"No, Momma, I haven't had time yet. My workload is just way too much. School's harder than I thought it would be. I study all the time."

"Not on the Sabbath, I hope," said Ruth smiling.

Colleen realized they could have an argument before they even got to the porch. That wouldn't do. She put her arm around her mother's waist and said as sweetly as she could, "I'll go to church with you and Starr this Sunday, I promise. Can we go in? I need to use the bathroom. It's been a long drive. Also, I have a present for you."

"A present? What on earth for? It's not my birthday for another few months."

Shepherding her momma onto the porch and into the house, Colleen said quickly, "It's just a little something. I have to pee," and she retreated down the hallway to the bathroom. She closed and locked the door. You have to lock doors with borderlines, she thought to herself. She sat on the toilet and opened her handbag. She had the two cell phones separated in different plastic bags. Her momma's was red. Fitting, she thought.

"Are you okay, honey?" her momma said from the other side of the door.

She's something else, Colleen thought to herself. "Yes, I'm fine. Be out in a minute." *Give me some space, bitch!*

Colleen tried to make herself pee. Not much there. She read the instructions for activation one more time and powered her momma's phone on. She checked again to make sure her momma's number was programmed into the other cell phone in the other baggie. Satisfied all was well, she flushed the toilet so her momma could hear the water running through the pipes and relax a bit. Bathroom functions, once they got past a certain age, had become one of the few private behaviors her mother allowed her daughters. Colleen checked herself in the mirror. She regained the resolve she was looking for.

Without asking if she wanted anything, Ruth had fixed Colleen some tea. Wondering if that might be a problem for later, Colleen decided not. Colleen then said, "Let me show you what I got for you." She pulled the red phone out of her bag and handed it to her mother.

Ruth said, "Why on earth did you get me one of these? I don't need a cell phone. Is this one of your father's ideas? Did you pay for it or did he?"

Boom. Lava had popped to the surface. Where'd she get the idea Daddy had anything to do with this? Colleen was not going into the core. *Not today.* She had practiced this moment. "Momma, Daddy has nothing to do with this. He knows nothing about it. This is a gift from me to you, so we can stay in touch more. I know you've been missing our contact, so I think this is a good way for us to be in touch with each other. It's not expensive at all, and I've programmed it so that you'll receive calls only from me. If ever you decide Starr should have one too, we can set it up so that only the three of us can call each other. It's a family phone, Momma. You're important to me. I feel awful we've kinda lost touch with each other. That's been my fault. I want you to forgive me, Momma. I need your forgiveness for not staying in touch and making you think I moved away from you and toward Daddy. You are the center of my world, Momma. This is a gift of redemption. Please accept my gift." *Take that into your self-centered heart!*

Ruth's face was streaked with tears. Colleen had gotten through. The lava had receded. Colleen had figured out the best way to get to her momma's heart was a path composed of stroking her momma's perpetual state of victimization, asking for forgiveness for trying to be independent, and offering a touch of family and redemption. Colleen knew how big a theme redemption was in Ruth's life.

"Please, Momma. Please take my gift. It'll help heal things."

Ruth felt comforted by her daughter's words. Maybe she hadn't lost her after all. "Of course I'll accept it, darling. I can't promise you I'll always know how to work it. I still haven't gotten used to cordless phones, and I'll never have a computer, but if it'll help us as a family, then, okay."

Colleen smiled at her momma and at herself and threw her arms around her momma. *Excellent.*

Ruth then said, "I'll be right back. I must get a tissue and blow my nose.

Colleen didn't object. Once her mother was in the bathroom, Colleen quickly took the tea her mother had fixed into the kitchen and poured it down the sink. She quickly rinsed the cup and dried it, placing it back on its hook.

Returning to the living room, she was sitting down when her mother returned to the room. Colleen said, "Come sit by me, Momma, and I'll show you how it works."

Ruth took the phone. "It's so small," Ruth said.

"Like I was when I was a baby, Momma."

Colleen showed her mother how to unfold the flip top. "Here's all you have to know. When you want to call me, you press number one. Simple, huh? And, there are no long distance charges, so our calls are free."

Colleen expertly manipulated the function button and played the tune she had set up as the ring tone. "Listen to this." She tapped the command button and the phone rang with the first few bars of "Amazing Grace" played on a haunting 12-string guitar.

Colleen watched her momma's incredulous and happy face.

"That's so sweet, darling. My favorite hymn."

"Our favorite hymn, Momma. This is my song to you. You'll know it's me whenever you hear Amazing Grace. No one else will call you and you'll know it's me."

"Okay, I accept," Ruth said with sudden finality. "I forgive you."

Colleen stared into her momma's eyes. She forgives me, she thought to herself. *Ain't she something?* She reset the phone to receive mode and was satisfied that it was all set. "That means a lot to me, Momma. Now, I have to go run an errand. I have to see somebody about my car. It's been acting funny, so a good BMW mechanic said he'd look at it at 11 am. I'll go do that and then come back, and we can have lunch together. Let's go have lunch at Captain Ratty's." Before her mother could protest, Colleen stood up, and pulled her momma off the couch.

"I'll call you in a few minutes on your new phone, okay?"

"Okay, darling," her momma said. "I'm glad we'll spend some time together this afternoon."

"Me too, Momma."

Ruth was thrilled with how that had gone. She had not lost her daughter. Her prayers had been answered. Lunch this afternoon. Church this coming Sunday. She was relieved and happy. Sonny had not won after all. She was considering what to wear to lunch when she heard Amazing Grace. She ran into the living room and picked up her cute little red phone. She flipped open the top and punched answer as Colleen had showed her. She put it to her ear and said "Hello."

The phone's explosion blew Ruth's head off.

Colleen tossed her own cell phone out of her car window over the bridge railing into the dark waters of the Neuse. *Redemption.*

Chapter 26

Dr. Cooper

February 2007

Worth insisted they drive his cop car to Chapel Hill, just in case they needed some of its potential. Like forcing their way through traffic or a student riot or something. Last spring the men's basketball team had beaten Illinois to win the NCAA National Championship. Students had stormed the center of town, setting trees on fire and rioting until the wee hours. The fire got so hot it had burned holes in the asphalt. Local residents had long since learned not to leave their cars parked on Franklin Street the night of a big game—even after a lesser win, cars might get flipped.

Worth and Calder knew they had to talk with Dr. Cooper to sort out some of the confusion about Colleen. First things first, though. Worth pulled into King's Restaurant in Kinston in route to Chapel Hill for a fix of what some said is the best pit-cooked barbeque in eastern North Carolina. He ordered two large chopped sandwiches with slaw and hot sauce, each with sides of hush puppies and two coffees. Worth couldn't talk either without eating while he talked or without thinking about his next meal while he talked.

"So what's your take on Sonny?" asked Calder. "Did his alibi stand up?"

After eating half his sandwich, Worth said, "Like your report said, he's a spoiled, self-centered twit."

"That's not exactly what my report said."

"I'm just boiling down the psychobabble."

"How much of a suspect is he?" Calder asked.

"He's always gonna be a suspect until somebody else gets my attention, but he seems like an unlikely candidate to cave somebody's head in. He's got a lot of anger, but my gut's telling me he ain't our guy. The biggest thing is his alibi did stand up. On the day Dr. Hughes was murdered, Sonny was at a croquet tournament in Asheville all the way across the state. At the time of her murder, he was feasting on squab and escargot at his hotel with ten other people. It's possible he could have figured out a way to fly to Ocracoke and back again within the time frame of the tourney and the time of death, but we can't find any records of any flights. He's rich enough to afford a no flight-plan covert trip, but I think that's a stretch. Besides, Sonny seems pretty pleased with the way things are going with his kids, at least with his oldest. The doctor in Charlotte who's working with him and his kids appears to be doing an okay job. Apparently, Sonny's got some way to go before Starr will hang out with him, but Colleen accepted his offer to pay for college and, he says, she is doing well academically."

"And Santos?"

"Well, now, our boy is a lying mutha. We got one of his prints off Dr. Hughes' CPU, which means his claim that he was never in her house is bullshit. Yeah, Johnny's sleazy enough to remain in the running. We got a search warrant for his house boat, and car, but found nada. We did find evidence on his computer system he'd been snooping into Hughes' financial files but nothing else. His ex-wife said he used to get rough when he'd been drinking, but she never felt like he tried to kill her. His alibi checks out too. He was drinking at Howard's 'til 1 a.m., but that doesn't mean he couldn't have ducked out for 30 minutes or so, done the deed, and returned. The night in question, Howard's had a band playing and the place was packed. He could have slipped out and no one noticed. The problem is there's no way Dr. Hughes would have agreed to meet him at night at her boat. I just don't have enough to prop up a murder motive under his sorry ass."

Sipping on his tea, Worth then asked, "What's this doctor like and how's this talk with her likely to go?"

"She's obviously worried. She continues to be very ethical about the whole matter and wants both of us to be clear that she will not reveal anything about her patient. As she put it, she's willing to listen, but she will keep a tight boundary around her patient's privilege. I told her you could tell her the name of our suspect as part of your investigation. Where this is gonna go after that is anybody's guess."

They pulled off Interstate 40 at the first Chapel Hill exit, making their way to Dr. Cooper's neighborhood. She was one of a number of psychotherapists in the small college town who had a home-based clinical practice. She lived in a beautiful, historic neighborhood within walking distance of the university campus. She saw them drive up and opened the door as they came down the private walk to her office off to the side of her house. Dr. Samantha Cooper was stunning to behold. She was about 5 feet ten, with blonde hair that was pulled back, but not too severely. She had piercing blue eyes and radiant white teeth and a very engaging, warm smile. She was wearing a soft, off-white blouse and a straight gray skirt that modestly accented her body. "She got legs," thought Calder, thanking ZZ Top for the right words.

"Hello, I'm Samantha Cooper," holding out her hand to shake Worth's hand.

He reciprocated and said, "Detective Brown, Doctor. Thank you so much for agreeing to see us."

Worth went in and then she turned and shook Calder's hand, and said, "And hello, Calder."

"Hi, Sam. Thanks for agreeing to see us on such short notice. And I echo Detective Brown's appreciation. I know this puts you in a bit of a tough spot clinically, but it may help his investigation."

Without any response to his comment, she said, "Please, come in. Can I get either of you some coffee, tea, or perhaps some water?" They walked into her warm and inviting therapy office. It was decorated in creams and various blues. There was a gorgeous and very expensive Hariz hanging on one of the walls and an intriguing oil painting standing on an easel. Calder stood in front of what was probably the primary patient chair. He wanted to be able to look at that painting. "No thanks," Calder said.

"Nothing for me either, Doctor," replied Worth.

"Please sit down. I will be as helpful as I can. Detective," she said as she looked straight into his eyes, "I appreciate what you said a few moments ago. This type of interview is potentially damaging to my relationship with my patient. If there were not a question of a murder, I'm afraid I would have fought very hard—legally, if necessary—to protect the privacy of my patient. I still might have to do that. Nevertheless, Calder has convinced me it makes sense for me to listen."

Before Calder could respond, Worth said, "Since we only have an hour, may I just jump right in?"

"Yes, please," she said.

Homicide detectives on an investigation weren't big on social graces. Murder was serious business, and Worth was serious.

"The person of interest in the murder of Mildred Hughes is Colleen McPherson, who was one of Dr. Hughes' patients for many years. Her therapy began when Colleen was very young, age 5 or so, and Dr. Hughes accepted the validity of a number of allegations of sexual abuse perpetrated against Colleen and her sister by her father and a number of other people. As Calder told you, he did an evaluation of the allegations and concluded there was sufficient information to indicate the girls had not been molested and possibly their therapy messed up the girls quite a bit. We think it's entirely possible Colleen read Calder's report and may have begun to do some reconsideration of her personal history. It is her father who is paying for her college education. There has been some reconciliation between Colleen and her father. We know from talking with Colleen she began seeing a different therapist when she came to Chapel Hill. Colleen would not tell us who her therapist is. That therapist just might be you."

Calder watched Sam's reaction to Worth's giving her Colleen's name, but Sam didn't flinch or react in a way that told Calder anything.

"How serious a suspect is this Colleen?" queried Sam.

"Very serious," replied Worth. "That's why we're here. I know you can't tell us anything, unless you develop sufficient concern that your patient might be a danger to herself or others. Right now, you're the only one of us in this room who knows whether or not you're treating Colleen McPherson."

What Sam was thinking was that she now knew Colleen, her patient, was a serious suspect in the murder of her former therapist, whose name her patient had withheld, and her patient had lied about her own identity. What Sam didn't know was why Colleen had masqueraded as Emma.

Calder could see Sam was deep in thought. "In light of what we've told you, can you tell us anything, Sam?"

"I'm thinking," Sam replied. "Can either of you tell me if this Colleen person has any siblings?"

Worth responded, "She has a younger sister named Starr."

In the middle of her next thought, Worth's cell vibrated. He checked the number. It was from Sgt. Willys, Worth's second in command. It had a text message Worth read to himself: *'Explosion at Ruth's house. Ruth may be dead. House on fire. Better roll.'*

Worth stood up abruptly and said, "Doctor, sorry to interrupt. There's an emergency pertaining to this case Calder and I must go to immediately."

Calder looked at Worth with a blank stare but stood up too.

Sam said, "Does it possibly have to do with this person Colleen?"

"Yes, ma'am, it does," retorted Worth. "That's all I can say for now, except Colleen has moved up towards the top of the suspects' list. If she is your patient, be careful. Let's go, Calder. We got to move. Thank you again, Dr. Cooper," and he went out her door.

Calder remained puzzled but knew enough to understand that a serious emergency had occurred. Calder then said, "Sam, I don't know what just happened, but heed Worth's advice. I'll call you if I learn anything that might be helpful. Call me if you need to. Thanks," and he bolted out the door. Worth had already backed his car around and had a blue light flashing. It was gonna be warp speed to somewhere.

Sam felt a natural protectiveness for her patient. She was also angry about Colleen's obvious deceit. Sam wondered, was her patient playing her like some chess piece, or was there a deeper disturbance in her psyche? She decided to call Colleen.

Colleen recognized Sam's number on her cell. She let Sam's call go to voice mail. *Now that's an interesting coincidence*, Colleen thought to herself. *Why's that bitch calling?*

Chapter 27

The Web

Calder got his door shut just as Worth gunned his car out of Sam's driveway. As Calder fumbled with his seatbelt, Worth said, "Text from Willys said an explosion at Ruth's, maybe Ruth's been killed. Their house is on fire. I just talked to Willys on the cell. Sheriff's deputies, my guys, the fire trucks and paramedics are there, and it sounds like it's contained, but we don't yet know who was in the house."

"Shit," Calder blurted.

It's about 125 miles from Chapel Hill to New Bern, mostly interstate. They got to the McPherson house in an hour and a half. It was a blue light special. Worth could drive. As they got within sight of the house, they could see some smoke coming from one side of the structure, but there were no visible flames. Worth spoke with Sgt. Willys several more times on the race to New Bern who apprised him of the scene's developments. They had found one adult female body with its head blown off, and it appeared to be Ruth. No one else was found in the house.

Upon arrival, Worth and Calder walked straight to the fire chief, who was talking with Sgt. Willys in front of the house. "Hi, Frank,"

Worth said. He nodded at Willys. "Chief, this is Dr. Miro. Calder, this is Chief Frank Davis. I think you know Sgt. Willys. Chief, can you fill us in?"

The Chief then said, "The fire is out. It appears to have been a contained explosion that blew out in all directions from what looks like the living room. It shattered the windows. The rural postman saw the smoke a little before 2 PM and called 911. This appears to be have been caused by a bomb of some sort. Since this isn't Baghdad, we don't have too many bomb experts in New Bern."

Willys then added, "As you told me, Sir," looking at Worth, "We do, however, have all the expertise we need at the army base at Ft. Bragg. Most of the U.S. military's bomb experts that go to Iraq and Afghanistan are trained less than two hours from here. I've called the base commander at Bragg, and he's got a team of experts on its way here right now. Should be here in less than an hour. "

"And the body?" asked Worth.

The chief looked at Worth and Calder and said, "We'll know for sure after the autopsy, but we've brought one body out so far. We think the victim was Ruth McPherson. It looks like the bomb blew her head off."

"Good God." Calder exclaimed. "What about the children? Was there anybody else in the house?"

"Of course somebody else could have been in there when the explosion happened, but we don't think so," said the chief. "The explosion was centered in one room, and we got here pretty fast. My men saw one body right away when they went in, so they pulled that out and looked for more. Except for the structural damage from the explosion, we managed thankfully to get the fire out pretty quickly. There's no indication of anyone else being in the house."

"Anybody see anything?" Worth asked.

Willys responded, "There aren't many neighbors. We've been canvassing the area to see if anybody saw anything, but nothing so far. We've also been making some calls to see if we can locate the girls. The postman heard the explosion and then saw the smoke plume, but he was down the road a good ways from here, so he didn't see anything. Unless we get a deer or a cow that can tell us something, it ain't likely we'll have a witness."

Worth and the Chief chuckled at Willys' gallows humor. Calder was not finding any humor in any of this.

The Chief then said, "If that's all, gentlemen, I've got to get back to work. Nice meeting you, Doctor."

"Nice meeting you, Chief."

"Thanks, Frank," Worth replied. "Let me know when the Army shows up," as the Chief walked away.

Willys then asked, "What's next, sir?"

"Keep working on locating the girls. Make sure you keep the few on-lookers who have shown up out of the yard and house, and don't let the television film crew go inside. Refer all reporters to me. Let's wait 'til the bomb experts get here and make their analysis, but take as many pictures as you can without disturbing anything further. Interview the guys who found Ruth's body and have them help you make some sketches of where she was located when they found her. After that, let's search all the rooms. We don't have too much daylight left, so let's use that to our advantage. How certain are we the victim is Ruth McPherson?"

Willys responded, "Although the body's pretty mangled from the shoulders up, it's the body of a middle-aged woman. Several of the fire crew are volunteers from around here, and they all think it's her. One even commented on her shoes. Ruth apparently always wore a particular kind of black slippers, like dancers wear, and that's what the victim has on her feet. You wanna take a look? Her body's been bagged, but the EMT van's still here."

Worth said, "Yeah, in a minute. Thanks, sergeant."

Willys walked off to attend to the many things Worth had ordered.

Worth then said to Calder, "You and I have both met Ruth. Wanna look at the body with me?"

"Not really, but I will."

Calder walked away from what he had just seen and felt like throwing up. There was no question it was Ruth, but her corpse was horribly damaged. It was a grisly mess.

"That's never easy. You all right?"

"Honestly, I feel sick, but I'm all right."

Worth's walky-talky popped. He said, "Yeah?"

Willys' voice responded, "Bomb guys are here, Sir."

"Be right there." He then said to Calder, "Why don't I get one of my men to take you to your office and I'll contact you as soon as I'm done here. Keep your head down and your eyes open. If it makes sense to you, try calling Dr. Cooper again. Our rushing out of there may have made her want to talk some more. I'm sure it scared her."

"You're right about that. Can I tell her it looks like Colleen's mother's been murdered?"

"Yes, you can. Tell her if Colleen's her patient, Colleen just might be responsible for two brutal murders. Emphasize that we don't know for sure, but it's a strong possibility."

"All right," said Calder. "I'll do what I can."

Worth then turned and walked towards two guys dressed in crisp army green striding towards him. With their help, he'd find out what blew off Ruth's head.

Officer Baker dropped Calder off at his office. It was dark and locked up when he got there. He let himself in, locked the deadbolt from the inside, and closed the blinds. Paranoia strikes deep. Into your heart it will creep. *Yes it will*, Calder thought. He laid his Glock on his desk and phoned Dr. Cooper. He left her a voice mail. His message asked her to call him back and that it was urgent.

Worth called Calder about an hour later on his cell and told him the bomb experts said Ruth's death was most likely caused by a cell phone that blew up right in her ear. They said it was probably detonated by another cell phone, using a kind of technology available on the Internet and that's in widespread use as IED's in the Middle East. Worth confirmed no one else had been in the house at the time of the explosion and he and his officers were working on locating the girls. He also said when they searched the house, they found some more voodoo dolls in a counter near the kitchen and some others, along with some drug paraphernalia, in a box hidden in what appeared to be Starr's bedroom. He said one of the dolls from the kitchen area had Sonny's name written on it and another one had "Miro" written on its arm. Both dolls had needles stuck through their hearts.

Calder didn't react right away to this last bit of news, which made Worth nervous.

"You hear what I'm telling you, Calder?"

"Yeah, I got it." His heart was racing.

"You still at your office?"

"Yeah. I put in a call to Dr. Cooper right after I got here. Hopefully, she'll call me back soon."

"You got your pistolero with you?"

"Yeah, I got it."

"I'm not trying to preach to you, but you and I both know you may be next. Get the Glock loaded and make it handy. Call me if you hear anything. Keep your eyes and ears open. I think one of our girls is a twisted sister."

Calder thought that, too. "Okay," he responded, "I'll do just that. Let's just hope I don't have to use it."

"Roger that, my friend, but, let's be glad you got it. You are in the middle of the kind of drama you evaluate."

The truth of the description startled Calder. "Okay, you got my attention."

"Good," said Worth. "Keep the Glock and your cell charged and handy. Call me after you hear from Dr. Cooper. Later."

"Later," said Calder as he closed his phone.

Even though Calder's message said it was urgent, Dr. Samantha Cooper didn't want to call Calder back, at least not right away. The visit today with the detective and Calder frightened her, and she knew her patient, regardless of whether or not she was a murderer, was not who Sam thought she was, and, of even greater concern to Sam, might not be clinically what Sam had been thinking she was. Sam came to the conclusion she needed to speak with Colleen, her actions motivated by her treatment application of the Hippocratic oath: first do no harm.

Chapter 28

Sketchy Evidence

Worth called Calder from outside Calder's office building. Without Calder knowing it, Officer Baker, at Worth's instructions, had been watching Calder's building ever since dropping him there.

Calder let his friend in. Worth brought a pepperoni pizza and some Pepsi. You can't find Coca-Cola in New Bern except on the black market.

"You got an appetite?" he asked Calder.

"Not really. I haven't heard back from Sam, and that's bothering me, but I'm just sitting here, stewing over everything, trying to figure things out and waiting for something bad to happen. I don't like this shit one bit."

"Me neither." Popping open a can of soda and helping himself to a slice of pizza, he said, "Tell me what that mind of yours been doing? Don't tell me you been consulting the OED again, lookin' up voodoo or death threats?"

Calder opened a soda and looked at Worth and said, "Okay. Here's where my mind has been going. We now have two victims who knew each other and were bonded together by the same case. One we know was the girls' psychologist who was murdered by a blunt object to the head, and the victim probably knew her killer. We think it was the person Dr. Hughes referred to as a 'friend' in her email to her son. We now know Ruth's head was blown off by a bomb. That means we have had two attacks to the head, which may be significant."

"Yeah," said Worth, chewing on his second piece, "and our killer, if it's the same person, and I think it is, is getting more sophisticated. It's one thing to crush somebody's skull with a bat or a club, but a bomb, now that's another matter indeed. We're now dealing with a bright, not necessarily smart, but resourceful killer. Crushing the doctor's head was up close and personal. Using a bomb is cold and distant."

Calder's stomach was settling down. He wasn't sure pepperoni pizza would help it. He added, "It may mean killing Ruth was more difficult emotionally for the killer, and she may have needed more distance."

"Why you saying *she*?"

"I hate saying it, but that's what my gut tells me. I think we're dealing with one killer, a psychopathic killer. There's no way Santos did these things. And I've really considered Sonny as a serious suspect. The decapitation thing is what's got my interest."

"You thinkin' about the decapitated baby in the drawing in the doctor's mouth?"

"Yep," Calder said. "That's way past coincidence. Our killer, consciously or unconsciously, has set a theme of decapitation, or at least a focus on the head, in this case right from the beginning and there's nothing subtle about it. If I stay open-minded, I suppose I should continue to think of Sonny as a suspect, but I don't anymore. Our killer has made assaults on the heads of two women who have been connected together for years around the issue of protecting the McPherson girls from abuse."

Worth leaned back in his chair and wiped some sauce off his lips. "You gonna eat any pizza?

"Save me one piece."

Happy with that response, Worth helped himself to another slice, and then said, "Not just from abuse, but from Satan. Which then raises the question of the decapitated baby. That was our first clue. I talked with Detective Smith who did the original criminal investigation of the allegations over ten years ago, and he confirmed what he told you. There was no forensic evidence, no blood, no charred ashes, no missing babies, nothing to confirm any of the wilder allegations made by the girls. Since there never were any missing or murdered babies in the McPherson case, or any physical forensic evidence for that matter, what does that drawing mean?"

Taking possession of his slice of pizza and setting it aside, Calder said, "I think it means whoever made that drawing wanted somebody to think there was a beheaded baby, or, more likely, the image of murdered, decapitated babies was an image created during her therapy. As you know, I was totally convinced Dr. Hughes' therapy of the McPherson children created this monstrous situation. I think it's probable either Starr or Colleen drew the headless baby during or after a therapy appointment with Dr. Hughes. As the SBI lab analysis indicated, I think at the very least it was created during the time the girls were in treatment with her and the so-called disclosure process was uncovering increasingly lurid, fantastic details."

"And, if you're right," mused Worth, "and the dots stay connected from the drawing of the baby in therapy, to the piece of the drawing in the doctor's mouth, to the crushing of the doctor's skull, to the decapitation of Ruth McPherson, it would appear that our killer puts the primary source of the blame for the headless baby idea on Hughes and Ruth."

"Maybe," Calder said. "But only if there's logic running through this killer's mind. I think the killer has developed an increasingly sophisticated theory that began with the child's drawing and culminated in Ruth getting her head blown off."

"As much as I hate to say it, Sherlock, Ruth's death hasn't culminated anything. We got evidence today somebody in the McPherson house has been thinking about Sonny's death and yours. We've had two terminations, commonly called murders, but no *culmination*. I agree with you that thinking about Santos makes no sense."

Worth continued. "Then there's Sonny. He has every reason to hate Dr. Hughes and Ruth. From his point of view, the two of them ruined his life as a father."

Worth shifted his weight in the chair and took another slice out of the box. "Sonny's too rich and lazy to do either of these murders himself. If he's the killer, it was by proxy. He'd have to hire assassins to do this. There's little reason to believe Dr. Hughes would have agreed to meet him—or one of his assassins on her boat at night. Besides, why would he have waited so long from the time of your report to her murder? The killer who went to her boat the night she was murdered probably was known to the doctor and was someone she trusted. The killer also had access to the drawing. Like you said, her email to her son indicated she was meeting a friend. Not likely Sonny could hire somebody who fit that description."

Calder then asked, "Did anything pan out with the search of the ferry logs?"

"Nada. The killer probably came to the island as a pedestrian, or if he drove, excuse me, if she drove, she used a fake I.D. The ferry between Hatteras and Ocracoke doesn't even require reservations for any vehicles. Over the past several weeks, we've circulated photos of the girls, Ruth, and Sonny among the ferry personnel at all three stations and turned up zip. If our killer was one of those four, he or she must have gone to Ocracoke on foot, and used a disguise."

"What about Dr. Hughes' bank records? Anything turn up?"

"There was nothing significant. She made a nice living from her clinical practice. Usual stuff: med school tuition payments, IRA's. Nothing that tied her to Santos, Ruth, Griff, or Sonny," Worth said.

Calder's cell phone vibrated as it sat on his desk. He flipped it open and recognized Sam's cell phone number. He said, "It's Sam," to Worth, and punched the answer button.

"Hi, Sam."

"Hi, Calder. It took me a while to call you back. I'm sorry for my delay."

"I'm glad to hear from you. Worth's sitting here with me in my office. If it's all right with you, he can hear my side of the conversation, or I can put you on speaker. Worth and I felt badly about the way we blasted out of your office, so I just wanted to make sure you were okay."

"Thanks. I appreciate that. Speaker phone's fine."

Calder punched the button. "Okay. We're on speaker."

"I'm okay, Sam said.

Worth chimed in, "Dr. Cooper, it's Detective Brown. I am sorry for the abrupt way we had to leave today, but there had been an explosion at Colleen McPherson's mother's house. Her mother was deliberately and violently murdered today. We are not certain Colleen is her killer, or that Colleen is responsible for the murder of her former therapist, but she certainly is a prime suspect. Can you tell us anything more?"

Sam took a deep breath. "Here's what I can say. I still cannot reveal the identity of my patient. At this point, I do not think I can breach confidentiality because I have no information obtained from my patient or my own clinical assessment that makes me think my patient might be dangerous, even homicidal. I am not in control of my patient, because I treat patients only on an outpatient basis. The information I've gotten from you so far is that Colleen McPherson is a prime suspect, but you are not certain she has committed two murders. My feeling is I must continue to think about and protect my patient's welfare."

Worth took a piece of paper and scribbled a note to Calder *'she's confirming she's treating Colleen!'*

Calder nodded his head in agreement. Sam told them without telling them.

Calder said to her, "So you're saying, at this point in time, you're not confirming your patient is our suspect, and you have no knowledge, based on your clinical experience with your patient, that he or she is dangerous, or possibly homicidal?"

"That's right," replied Sam. "It is my understanding North Carolina does not have a specific law that requires psychologists treating individuals on an outpatient basis to act on a Tarasoff-like duty to warn. Even if we did have such a law, based on my treatment of my patient, I am not at that point regarding my patient. On the other hand, if a psychologist learns her patient has committed a crime, such as a murder, there would be no confidentiality. Have you learned anything in your investigation that would help me?"

"Not at this time, Dr. Cooper," replied Worth. "I think you should take whatever precautions you think are necessary for the well-being of you and your family, as well as your patient, but we have no specific information that indicates you specifically are in any danger. Do you have time for a general clinical question?"

"I don't know if I can answer it, but, yes, I have time."

Worth asked, "How rare is female perpetrated matricide?" Worth looked at Calder and raised both his eyebrows a couple of times to signal he was pleased with his question and wanted his friend to be impressed.

Calder scribbled so Worth could see it, 'Not bad for a cop!'

Sam replied, "I honestly don't know, but very rare, I would think. Calder, do you know?"

Calder said, "I don't know either, but I'm gonna try to find out. What Worth's saying is that might be what we have in our case. The victim today had two daughters, and one of 'em might have killed her mother."

Sam said, "Well, I have to go. Thanks for calling me earlier, and you'll keep me in the loop I assume?"

"Yes, we will, Sam," Calder replied. "And please do the same for us if your view of your patient changes. Take good care of yourself."

"So long, Dr. Cooper," added Worth. "Let us hear from you if you think we need to."

"Goodbye," and Sam hung up.

Worth said to Calder, "She's worried."

"I would be too, if I was in her shoes. She hasn't given up on Colleen either. No self-respecting therapist would."

Chapter 29

Takin' Care o' Business

Colleen pulled her car off the road into an isolated part of the woods. She sure liked her Beemer. It would get her back to Chapel Hill before anybody knew she wasn't there. Still, she needed to look at her play book one more time before she burned it. She kept it hidden under the spare tire in the trunk. This notebook had become her journal midway through her work with Sam. It was where she sorted things out. It was where she sorted out how many people betrayed her in how many ways and what it would take to make things right. It was where she formulated her plan. Those persons found guilty of betrayal were listed: Sonny, Mildred, Calder, Momma, and Starr. She also had written: 'Jury still out – Sam?'

Colleen sat down on the soft pine needles and contemplated things. She and Emma agreed they needed Calder, at least for now. Besides, Starr was fixated on him. When Daddy died, she and Starr would be Daddy's heirs. They would be stinking rich. If Daddy crossed the river Styx sooner, rather than later, she surmised she and Starr would move up in the natural order of things. *Granddaddy would take care of us.* Starr, on the other hand, was getting a little too close. The little twit was getting suspicious. It was her bullshit craziness that kept Momma sick and sentenced them both to the lifetime of therapeutic hell with 'the-rapist,' Mildred. Colleen loved the irony of the word when you broke it apart.

Colleen took her pen and crossed out Mildred and Momma. She closed her eyes and went inward to find her conviction. When she opened her eyes, she lit a cigarette and took a long, slow drag. Exhaling, she crossed off Starr.

Using a branch, she dug a round, shallow hole in the earth and put her journal in it. After soaking it with lighter fluid, she tossed her cigarette butt on the notebook and tended the fires of hell until all was consumed.

Chapter 30

Momma's Funeral

Tracking down the McPherson girls took some time. At the request of the New Bern Police Department, the Chapel Hill police located Colleen at her off-campus apartment in Chapel Hill. A police social worker informed her of her mother's death. The social worker noted that when she told Colleen her mother had been killed, Colleen stared blankly into space, and refused any crisis aid. Starr was at the mall in New Bern with a classmate whose mother called her daughter on her cell. The friend's mother saw the news of the fire on television and knew right away whose house it was because of the location—and the ten-foot cross in the front yard. She located her daughter and Starr right away. Starr called Colleen, who drove to New Bern to be with Starr at her friend's house. It was Colleen who told Starr their momma was dead. That somebody had exploded a bomb in their house. The police said they couldn't go to their momma's house because it wasn't safe. Her friend's momma left the two sisters alone in the den to talk. Starr wept uncontrollably. Colleen held her and rocked her, as she had done many times before.

"Who would, like, do this to Momma?" Starr demanded of her sister. "She's not dead," she blurted out, and fell into deep sobs again.

Colleen held her sister and stroked her hair. "The Devil did this, precious. It was pure evil. Nobody human disliked Momma. She was a saint. It had to have been the Devil, punishing Momma for all her good deeds."

Starr looked up at her sister and said, "Daddy hated Momma. Momma said Daddy was a sick man who did sick things to me and you. Momma and Mildred said Daddy was, like, an agent of the Devil. Daddy killed Momma and Mildred, didn't he?"

Colleen had thought about this question for a long time, because she knew her sister would ask it. Their momma and Dr. Hughes had instilled in Starr an unshakable belief their father was a monster. Starr was convinced, and eventually became very convincing, that her daddy and many others sexually molested them in dark caves or on altars, and filmed all their sadistic activities. Starr's own sad and morbid life was anchored in a set of memories of things that never happened, yet she could recall these events in bloody detail.

"I don't think so, sweetie. I don't know who did this, but I don't think it was Daddy. There was a time when he probably felt like killing her, but I don't think he's capable of doing something like this."

Starr lay very still in her sister's lap. "Daddy killed Dr. Hughes, too, didn't he?"

"I can understand why it might look that way. I thought about it, too, right after she was murdered, but I've come to believe that he didn't. I even asked him."

"When did you do that?"

"Right after it happened," said Colleen. "I wanted to know, and you know how good I am at telling when somebody's lying, sweetie? Well, I could see it in his eyes. He was hurt by my question. He said some pretty nasty things about her, and told me he once thought about trying to sue her so she'd lose her license, but that was the worst thing he could imagine doing to her. Daddy didn't kill Dr. Hughes."

"Do you think the same person killed both of 'em?"

"Yes, I do, but I don't think it was a person. I think it was Lucifer or somebody working for him. Momma and Dr. Hughes were good.

This was the handiwork of evil. Daddy's got his faults and weaknesses, but he's not evil."

"How come you don't believe like Momma and I do that he did all those things to us?"

"I asked him that too," said Colleen. "I asked him that the first time I saw him when the court ordered us to go for visitation. You were with Grandpa, and I looked Daddy straight in the eye and said, "Did you fuck me and my sister?""

Starr and Angel sat up. "What'd he say?"

"He got very angry. He got so mad he couldn't talk. He rambled on about how all the allegations were used against him and how he had to stop seeing us. Then he left the room we were in and smoked a cigarette outside and came in a little calmer. Then he started crying. They looked like real tears. He told me about hiring his attorney to get us back and hiring Dr. Miro. He still doesn't know we read the report. I don't know if Momma knew either. I believed him. Or maybe I wanted to believe him. Anyway, at that moment, I forgave him."

Starr was puzzled by that. "Forgave him for, like, what? If you didn't believe he'd done all those things, what did you, like, forgive him for? For, like, being a rich asshole?"

Colleen turned so she could look straight into her sister's bloodshot eyes. "I decided my life was going to be better if I had a relationship with him. I forgave him for whatever he did or didn't do. I knew I'd never know. But most of all, I forgave him for leaving Momma, leaving you, and leaving me. I decided to get off the road to perdition."

"Huh?"

"It means living in a constant state of damnation. My life's better now."

Starr thought that was an odd statement. Angel agreed. Momma had just been killed and their dear therapist who had guided them through so much turmoil had been killed last year, and her sister was saying her life was better now.

Sensing her sister's change of mood, Colleen said, "We gotta plan Momma's funeral."

"I don't want to," said Starr.

"It's not a question of whether we want to or not. Either we do it the way Momma would want it, or the funeral home will do it in some tacky, expensive way. And we sure don't want any snake handlers or tongue speaking. Be just like one of Roy Purdy's relatives to show up and fuck things up. One of Grady's funeral home vultures already has called and they've taken Momma's body from the morgue to Grady's. We have to plan it. We have no choice. Momma's counting on us."

"Are you sad?" asked Starr.

Caught off guard by this question, Colleen flinched. Starr and Angel could feel it. Colleen responded, "Yes, darling, I am very sad, but now's not the time for tears. There will be plenty of time for grief later. Now we must be strong. We must stand up and help Momma move on to a better place."

Colleen smiled that fetching smile. Momma would have liked her funeral, she thought to herself. The vase for Momma's ashes she and Starr picked out was pretty. Mr. Grady, the mortician, always did a nice job. Colleen thought about her mother's body. Too bad they had to have her cremated, but the damage was probably too severe. Colleen recalled her momma's nice face and figure. Always just so. Her momma always wanted to understate things, especially her breasts. Colleen knew Momma always wanted sex hidden. She recalled what Momma used to say – don't want to give a man the wrong impression. Leads to bad thoughts, particularly when there's brown liquor involved. Corn squeezin's one thing. That can lead to trouble. Brown liquor means lust and violence.

Colleen always figured her momma was referring to Colleen's granddaddy, Reverend Roy, but she was never sure what her momma had been through. Momma always sounded like she knew about the dangers of sex and drinking. She now lay there, peaceful and pulverized.

Colleen looked about. Starr was a study in black. She didn't own clothes of any other color. Starr was in perpetual mourning. Colleen thought, the funeral's right, though. Mr. Grady had his two fine limousines, all black and chrome. Cemetery steeds. In high school, Colleen's cousin, Woody, had once purchased a used limo from Mr.

Grady and turned it into the finest party wagon ever seen around Craven County. Colleen always loved the name of the county. Craven. Cravin' for what? Woody's ride affectionately was known as the Death Wagon. Though nobody died, there sure was a substantial amount of unconsciousness reached by its stoned and inebriated occupants. Colleen had missed a lot of high school football games while in the back of that wagon.

For a winter's day, today was hot. Colleen recalled the many funerals she'd attended as a child. Seemed like everybody got buried on a sweltering day. Maybe God divined to turn up the heat for Southern funerals. Made things slow and wet. Sultry. Colleen had picked up one of the hand-held fans from the basket by the front door. Momma always liked these funeral hand-fans, mused Colleen. Colleen looked at hers. A picture of Jesus at Gethsemane attached to what looked like a tongue depressor, with a tasteful advertisement of the funeral home at the bottom. Mr. Grady figured you'd take it home. Good for business. A never-ending business at that. Future assured. Be a good career move if it weren't for the dead folk. Colleen surveyed the crowd. A good crowd. Momma's church folk. All her family's here, too. Momma's folks lived all over eastern North and South Carolina. Given that Momma had almost no ongoing relationships with most of them, it was a good bet that the family was anticipating some good funeral food. Half of them don't fit under the tent, she observed, since there's so many, and since some of Momma's kin are too fat to fit under any tent. Colleen snickered to herself. Still, maybe things would have been better with a bigger tent. Too warm a day to stand there grieving. Colleen figured this would be over quick.

Nobody understood why Momma had to die so young or so violently. Rumors were flying among the relatives and within the community. There was consensus that her vicious murder was the Devil's deed. Colleen saw Aunt Essie was waving for things to begin. The Reverend Jamieson opened the good book. Time to be sad. Swing low, sweet chariot.

Starr couldn't take her eyes off her sister. Angel kept muttering to Starr that something's not right with Colleen.

Colleen was well aware of her sister's piercing stare. *That's gotta stop!* She was also aware of another set of eyes.

As inconspicuous as an impeccably dressed, 250 pound, six foot two, black man in shades can be at a lily white funeral, Worth discretely watched both sisters.

Chapter 31

Ancient History

May 17, 2007

Colleen hadn't told Starr about her apartment in New Bern until after their momma was killed, but Starr had figured it out already. She had her network of homies all over town, and one of 'em told her he'd seen Colleen carrying some groceries into an apartment on Chatham Street, probably right after she rented it. Ever since her momma's funeral, Starr had been thinking about her sister and things she said and didn't say. Out of curiosity, she'd secretly made a copy of the apartment key from Colleen's key ring on one of her sister's infrequent visits to see her and their momma.

Now that Momma was dead and buried, Starr faced her new life with dread and cold vengeance. She was expected to stay with Aunt Essie and finish junior college. If Momma was a saint, Aunt Essie was Mary herself. Her aunt already told her she had to stop wearing black now that the funeral was over and she had to observe a curfew. It wasn't going to work for her to stay at her aunt's, so she had begun thinking of a way to scam a bed at Colleen's.

Starr took a long hit off the joint. Billy always had dank shit. Good marijuana brought calculating clarity for Starr. It settled down the demons. Angel did not consider herself a demon, so she was very excited. She loved espionage shit. Starr had borrowed some normal clothes to wear from her friend Sarah so she wouldn't stand out in her usual darkness. A simple, white t-shirt and faded blue jeans made her look like a typical teen. Starr wasn't keen on having to dress this way, but Angel thought of herself as Mata Hari. Starr had begun thinking about what Colleen said about their daddy.

Starr stood across the street and watched the patterns of people going in and out of her sister's apartment building. The doorman was kinda lame. She noticed sometimes he left his desk to stand outside to smoke. She stubbed out the joint and put the roach in her pocket. She timed her move so she walked in at the same time another resident, an elderly woman, was coming out with her grandkids. A glacier moves faster than an elderly person using a walker, so Starr was able to slide right in as everyone, including the doorman, helped the lady manage the walker over the rugs, the threshold, the sidewalk and the curb. Walkers were only a good idea in theory. They were a disaster on anything but a smooth surface.

Starr knew Colleen was off with their daddy looking at some land and wouldn't be back 'til dark. That gave her about five hours. Starr entered her sister's apartment. Man, this is, like, weird, she thought. What's up with all this child décor? Starr was beginning to wonder if Colleen had had a baby or something.

Starr wandered around and picked up the sketch book. This is the kinda shit Dr. Hughes made us do, she thought. She leafed through the pages. Goats, crosses, penises, bonfires. People think I'm fucked up, thought Starr. She got to the picture of a fiery explosion. It wasn't a bonfire. It was an explosion. Starr dropped the book and sat very still. No fuckin' way. No fuckin' way. "What does that mean?" Angel asked. Starr ignored her and caught her breath. She focused.

Starr was a master at concealing things. You had to be at Momma's house. Hiding her dope, her eating disorder, and her contraceptives, not to mention most of her music, had made her clever. This meant she knew where to look and how to look. She went right to her sister's bedroom closet. She looked for telltales first, because that's what smart spies do, she thought. They put in place small objects, like hairs, thread, and pieces of invisible tape that, if accidentally removed, let the hider know there's been a snoop. There was one. One shoe crossed over another on the floor of the closet. Left over right, heel reversed. Got it. Shoebox exactly two inches from each side of the corner walls. Number two. Rug swatch under the shoe box. Scotch tape on right side, sticking to the baseboard. Number three. Clever girl, Colleen, but I'm your sister, Starr thought to herself. We both hid parts of ourselves. What have you hidden?

Starr crouched down and memorized what she saw. She methodically worked her way through the telltales and lifted the rug. There it was, my precious, she said to herself. She felt like Gollum about to find the ring. Starr lifted open the small door Colleen had cut and crafted to fit in the closet floor. The space was about the size of a medium suitcase. It contained several drawings like the ones in the sketch book, but much older looking. Kinda faded. There was a file folder too, with a label on it in a handwriting Starr did not recognize. There was a bunch of video tapes with her and Colleen's names on them. There was a blonde wig. Underneath was a notebook. Starr lifted everything out and sat on the floor.

The drawings were of mutilated babies. Several of the drawings had been cut into pieces, maybe with a knife or scissors. Starr didn't know about the drawing found in her therapist's mouth, because the police had kept this detail to themselves.

She set the drawings aside and looked at the file. Its contents were about Colleen and her. There were copies of letters in it that went back to the year Starr was born—1988. There was a copy of that asshole doctor's evaluation—Dr. Asshole Miro and his bullshit, retrospective, ass-kissing distortion of her family's history. There were notes of various appointments she and Colleen had with Dr. Hughes. Starr realized she was looking at Dr. Hughes' handwriting about her sister and her. Colleen had Dr. Hughes' file.

Starr dropped the file and grabbed the spiral notebook that said UNC Tar Heels across the front. Colleen had written her name on the first page. It had a calendar in it with dates of appointments with somebody named Sam. Bet she's fuckin' him, thought Starr. Sex by appointment. Don't they call that hookin'?

The notebook also had notes in Colleen's neat script that talked about herself, MPD, dissociation, and alters. There was a line that read "Momma b-line?" There was another entry that said "an archeological dig into my soul." There was an obituary of the actress who played Tony Soprano's mother. There was another entry that asked, "Does the soul have boundaries?" There was a page with geometric drawings on it. A square with the names Momma, Daddy, Mildred, and Emma at each corner. There was a triangle that had Mildred, Momma, Daddy at each point. The whole section with these notes was called "Emma's therapy." "Who the fuck is Emma?" Starr wondered out loud.

The last two things Starr found immobilized her. One was a schedule for the NC ferry system. The portion about the schedule from Cedar Island to Ocracoke was highlighted in yellow. Colleen had written "Emma goes to the beach" across the top of the ferry schedule.

Starr could hardly breathe. She felt like throwing up. She knew she couldn't do that. Colleen would be able to smell she'd been there. The last thing Starr found was a sheaf of papers held together by a paper clip. It was a bunch of shit downloaded from various websites about C-4 explosives. She had to get out of here. She couldn't move. Everything suddenly went black. Starr collapsed.

Calder sat at his computer doing a most modern task, sorting the wheat from the chaff of his e-mails. Even with spam, spyware, firewalls, and pop-up blockers, he got so many professional-related e-mails he couldn't get anything else done if he read them all. Sometimes the subjects being discussed or argued were compelling, and he'd fall into the chatter, but he deleted the majority. Calder thought the Internet was one of the coolest things ever invented, but it was a mixed blessing some days.

His secretary buzzed him on the intercom and said, "There's a Ms. Starr McPherson here to see you. She knows she doesn't have an appointment, but she says it's urgent."

Calder's mind spun in fifty different directions. He hadn't anticipated this. He picked up the phone so he and his secretary could talk privately. "Is she right there with you now?"

"Yes," said Carol.

"Is she alone?"

"Correct. She also said she had some things she found at her sister's apartment she wants to show you and asked me to give you a sketchbook so you can see why she needs to talk to you. She also said for me to tell you she was scared."

"Please tell her to have a seat and I'll be with her in a few minutes. Get your cell phone and bring me the sketchbook and politely excuse yourself to the ladies' room and call Worth. Tell him what's going on. He'll know what to do. But whatever you do, do not go back into your office or the waiting room. This girl could be a murderer."

"I can do that," Carol said coolly.

A few moments later, Carol knocked on Calder's private office door and handed him the sketchbook. It was an artist's sketchpad covered in heavy gray paper bound by a black binding.

In a stage whisper, Calder asked, "Is she carrying anything?"

"A backpack she was wearing when she came in," Carol said. "She took this sketchbook out of it, but I could tell by its weight there's other stuff in it."

Calder said, "Call Worth as fast as you can."

Carol spun on her heel and walked across the hallway to the restroom. Calder heard her lock the door. He shut his own door. He laid the notebook down and pulled his Glock out of his briefcase. He checked the chamber to make sure there was no round in it, popped out the clip, re-inserted it and laid the gun on his desk. He opened the sketchbook and scanned its pages. There was one page marked with a paper clip. It had a crude sketch of an explosion. He could see the other drawings were child-like sketches of sexual anatomy, crosses, devils, and bonfires. There were mutilated babies, some with no heads.

His cell phone vibrated in his pocket and he saw it was Worth. Calder answered it and Worth said, "I'm at the basement door." The man was fast.

Calder told him the code to let himself in, and Worth said, "Carol told me what's going down. I told her to stay in the bathroom 'til we get a handle on this thing. What's your thinking on this? This girl in your waiting room with a backpack just may be our killer, so this ain't no time for heroics."

Calder responded, "I'm gonna go see her in the waiting room. She says she's brought me some things from Colleen's apartment. I'm looking at a sketchbook with SRA symbols and a fiery explosion. Starr told Carol she found it at her sister's. It looks like sketches from the mind of our murderer."

"The problem is, my man, we don't know which one of these sisters is calling the plays," warned Worth. "This could be a move to throw us off her trail and frame her sister." He was whispering now, "If she is the one, while it's not likely she would blow you and herself up, we cannot take any chances. Okay, I'm outside your office door. You got your Glock?"

"Yeah, loaded."

"Chamber a round and place it at your waist at the small of your back."

Calder pulled the slide, inserting a bullet into his gun. "Got it."

"Calder, here's the plan. Walk into the waiting room as you normally would. Don't turn your back on this sister. As you enter from the hallway, I will step into the room before she has a chance to react. No heroics, buddy. This may be one dangerous bitch."

"Roger that, Detective." Calder said, "I like having the cavalry in my office."

"This ain't funny, homeboy. One of these sisters is murderously sick. Right now, we findin' out which one. I don't want you to become vic 3 as our problem solving method."

"Me neither. Let's do this before she gets too nervous. I've kept her waiting long enough."

"Okay, I'm ready. Be careful, C-man."

"Will do."

Calder put his gun in place as Worth had instructed so he could draw it with his right hand. At Worth's insistence, when he was learning to shoot, he had practiced how to draw and pull the slide on his Glock in a single motion. What he'd never done was chamber a round and carry it the way Worth had instructed. He also had never shot anybody. He hoped today wasn't the day to find out if he could do it. He took a deep breath, grabbed the sketchbook, opened his office door and walked down the short hallway past Carol's office, into the reception area. Starr McPherson was pacing in a small circular motion. She had a backpack on the chair about two feet away from her. Calder decided he didn't like strangers with backpacks anymore, unless he was in Glacier Park hiking or skiing in Colorado. Fear and perceived threat had become the new normal.

"Ms. McPherson, I'm Calder Miro. My secretary said you had something of an urgent nature. May I ask what is so urgent?" Calder's insides were urgent. No, they were way past urgent.

Starr McPherson stopped her pacing and looked at Calder, who thought she looked nervous as a cat. As soon as she saw Calder, she took a step in his direction.

Worth swung open Calder's door and stepped inside just behind Starr. His entrance was so sudden, it startled Calder, who knew it was going to happen. Starr froze in her tracks and turned to look at Worth, who stood right behind her, said, "Ms. McPherson, I am Homicide Detective Brown of the New Bern Police Department. I am sorry if I frightened you, but I would like you to allow me to examine your backpack. And," he emphasized, "I would ask that you not put your hands in your pockets."

Starr turned back to look at Calder and stammered, "Dr. Miro, I know, like, I know this sounds weird, but, but I think maybe my sister killed Dr. Hughes and Momma. I just came from her apartment and I found all this stuff that, like, totally freaked me out. I didn't know where else to go. Everything's so fucked up now."

Based on the watery mixture of fear and desperation he saw in her eyes, Calder wanted to believe her, but he knew Worth was right. Despite her age, Starr could be a frightened child or a homicidal psychopath. Maybe both.

Worth's voice boomed again, "Ms. McPherson, may I search your backpack?"

Calder knew that was going to be the last time he asked her. Starr's head did a funny movement, like the one people do when they try to clear the cobwebs out of their brain, and she whispered "Sure."

Worth said, "Please have a seat and keep your hands where we can see them."

Starr crumpled in a heap into the overstuffed chair in the corner and Worth began examining the contents of her bag. He kept one eye on Starr as he did. The first thing he pulled out was another sketchbook, much older, yellowed and worn than the one Calder had just looked at and a manila file. The sketchbook had a watermark on the front that said 'A.L. Dunn.'

"I found those things in Colleen's closet," Starr said.

Worth had gone through all the closets at Ruth McPherson's house, so he knew this stuff was not there then.

"What closet? Where?" he demanded.

Starr told them of her sister's apartment in New Bern and its address.

Worth instantly called his fellow investigators on his two-way and told them to get an unmarked watching Colleen's apartment building.

Worth removed a spiral college notebook. As he did so, Starr uttered, "I think, like, a lot of the stuff is from Dr. Hughes' office." Tears began to pool in her eyes. Angel watched all this with fascination. She loved the attention these two ripped men were giving her.

Calder had never met Starr before. Her mother had been a fierce protector. He always imagined Starr as the most damaged of the two children, not only because she was the younger, but because everyone talked about her that way. Starr was described by most who knew her as a psychiatric train wreck. She dressed the part. She looked like a female version of The Cure's Robert Smith. Calder looked into her blue eyes, searching for the rage he knew she must feel towards him for the conclusions he reached about her therapist and her parents. He searched too for the rage and lunacy that would lead a person to kill. What he continued to see was fear and desperation that was resigning into despair. Calder's insides were beginning to settle down.

Starr returned his gaze. "Dr. Miro," she said, staring back into his eyes. "Are you afraid of me?"

Her perceptive question startled him, but again, given that he had admitted to himself his churning guts went past emergency status, maybe he wasn't being as cool as he thought. "No, ma'am, not anymore. I was for a few minutes, but now I am afraid for you." Good recovery, he thought to himself.

Her question to Calder prompted Worth to stop his search of her bag and focus his intense brown eyes on Starr and her hands. Worth interpreted her question to Calder as cool and challenging. He slid his gun hand under his jacket.

Calder knew if she made a sudden move, Worth would respond in a split second.

Calder's clinical training kicked into gear. Starr was not his patient. She was not here to be evaluated. Although he wasn't sure why she'd come to his office, by all appearances, she was a desperate teenager who was facing the possibility her sister was someone she didn't know, and probably never had known.

"Miss McPherson?"

"Yeah?" she asked.

"I want to level with you. I was afraid. I was very afraid. I assumed, and still do, you might have a lot of angry feelings towards me that are very understandable, given my role in your family's life. When my secretary told me you were here, without an appointment, I could not guess your motives. I know two people whom you loved have died horrible deaths. My first instinct was to protect myself, my secretary and my office and all the other people in this building. Now, I want to protect you. I think you need some protection."

Satisfied with his search of the contents of her backpack, Worth gave Calder a slight nod that signaled he agreed with Calder's assessment. Worth was convinced this young woman-child wasn't going to blow everybody to smithereens.

"Let's go into the conference room, where we can sit down and talk," as Calder gestured them down the other hall. "You two go on in. I'll be right there." He hesitated a moment so there was no chance Starr might see the weapon tucked into his waist at the small of his back.

Calder swung by the restroom and knocked softly on the door. "All clear."

Carol stepped out and said, "Whew! Nobody's ever gonna accuse you of being a boring boss."

"You okay?" Calder asked. Assured that she was, Calder smiled and said, "I need for you to do one more thing and you can go home. I gotta get in that interview. Please call every number we've got for

Dr. Samantha Cooper and find her if you can. Call her cell, her office, her home. Have her call me back on my cell if you have to leave a message. Tell her it's extremely urgent. If you get her before you leave, please come interrupt the interview and get me."

"I can do that," Carol replied.

He walked back to the conference room where Starr and Worth sat at the big table. Worth had placed all the materials in front of her and a tape recorder on the table, which was turned on. He also wore a pair of latex gloves. Worth handed Calder a pair and nodded.

Worth began, "This is May 17, 2007. This is an interview with Starr McPherson. With me is Dr. Calder Miro. Ms. McPherson, please start from the beginning and tell us how you came upon these things you have in front of you and tell us what they are, or what you think they are. You know you are being tape recorded and you know you are not under arrest and are here of your own free will and we are not forcing you to talk with us, correct?"

"Yes, sir," she said. Angel almost giggled. Worth opened Dr. Hughes' clinical file on the table. Under Calder and Worth's questioning, Starr began a journey down a twenty-year path of ancient history that began in 1985 when her mother and father married and led her and, ultimately, Worth and Calder, to the concealed compartment in Colleen's closet.

Worth rolled his chair back from the conference table. He called Sergeant Willys. "Willy, put eyes on Colleen McPherson's apartment asap." He gave Willys the address. "Call the Chapel Hill PD and check to see if they've had any luck locating Colleen. Get Murphy in the D.A.'s office to work up search warrants for the address I just gave you and her Chapel Hill apartment. We're gonna need an arrest warrant. Tell 'im I'm bringing the probable cause evidence in a few minutes."

After Starr finished her narrative, she was broken again. A splintered shipwreck. Her sobs were deep and inconsolable. Filling them in on her mother's and sister's lives since Colleen had reunited with their father and gone to college led Starr to the same conclusion reached by Worth and Calder.

Still, there was the loose end about the voodoo doll. Worth was convinced it was Starr who did that. He asked, "What made you put the voodoo doll on Dr. Miro's door?"

Drained by the telling of her narrative, she hesitated a moment in surprise, then said, "I guess I, like, did it because I was so mad at him, at you, Dr. Miro for what you said in your report."

"So you read his report?" asked Worth.

"Yeah, Colleen and I both did. Like, right after Momma got it. We, like, kept it a secret for a long time. We never even told Momma."

Calder then asked, "Did Colleen know about your putting the doll on my office door?"

"Yeah, I told her I was gonna do it. I think she thought that was totally awesome."

"Why do you think that?" asked Calder.

"'Cause she, like, didn't try to stop me. I thought she would have, but she didn't. She was, like, always trying to put the brakes on many of my crazy moves. My house had two mommas."

Not anymore, Calder thought to himself.

Chapter 32

What I'm Looking For

Colleen arranged to borrow a friend's car, leaving her BMW parked in front of her Chapel Hill apartment. She dressed as conservatively as her wardrobe allowed. Wearing her favorite wig, the long blonde one, accented by black rimmed reading glasses, she headed out. She looked more like a business professional than a college student. The detectives from Chapel Hill Homicide watching Colleen's apartment at Worth's request didn't react to her departure.

Sam finished her day's clinical notes. She had left another call on Colleen's cell voice mail, but had not heard from her. She was worried but didn't know what else to do. Sam walked across the first floor of her house into her kitchen and began sorting through the mail. She saw that her home phone answering machine on the kitchen counter was blinking to indicate a message, but she had not left her home number for Colleen. She pushed the play button. It was Calder's secretary, asking her to call Calder and it was urgent. Sam had left her cell phone on her office desk. As she turned to retrace her steps, she heard a creak of the wooden floor in the hallway. *Oh my God*, she thought to herself. She knew she had no other patients to see. She had forgotten to lock her office door. Before she could decide what to do, a blonde Colleen stepped suddenly into her kitchen from the hallway door. Colleen was pointing a silver pistol at Sam.

"I've come for my file, Sam."

Sam gulped. She stared at the shiny gun for a moment, then at her patient. "Colleen, let me help you." It was a plea.

"Call me Emma, please, doctor," retorted Colleen. "How do you like my new look? Bad, huh? Now we're both righteous blondes. Let's go get my file. Time's a-wastin.'" There was a cruel coldness in Colleen's voice Sam had never heard. Colleen waved her gun in the direction of Sam's office. She stepped closer to Sam and made space for Sam to lead the way.

Sam complied. Her mind was racing. *Think, think*, she was admonishing herself. Sam had worked with dangerous patients in a prison setting, but never had her life been threatened. Once in her office, Sam tried again to connect with her patient.

"Emma, please don't do this." Sam was hoping she could reach through this young woman's psychopathology. "I can help you if you'll let me. Let's sit down and talk. I know you're angry. I know you're scared. I imagine you're feeling vulnerable and trapped. Please give me the gun. Please don't make things worse than they already are. I can help you through this." Sam was trying to look into Colleen's eyes, but Sam was feeling increasingly frightened by Colleen's gun.

Colleen smiled. She liked how this was going. "Sam, let's cut the shit. I overheard the message you played. You been playing me too, Sam. Chatting with Dr. Miro and his detective friend, have we? Violating my confidentiality? Naughty, naughty!"

"Colleen, I…"

"It's Emma, bitch," Colleen screamed. "What part of 'Call me Emma' don't you understand." Cutting Sam off with her retort was not a question. "We don't have time for therapy. Therapy is over. Let's consider this our termination session. Therapy can be terminal to your health, you know. We're bringing closure. I got what I needed. You were helpful and we're done. Get my file and come with me. We're going for a ride."

"Emma, where are you taking me?"

"Down the road to redemption, Sam. The archeological dig of my soul has uncovered a paved road that leads from here to Craven County. I'm cravin' to show it to you firsthand. Now let's get going. I'm gonna let you drive." Colleen snatched Sam's cell off her desk. "We'll listen to your messages as we drive."

Sam's hand was trembling as she retrieved Colleen's file from the cabinet under her desk.

"I'll take that," demanded Colleen. She pointed the gun at Sam's face and slid the file into the large shoulder bag she was carrying. "Now let's go. If you make any effort to let anybody know some shit's going down, I'll blow your head off."

Chapter 33

Insane

May 17, 2007

Worth arranged for an officer and a social worker to take Starr to her Aunt Essie's house. He instructed the officer to sit on the aunt's place. Worth was taking no chances. The fact he didn't know where Colleen was pissed him off. The fact he didn't know her next play worried him. Starr had given him a key to Colleen's New Bern apartment. He put a BOLO for Colleen through his communications center. Willys informed him that Colleen's car still sat in front of her place in Chapel Hill. At Worth's request, uniformed officers convinced the building superintendent to let them into her apartment. No one was home.

Calder said, "Why don't you drop me off at my office?"

"Nada," responded Worth. "Our little Miss Murder She Drew might still have plans injurious to your welfare. You be sticking with me. Besides, I normally wouldn't want a civilian with me in a situation like this, but, C-man, I figure I might need your help, in case when we do find her, she takes a flip into the deep end. The pool in our killer's head ain't shaped like everyone else's."

Worth took the evidence by the D.A,'s. ADA Murph was easily convinced by Worth's statement of probable cause and the emergent nature of the situation. He executed search and arrest warrants, and got a judge to sign them.

While Worth papered the case, Calder called Sam again. He got her voice mail on her office and cell. Her home phone was answered by Meghan, one of her children. Meghan said her mom's car was there, but she wasn't home. She said she might be out for a walk, but she hadn't left a note like she always did.

Worth's cell vibrated. Text from Willys. *Colleen's home. Older blonde female with her.*

Worth called Willys back. "Willy, did they go into the building?"

"Roger that. We think it's our suspect, sir. Both subjects were female, both blondes. One early twenties, black rimmed specs. Other mid forties maybe. They were driving a white Toyota Camry, registered to a Michael Lee Klein in Chapel Hill. We didn't recognize her at first, but the lights in her apartment went on right after they went in. Don't know who the older woman is, sir."

"I think I do, Willy. I think it's Dr. Cooper, Colleen's therapist from Chapel Hill. Tall, maybe, 5 foot 10, attractive, hair maybe pulled back?"

"Roger. That fits. Is our suspect blonde, sir?"

"She is today, Willy. At least, that's what it looks like. Get the crew there with you. I think we have to assume this is a hostage situation, and the doctor's presence may be under duress. Covert eyes on all the way around. Calder and I are on the way. Let's just hope we can defuse things before she decides to pop another doctor."

Calder was warming a bench in the hallway outside the D.A.'s office. Worth stepped out at a rapid pace. "Let's roll, C-man. It looks like our little murderer has come home to roost. And she brought a guest."

"What do you mean?"

Worth filled him in on what Willys described.

"Shit," Calder blurted. "She brought Sam with her?"

"Looks that way. Might not be, but that's how we gonna play it anyway. We gotta move."

As they half sprinted down the marbled floored hall, Calder told Worth about his conversation with Sam's daughter. He added, "No way Sam would come here voluntarily."

"Why you think that? She might still think she can help our psycho."

"One," Calder replied, "She hasn't called me back. Two, she's too devoted a mother to break her communication routine with her children. Three, she's not the type of clinician that would breech boundaries and ethics to make a house call. What I don't get is why Colleen would see any advantage in taking her hostage."

"You be attaching rational plan to this bitch's actions?"

"Good question," Calder responded. "If she's psychotic, maybe not. If she's a psychopath, maybe so."

Worth's demeanor changed and he picked up the pace. They had taken the stairs instead of the elevator. He had that look Calder had seen before. Intense focus. Little speech. As they slid into Worth's ride, Worth used his extra, a Beretta, to anchor the file on the seat beside him. "Grab that vest off the back seat and suit up. We be climbing out of the trenches soon."

As Calder closed the car door, Worth snatched the portable walkie-talkie from its holder on his dash and barked,

"Units 202 and 203. Brown here. Copy?"

A bit of a squelch pop, and a voice said, "Roger that, sir. Both units standing by at rendezvous point as ordered, sir. Over."

Worth pulled into a side street so his driver's window was next to Willys' driver's window. An auto face-to-face. Worth had punched in the location schematics on his laptop and was studying the lay of the land. Both men lowered their windows.

"Evening, sir."

"Evening, Sergeant. Evening Officer Anderson." Anderson was Willys' partner for tonight. "You two ready for this?"

"Yes sir."

Calder noted to himself that Willys had the same serious look as Worth. Game face. Calder struggled to find his own game face, but the only faces he imagined were Colleen's and Sam's.

Worth looked at the precise details of the location and layout of Colleen's apartment building and the surrounding streets and alleys. The computer gave him data on entrances and exits, as well as the locations of stairwells. He punched the talk button again. "Unit 202, I want you and Officer Baker to cover the back entrance. It's on Caswell. Come in slowly from 8th. No lights. Slow rolling. Use the building next door to shield you from her window, just in case she's looking out. Stay cool 'til we get to her front door. Everybody vest up. Calder and I will go on foot to the front with Sgt. Willys. When we get to her apartment door, I'll signal you to move to the back door. Do it casually, on foot. No SWAT bullshit. If she should somehow try to escape out the back, I want you two to make a nice, clean, non-physical bust. No bruises, no tackles. If she comes your way, I want you to pretend you're arresting-- Baker, who's your favorite female country singer? Quick, tell me."

The radio popped, and Baker blurted out, "Shania Twain, sir."

"If our suspect comes out the back door, I want you two to act as if you're arresting Shania," Worth responded. "I don't think the suspect will show up at the back door, but if she does, cuff her with dignity and respect. Copy?"

"Copy that, sir. Man, I'd hate to have to arrest Shania," Baker said. Baker was one of the few female beat officers in the department, and Worth knew she was better in most situations than all the males in the department, except Sergeant Willys.

Worth chortled to himself as he and Willys cut a glance at each other. Then Worth looked at his rearview mirror. Calder leaned forward so he could see out of the right side mirror and noted that two New Bern PD squad cars had crisscrossed into streets behind them, positioned as ordered. Worth said back into the radio, "Yeah, I would too. A lot of honky tonk singers should be arrested for perpetrating that so-called music, but not her." Before anyone in the other car could respond, Worth said, "Keep your comments to yourself. We ain't got time to debate why God allows some kinds of music into the air. You in place, unit 202?"

"Roger that, sir. One question, sir."

"Go ahead."

"What if she comes out with a weapon, sir, like a gun or something? How much latitude does she get, sir?"

"Normal rules of engagement if she's armed, but let's try to take her down so no one gets hurt. Not you, not her, not a stray citizen. Copy?"

"Copy that, sir."

Worth said to his wingman, "Willy, you and Anderson park out of sight and come in on foot from the south. Calder and I will scoot along side those bushes from the north."

"Yes, sir."

"As soon as we're all in position, Anderson, you stay with the doorman while Sergeant Willys, Calder, and I go up. You can see the stairwell from the foyer. After we make a few introductory remarks to the doorman, position yourself so you watch the doorman and the stairs. I don't want him announcing our arrival. Make sure he knows not to. A little dinero from Ms. Newly Rich might make him a look-out. Copy that?"

"Roger that, sir."

"If by some twist of fate our suspect scoots down the stairwell, you are to keep her from leaving the building with the same finesse and grace Baker knows she's gonna do if our suspect comes out the back door. Everyone clear? This has to be clean. Her granddaddy will throw more lawyers on us than dopers at a Dead concert."

Two sets of affirmatives snapped out of Worth's radio.

For reasons that weren't obvious, after Colleen finished her sophomore year at Carolina, she had moved back to New Bern for the summer and taken this apartment, probably with money from her daddy. As Calder listened to Worth's commands to his officers, he also realized Worth did not want a screw-up during the arrest that might allow her to walk on a technicality. She was, after all, the granddaughter of one of the country's richest men.

Their entrance into the building went as planned, and the doorman was agreeable and cooperative. Worth and Calder took the elevator to Colleen's apartment. Sgt. Willys took the stairs.

Chapter 34

Make My Day

As Worth and Calder were having their face-to-face chalk talk with Willys and Anderson, Colleen was having her own word of prayer with Sam in her apartment. Once they arrived, Colleen had fixed them some tea, but Sam's was laced with 60 milligrams of Flurazepam. When taken as prescribed, it was a gentle, but effective hypnotic sedative. 60 milligrams was a knock out punch. She masked its taste with honey.

Colleen sat across from Sam, whose typically perfect posture was dissolving into a slouch from the effects of the drug. Sam became one with a buttery leather easy chair. Colleen read her file, occasionally out loud, and strafed questions and comments at Sam, while still waving the gun. Colleen's stare between accusations sent shivers through Sam's body. Fighting hard to stay alert and responsive to her patient, Sam slid slowly into unconsciousness. She mumbled, "Drugged." The last thing she saw before falling asleep was a doll house and some small chairs at a table that might normally be in a pre-school. *That's odd*, she thought, and then it was lights out.

"Smart girl you are, Sam." Colleen pulled out a pair of handcuffs and locked Sam's wrists together behind Sam's back. She encircled her ankles together with several turns of duct tape, and taped Sam's mouth. "Loverly, just loverly." Colleen then dragged Sam out of the chair to a corner of the room to the right of the entrance door and propped her into a corner. Colleen savored the moment. Sam's body was positioned just like Mildred's before the *coup de* grace. "Now that was a home run," Colleen said to herself. She covered Sam from head to toe with a fuzzy Carolina blue blanket that said "Ram's Club" in bold black and white letters. Colleen slid the doll house and an easel in front so the whole corner looked like a child's play space. In a high-pitched, squeaky voice, Colleen said out loud, "Okay, Emma. Okay Wendy. Front and center. Scene change! This ain't no dress rehearsal!"

As they rode up the elevator, Calder looked at his friend, Worth, and thought to himself, this must be scary to Worth, but if it was, there was no trace of fear coming from his buddy. Calder had fallen asleep the previous night thinking about the psychological state of mind it would take for someone to do what the murderer had done. Killing her therapist was one thing. Now that he knew for sure, Calder guessed Colleen, working off his report and working in therapy with Sam, over time focused a lot of hatred on Mildred Hughes. But daughters just don't kill their mothers. Matricide by daughters was too unnatural, and as they walked towards her apartment, Calder's stomach declared another state of emergency. The violence of each of the murders was chilling. Both Calder and Worth were hoping against hope Colleen had not harmed Sam.

Worth quietly spoke into his radio, activating the actions of the three officers at the street level. "We're on her floor and going in. Secure your positions now." He turned its volume to vibrate and clipped the walkie-talkie to his belt. He placed his right hand in his jacket pocket. Calder could hear the safety switch come off his Beretta. Sgt. Willys joined them from the stairwell and unsnapped his sidearm and took it out, holding it by his side. Responding to a nod from Worth, he flipped on a microcassette tape recorder in his front top pocket. "Stay behind me," Worth said to Calder. Worth buzzed her doorbell. They knew Colleen would think it odd for a visitor to show up without calling first. They were off the normal protocol of most apartment buildings, but Calder also knew Worth and Sgt. Willys weren't going to wait too long for her to answer the door before they kicked it in. Calder had forgotten Starr gave Worth a key.

After two presses of the chime, they heard a small, sleepy voice say,

"Who is it?"

Since all the doors had security peep holes, they knew she could see Worth and Calder if she wanted to. Sgt. Willys had flattened himself out of view, at least as much as a donut- and barbeque-lovin' man can.

"Ms. McPherson," Worth said. "It's Detective Kenilworth Brown and Dr. Calder Miro. We're sorry to disturb you at this hour, but we'd like to come in and talk with you."

To their surprise and relief, Colleen opened the door. She was barefoot and wearing an expensive, lavender silk nightgown that radiated sensuality and comfort. Her breasts were mostly exposed and she made no effort to cover herself. Her hair was its normal auburn color.

Colleen said, "Please come in. Who is it you're looking for? A Ms. McPherson, you say?"

She took a casual walk to a luxuriant leather easy chair, where she curled up, with her legs and feet tucked under her. She pulled a small teddy bear to her chest. There was a full mug of what looked like hot tea on the table beside her. It looked like she had just awakened. The lighting in the room was dim. There was an eerie dreaminess to the whole scene. There was a drawing pad and a clay pot full of pens and crayons on the floor beside her. Her apartment was like her pajamas—comfortable and sensuous, but there was a striking incongruity about it too. Where an adult would normally put a dining room table and chairs, there was a small child's table and two small chairs. A doll house and easel framed what was perhaps a play area. A blanket was draped in the corner behind these items

Worth followed her in, and Calder followed him. Colleen did not react in the slightest to the appearance of Sgt. Willys, who quickly entered and positioned himself in a manner that allowed him some distance from all three of them and did not permit Colleen to see his revolver in his hand by his side. He had an unobstructed view of Colleen. Or shot, if necessary.

Calder pondered her curious response to Worth's request to speak with her, because it sounded as if she was pretending not to be Colleen McPherson. As these recent months had passed, and she came into focus as a prime suspect, Calder had marveled at her capacity for cleverness, and was well aware that her personality was possibly composed of some serious psychopathic characteristics. Among their many talents, psychopaths could be witty, charming, often physically attractive, very likeable, seductive, and manipulative, but incapable of empathy. Despite Dr. Cooper's superb analytical abilities, Calder thought Colleen had conned Dr. Cooper. Right now, Calder was full of skepticism and curiosity. To his left, as he scanned the room, Calder noted the corner of the apartment containing an easel and doll house with a fuzzy blanket behind them. He didn't see Sam anywhere. This isn't good, he thought to himself. Because she had allowed them in with such a disarming manner, the anxiety in Calder had dropped a few points and his heart wasn't pounding so much, but his heart rate rocketed again when he didn't see Sam. Calder realized how much he cared about Sam. Maybe cared too much, given her marital status. His clinical and forensic radar had turned on automatically.

Worth came right to the point. "Ms. McPherson, we are here to arrest you for the murders of Dr. Mildred Hughes and Ms. Ruth McPherson." He handed her the arrest warrants and the search warrant. Colleen placed these on the arm of her chair without looking at them. Worth said, "You have the right to remain silent. You have the right to an attorney. If you cannot afford an attorney, one will be appointed for you. Anything you say, can and will be used against you in a court of law. Do you understand?"

Colleen didn't move. In fact, she didn't react at all. Several seconds passed.

Worth stepped a little closer to her. Willys' gaze was locked onto her hands clutching that bear. He had not relaxed.

Worth looked at Colleen and said, "Ms. McPherson, do you understand? We are here to arrest you for the murders of your former therapist, Dr. Hughes, and your mother, Ruth McPherson." We are also here to speak with Dr. Cooper. We know she came here with you. Where is she?" Worth followed this with a simultaneous command into his radio, "I want all three of you up here, pronto, but no noise. Do not wake up the rest of the building. Keep your side arms in their holsters."

Colleen remained still. She put the bear in her lap and Willys shifted his weight slightly. Calder was again distracted by the reappearance of her perfect breasts, and realized he would have made a lousy cop. Colleen was stoked by Calder's breathless stare.

Colleen's outward, non-reaction was creating a creepy atmosphere. They all believed this woman had viciously, violently killed both her psychologist and her mother. Her non-reaction was unexpected and deeply troubling. Calder knew they had entered into the realm of some deep psychopathology. She was greeting them with calm and seductiveness. Worth and Willys grew anxious and coiled.

The other three officers entered the room. Colleen didn't flinch. She did say, "Hi everybody."

The dreamy, creepy tempo switched in a flash. Something moved in the corner behind everyone. Sam had shifted her legs. One of her feet was lodged in a fold of the blanket. Her movement pulled the blanket, revealing her face and one foot. One of the tiny dolls in the doll house fell over. As Calder spun to react to the sudden appearance of Sam, Colleen screamed, "Bitch!" and whipped her small caliber pistol from the insides of the bear directing its barrel towards Sam. Without thinking, Calder spun his body in Sam's direction. Colleen's shot hit him in the back, in the space not covered by the vest Worth made him wear.

Worth lunged at Colleen. Before Willys or any of the other officers reacted, Worth twisted the gun out of her hand, tossed the bear on the floor and pinned Colleen's neck into the back of her chair with his big black hand. He looked deep into her deranged eyes. "You're done killing folk. Cuff her, Willy."

With the cuffs in place, Worth let go of his grip. Anderson called for an ambulance. Worth handed off Colleen's care to Willys and knelt beside Calder who was lying face down. The wound was just above Calder's right shoulder blade. There wasn't much blood and Calder was conscious and breathing. Baker slipped a pillow under Calder's head. "Just lie still, C-man. EMT's on the way."

Calder tried to look in the direction of Sam, who was being attended to by Anderson and another officer. "How's Sam? Is she okay?"

Anderson checked her vitals and gave Worth a thumbs up signal.

"We'll know more when the EMT's get here, but she seems all right, but out cold. Probably drugged. She's alive. That's the good thing. So are you. That's another good thing."

Calder breathed a sigh of relief. He looked at Worth. "Who said you couldn't hit a moving target?"

"Well at least she didn't hit your humor, but if you was trying to be speedy and dodge that bullet, you got some work to do on your moves. From where I stood, looks like you did what you wanted to do." Worth replied.

"And that be what?" muttered Calder, who was beginning to feel some real sharp pain.

Baker applied a pressure bandage beneath the vest, underneath Calder's shirt.

"Look to me like you be putting yoself in harm's way for the lady doctor. That be some chivalry plus."

Calder grimaced. "Where am I hit?"

Worth said, "It looks like you got lucky. Maybe right above your scapula and below your clavicle. There's not too much blood."

"You're so comforting. I'm feeling better already."

Baker snickered.

Worth cut her a look and said, "Got to work on my bedside manner. The location of this wound probably means you'll have to let go of the dream of pichin' relief for Boston."

The EMT crew arrived. Assured his friend and Sam were all right, Worth turned his attention back to Ms. Wacko.

"Baker, I want you to go into Ms. McPherson's bedroom and find her a robe or something suitable for her to put on. Then I want the three of you to search this place from stem to stern."

Colleen asked if she could drink her tea.

"No ma'am. This is not a tea party."

She looked at Worth and said, "I like tea parties. My name is Wendy Donovan. I'm afraid I don't know the two people you say were murdered. If you think my last name is McPherson, I'm sorry to say there must be some kind of mistake. My last name is Donovan. Like in 'Sunshine Superman.'" She spoke in a childlike voice and almost sang her words.

Officer Baker came out of the bedroom with a selection of undergarments, a sweater, jeans, and some socks and running shoes. Worth said, "Ms. McPherson, or Ms. Donovan, I want you to put these items on, in the presence of Officer Baker."

Colleen looked at the handcuffs. "They're shiny," she quipped. "I'll get dressed. Officer, if you'll follow me, we can pick out something nice. Maybe something in arrest-me red. Isn't that funny?"

As she stood up, she said, "Can I get one of these bracelets off for a few minutes? It will be hard to put on my clothes otherwise. I suppose someone could dress me. You perhaps," looking at Worth.

Worth answered, "You may have one wrist free briefly, Ms. McPherson, but you'll have to wear what Officer Baker has selected because I cannot allow you to go back into your bedroom or any other room of this apartment until we search it, and that will take some time. Baker, find some other shoes. I want those running shoes to go to the lab."

Officer Baker gestured for Colleen to move towards the bathroom. As Colleen moved out of the living room area where they were all standing, Worth said in a stage whisper to Baker, "Do not let her out of your sight for a nano-second. You go in the bathroom with her. No make-up, no going into drawers, no nothing. Keep the door cracked. Got it?"

Baker nodded and stepped in behind Colleen. Willys followed them both and stood quietly in the hall, just outside the bathroom.

The other officers were beginning their search. It was not a toss, but a methodical search.

The EMT's carried Calder and Sam out on rolling stretchers. The EMT leader told Worth Sam's condition suggested a drug overdose, but she was stable and not in any distress. He also confirmed Worth's assessment of Calder's gunshot wound. It missed the primary arteries, veins, and bones, but may have grazed a rib. "He's gonna be okay, but sore," he said to Worth.

Baker got Colleen dressed and re-cuffed without incident. As Baker and Willys led Colleen out of her apartment, she stopped at the threshold, and looked back at Worth. She said in a gently Southern manner, "Thank you all for coming." Baker and the other two officers took her to the squad car. Colleen had insisted on taking her bear with her, but Worth wouldn't allow it. He wanted to dust it and scan it first. Maybe she'd hidden other objects within its innards.

After getting things squared away at the station, Worth checked on Calder and Sam at Craven Regional Medical Center, where they were hospitalized. Sam remained stable and just needed to sleep it off. Her husband was at her bedside. Worth spoke with him briefly, gave him his card, and then Worth dropped by Calder's room. The bullet went cleanly through. Willys found it in the wall of Colleen's apartment. Calder was woozy but awake. Calder saw Worth and faintly smiled. He gave Worth a peace sign. Worth responded with an upheld black power fist.

"How you be, man," asked Worth.

"I've been better. How's Sam?"

"She's fine. Ms. Wacko slipped her some benzos, but she'll be okay. Her husband's here. She'll probably go home tomorrow. I hope to take a statement before she leaves for Blue Heaven. So, C-man, you feel like talking a bit?"

"Maybe a few minutes. I got pain meds coursing through my 'bod-ee,' and I can feel a deep sleep coming on. Jones coming down. I got a basketball Jones," he sang.

Worth realized Calder was stoned, but decided maybe he'd venture a few questions. "Okay, this is where I truly get to practice my bedside manner. Before you took one for the team, or took one for the beautiful doctor, what the hell did we walk into?"

"I dunno. I think you got yoself a double murderer who's gonna claim inanity, I mean, insanity. I think she panned, planned being arrested with the same thoroughness she planned those murders. I think she's gonna claim she's a multiple, and try to tip toe through the tulips."

Calder's eyes were at half mast.

"You think she's insane?"

Calder mumbled, "She got it worked out." Then he snored.

Chapter 35

Stone Free

"What did you mean, she got it all worked out? Seven of us were present when she tried to shoot Dr. Cooper."

"When did I say that?" Calder asked.

"Back when you was under the influence of poppies."

"Well, if I said it, it was brilliant, don't you think?" Calder laughed at Worth's look of annoyance.

"I do have a theory," continued Calder. "I think Colleen can use her therapy with Hughes and her therapy with Sam to create either reasonable doubt or a successful insanity defense. Her actions with Sam and with us when we went in all appear more than a bit nuts. The District Attorney's gonna need to find a really good person to evaluate her."

"That you, white bread!"

"I'd love to, but I've been involved too much already. I don't think I'd be asked, but I'd decline if I were."

"The term you just used—'nuts'—is that a DSM-IV category?"

"It'll definitely be in edition five, right behind 'bat shit crazy' followed by 'the lights are on, but no one's home.'"

Worth said, "The demolition guys confirmed the explosive that blew Ruth's head off definitely was the same type of technology that's available all over the Internet and is being used to blow our guys to kingdom come in Iraq. There weren't enough fragments to piece together, but I wonder if it wasn't Hughes' phone? The materials Starr found in Colleen's closet had enough of the specs about this technology to tie Colleen to the device."

"If she was searching the Internet for C-4 and how to make a cell phone into a bomb, how come Carnivore didn't pick her up?"

Worth stared at Calder. "Well, well, well. How did C-Man come to know about Carnivore, our nation's super secret system for tracking potential criminals and terrorists?"

"I got high friends in low places," Calder replied, thinking about Tek, who smoked more weed than the Marley brothers.

Worth added, "Well, it's a good question. Getting the tech info about how to rig a cell phone is one thing, but actually obtaining the C-4 is quite another. That took some connections. Once I learned it was a cell phone, I figured she used Dr. Hughes' cell to do the deed."

"Do you think Colleen had help?"

"If not help from someone who knew what she was doing, she had to have connections to get the material. It ain't like making a bomb outta fertilizer. This shit's in a class by itself. And, one other mystery was solved."

"What was that?" queried Calder.

"Seems Ruth had been stashing all her cash in this movable altar she had in her house. Looks like she always got paid in cash. Once we went over her house again a second time, Baker found this sliding door in the back of the thing and there was about four hundred thousand in there. The altar was in a breakfast nook, so it wasn't damaged by the explosion or fire, but all the money got soaked by the fire hoses. We're not sure if she had a will or not, so Starr will probably get it, but I have some vague memory from another case I had there's some state statute that addresses what happens to a person's property when they die without a will. Why would she keep all that money stashed and not use it on her kids, her house, or herself?"

Calder responded, "Honestly, who knows what Ruth was thinking. Some people, especially when they grow up feeling deprived of certain things they wanted or needed—love, food, money, or whatever—develop a pathological drive to hoard stuff. In Ruth's case, it was obviously money. Maybe she had a plan for it. I guess we'll never know. We do know both girls knew their momma hadn't been telling them the truth about never getting any money from their daddy. I wonder if either one of them ever discovered Ruth's bank?"

There was a knock at Worth's door. "Yeah?" he said.

Officer Baker stuck her head in and said, "We found some more things from Dr. Hughes' file in Colleen's apartment and Colleen's prints and hair are all over them. We got a solid match on her prints from the books and stuff her sister found, Detective. Turns out, too, her apartment is rented to Windy Donovan."

"Okay, that's progress. And give her this damn bear back, before Calder gets attached to it. We don't want to deprive prisoners of their constitutional right to bear bears."

Baker laughed, as he tossed her the bear. She remained at the door.

"What?" said Worth.

"There's one other development, sir."

"And that is?"

Baker said, "Her attorney has called and is on his way."

"Well, that didn't take too long. Who is it?"

"Tom Mesereau," she said. "I think he's the guy who defended Michael Jackson."

Worth sat upright. "You yankin' my chain, Baker?"

"No, sir."

Worth and Calder looked at each other.

Important, if true.

Chapter 36

Post Mortem

Colleen's attorneys put her case squarely in front of the media. When you got big money and old, big money, a person suspected of a crime has a constitutional right to a fair trial by media. The State's evidence was airtight—until an expensive, talented defense team blew a big hole in the case and let the air out. By the time the trial started, Colleen's defense team consisted of six lawyers, three investigators, three jury consultants, a media consultant, a mitigation specialist, a forensic psychologist, and a forensic psychiatrist. A lab of forensic scientists huddled in the wings.

Colleen's attorneys initially claimed she was not competent to stand trial, so there were a few rounds of competency evaluations back and forth between her experts and the State's. She was eventually determined to be competent and was sent back to Craven County for trial. Her lawyers asked for a jury trial and entered a plea of not guilty by reason of insanity. North Carolina is one of the states that allows for such a defense, based on the so-called "*M'Naughten* test" of insanity. Colleen's attorneys were hoping to be successful in convincing the jury that she was "laboring under such a defect of reason, from disease of the mind, as to not know the nature and quality of the act [she] was doing, or, if she did know it, she did not know it was wrong."

Calder's wound healed nicely. Calder and Worth were called as prosecution witnesses. So was Dr. Cooper, but she was not helpful because her heart simply wasn't into testifying against her patient. Under cross-examination, Colleen's attorneys were able to create considerable reasonable doubt, based on the early stages of Sam's therapy with Colleen, who was treated for almost two years as a person named Emma. Starr was called too, but she emotionally collapsed a few days before her scheduled testimony and was psychiatrically hospitalized. Her father declared she would never testify and no one could ever try to make her. Sonny was called as a witness for the defense. So was Griff. The jury was moved by their impassioned pleas for mercy and compassion. Griff made an imposing witness and media magnet. The local, state, and national media were all over the case.

The surprise witness for the defense was Colleen herself. There was considerable confusion about who was to be put under oath. Seeking the death penalty, the State indicted Colleen for both murders and its case was filed as the *State of North Carolina v. Colleen McPherson*, but Colleen's lawyers argued she needed to be sworn as Wendy Donovan, since this was who she recognized herself to be. This strategy became effective theater. The trial judge had the jury going in and out of the courtroom so many times to keep these arguments from being heard by the jury, the courtroom deputies joked among themselves about putting a revolving door on the jury room.

Neither the judge nor the jury was amused. The judge kept Court TV and cameras out of the courtroom, but the courthouse was packed every day. The trial never became a circus, but Colleen's team of lawyers and consultants managed to create enough chaos in the courtroom and the media to mimic what they believed was Colleen's actual state of mind. New Bern became a collective multiple personality. Starr's collapse and hospitalization were used effectively to engender sympathy for both sisters. By the end of the trial, the buzz in the bars, restaurants, and churches around New Bern and across the state was that most people felt sympathy for Colleen.

Colleen was evaluated for the prosecution in the forensic unit of Dorothea Dix Hospital, the state hospital in Raleigh. There was some effort made to make her case a federal case because of the weapons and technology in Ruth's murder, but the defense was successful in keeping it in the state court. Colleen was evaluated for the defense by a forensic psychologist and a forensic psychiatrist, both of whom were among the best in the country. Calder thought they were good choices. Their conclusions were that Colleen suffered from a dissociative identity disorder and was most likely insane at the time of the offenses. The State's experts concluded she was a psychopath who was malingering her dissociation. All in all, the battle of the experts went about the way Calder had expected. More to the point, though, Calder thought it went about the way Colleen had planned it.

Colleen's defense team used power point slides, enlargements of documents from Dr. Hughes' records and Colleen's journals, samples from Dr. Hughes' video tapes of the little McPherson girls, testimony from their forensic experts, and documents from Dr. Cooper's treatment records of Colleen, which the trial judge, over Dr. Cooper's own lawyer's objection, ordered her to release. Colleen's defense team made a solid evidentiary showing that Colleen McPherson had been insane for a long time, well before either of the two murders. To Worth's and Calder's minds, the district attorney made a huge mistake when he rejected the idea of showing the jury how Dr. Hughes' therapy had harmed both girls. The D.A. thought the concept of the iatrogenic effects of therapy would be lost on the jury and would sound like he was blaming one of the murder victims. It was painful for Calder to think the jury might see the girls' videos and find them credible. But, justice is blind.

The trial lasted three weeks, but the jury wasn't out very long. A jury of Colleen's peers made its decision in three hours, reaching a verdict of not guilty by reason of insanity.

When the verdict came in, Worth reacted with disgust, for he knew Colleen had scammed the system with the best help money can buy. Calder was more philosophic, and despite his explaining to Worth sometimes you're the windshield, sometimes you're the bug, it didn't change Worth's attitude.

The sentencing hearing was held about a month later. In North Carolina, when a defendant is found not guilty by reason of insanity, the relevant statute calls for an automatic commitment to a forensic unit in the state mental health system, which meant Colleen was sent back to Dorothea Dix Hospital in Raleigh for an initial commitment of fifty days, to be reviewed ninety days afterwards, reviewed again one hundred and eighty days later, and once a year after that. Theoretically, Colleen could remain in the State's forensic psychiatric care for the rest of her life. The standard for release from this forever commitment is that the Respondent (the patient) has to prove she is no longer mentally ill or no longer dangerous to others. The burden would be on Colleen to prove her readiness for release, not on the State to prove the criteria are met.

The two friends sat at the bar, drinking Grolsch and Guinness. They were conducting a post mortem on the case, and actually got some sympathy from Maggie, the green-eyed, Irish goddess. Worth figured Colleen would ultimately convince the State's review panel she was not dangerous, because she no longer wanted to kill anybody, and was no longer mentally ill, because Worth and Calder thought she never had been. Calder agreed. Both decided that had been her plan. With her family's political clout and pressures on the D.A.'s office from the community, the only thing they couldn't agree on was how long it would take her to get out. Worth bet Calder five years. Maggie weighed in and wagered seven.

Calder clinked his glass on Worth's and said, "Politics and justice never collide."

To which Worth responded, "If you believe that, I be yo white ass fairy godmother."

Calder chuckled and threw some more sarcastic wood on the fire: "I liked the way the community pressure didn't get to the D.A."

Taking a big pull on his beer, Worth swallowed and said, "In this case, justice was not only blind, it also was invisible."

Calder drained his pint of Guinness, nodded at Maggie who had signaled him if he wanted another, and said "Murderers never smile in the courtroom. It'll be a long time before we see that again."

"It was a Mona Lisa moment, C-man."

The sympathy defense worked with Maggie, too. She even volunteered she got off work early that night and would be willing to go to dinner with them, if they promised to behave themselves. Worth and Calder looked at each other, clinked their steins again, and winked. Simultaneously, they looked at Maggie and said, "Of course."

Worth was grinning that big grin of his. Calder grinned too, hoping he or Worth could show her some bass guitar walkin' blues and blues sex. Calder corrected himself. He meant sax. Worth played the sax. Calder meant sax.

About the Author

H.D. "De" Kirkpatrick is a licensed psychologist in private practice in Charlotte, North Carolina, where he specializes in clinical and forensic psychology. He has a doctorate in psychology and also holds a diploma in forensic psychology from the American Board of Professional Psychology. He has authored or co-authored a number of professional articles in the field of forensic psychology. This is his first novel. His hobbies include tennis, learning the electric bass guitar, and cooking. He lives with his wife, Katie Holliday, a family law attorney, in Charlotte.